Lost American Fiction

Edited by *Matthew J. Bruccoli*

The first title in this series, Edith Summers Kelley's *Weeds*, appeared in 1972, and, subsequently, became the start of the Lost American Fiction series. Its reception encouraged Southern Illinois University Press to mount a series that would republish obscure or unavailable works of fiction that merit a new audience. Since 1972 fourteen volumes of Lost American Fiction have appeared—in hardbound from the Press and in paperback from Popular Library, the co-operating publisher.

The editor is frequently asked about the basis for selection. Obviously, there can be no clear guidelines, for the decisions are largely subjective and impressionistic. The only firm rule is that a book considered for inclusion in the series must have been originally published before World War II. Our chief consideration, of course, has been literary merit. Another quality we are looking for might be called "life": does the work live?—does it have life of its own?—does it present human nature convincingly? A third test for including a work in the series is its literary or social value: does the work illuminate the literary or social history of its time? The fourteen volumes chosen so far do not represent one editor's judgment; five were recommended by friends, our co-operating publisher, colleagues, even strangers who wrote enthusiastically about the series.

At this point the editor and publisher feel that the Lost American series has largely achieved what it set out to do. Fourteen novels have been given another chance, and some are clearly finding new audiences. The paperback reprint arrangement with Popular Library is making the books available to a wide readership. To be sure, some will vanish again. We cannot claim that all of the titles are lost masterpieces, but we believe that a few are. Perhaps the most meaningful fact about the response to the series is that there has been considerable disagreement from readers about individual titles. We never expected uniformity of response. That readers would find the Lost American Fiction books worth reading and would be prompted to make their own re-appraisals is all we wanted.

M.J.B.

QUEER PEOPLE

PEOPLE

By CARROLL *and*
GARRETT GRAHAM

Afterword by
Budd Schulberg

Southern Illinois University Press
Carbondale and Edwardsville

Feffer & Simons, Inc.
London and Amsterdam

C, 2

This edition printed by offset lithography in the United States of America

Designed by Gary Gore

Library of Congress Cataloging in Publication Data
Graham, Carroll.
  Queer people.
  (Lost American fiction)
  Reprint of the ed. published by Vanguard Press, New York.
  I. Graham, Garrett, joint author. II. Title.
PZ3.G75673Qu 15 [PS3513.R1476] 813'.5'2 76–3478
ISBN 0-8093-0784-7

BL

NOV 15 '80

FOR BROWNIE

*"For I am Jurgen—a
monstrous clever fellow
—and I will taste any
drink once."*

JAMES BRANCH CABELL

QUEER PEOPLE

An irresponsible youth, reporter by profession, drifts to California in search of anonymity and finds his element amongst studio people—with their own relentless search for diversions in booze and temporary affairs—and is not shaken even when he finds himself the center of a murder investigation.

CHAPTER ONE

AND so the film star called the bootlegger.

It was the only logical thing for Gilbert Vance to do.
All in one day, his wife had left him, Colossal Pictures
had renewed his contract, his mistress had returned unexpectedly from location, his lawyer had informed him
that a charge of driving while intoxicated had been
"fixed," and his tests—both film and Wassermann—had
turned out favorably.

He had rather expected his wife to leave him, and he
had been hoping that she would do it sooner. He had
not been quite so sure about the contract, and it was
naturally a source of immense relief to know that his
magnificent salary was to continue for another year.
But his joy was complete when Peanuts Oliver turned
up in Hollywood. She was to have been away two weeks
longer, and she would have been had her director been
content with mere perpetual intoxication. But when
he lapsed into delirium tremens, the company decided
that while this would probably make no difference in
the quality of the production, it would be a good ex-
cuse to call the troupe home and save money.

All of these things, naturally, called for a party.

Almost simultaneously with the arrival of the
bootlegger, guests, guided by that occult sense which

most Hollywood guests seem to possess, began to drop in.

Joe Greet, directing a comedy at Culver City, heard of the budding brawl in some mysterious fashion, dismissed his mimes for the afternoon, and hurried to Vance's home.

A leading man, apprised of the festivities, rushed over from the studio, without bothering to remove his grease-paint or change from the evening dress in which he had been performing.

Wind of it eddied to the Y.W.C.A. Studio Club. A bulletin was posted in the lobby for all hands to stand by the telephone and await invitations.

A blond young extra man driving by the house was seized because he could play the piano. He sent for his heart of the moment, a tempestuous Mexican girl who had lately abandoned a Tia Juana honky-tonk for a career on the screen.

There came divers others—scenario writers, a director or two, a minor studio official, two gagmen, extra girls, a real estate salesman, a casting director, and an unemployed press agent.

It assumed the aspect of particularly high festivities as the guests began to plow steadily through Gilbert Vance's Scotch. As the afternoon shadows lengthened and the din increased, an untrained observer might have thought that the utmost had been achieved in Hollywood wassail.

But the guest who was to prove the party's most spectacular member had not yet arrived. He had not

even met any of those present. They had never heard
of him.

II

Hollywood had no adequate means of coping with
Whitey, nor Whitey with Hollywood. His invasion was
in the nature of a surprise attack—a surprise to both
Hollywood and Whitey.

He alighted from a Santa Fe transcontinental train,
dusty and bored with three days of staring at Kansas,
New Mexico and Arizona.

A taxi-driver seized his bags (one of which had been
borrowed from a friend without permission) and
whisked Whitey to the Rosslyn Hotel in downtown Los
Angeles.

Whitey registered, somewhat grandiosely, as Theodore Anthony White, indicated Chicago as his place of
residence, bought copies of all the afternoon papers,
and followed the boy to his room.

After a bath had removed the railroad grime from his
chubby body, Whitey settled down to survey his prob-
able future in Los Angeles.

Unpacking his bags was no great task. They con-
tained another suit, a battered pair of tan shoes, bedroom slippers belonging to the friend who owned the
bag, an old and frayed beach robe, a bathing suit two
sizes too small for him, manuscripts of five unfinished
short stories, a deck of marked cards from which the
seven of spades was missing, a snapshot of himself and
a plump maiden taken on the beach of Miami, two

volumes of James Branch Cabell and a copy of Hecht's *Count Bruga*, an assortment of rumpled linen, a revolver which he had removed from the body of a slain Chicago gangster, shirt and shoes to go with evening dress which he did not possess and divers odds and ends, including an empty gin bottle, the last contents of which had been consumed as the train passed through Hutchinson, Kansas.

Whitey, to his knowledge, had not an acquaintance in town and was heartily glad of it. In his roving career as a newspaperman he had touched upon such ports as the Denver *Post*, the New Orleans *Times-Picayune*, the Omaha *Bee*, the Chicago *Herald-Examiner*, the Washington *Star*, the Cleveland *Plain-Dealer* and, returning to Chicago, the *Tribune*.

Until this day he had let Los Angeles remain unsmirched by his presence. He had fled to it now because the police had frowned upon a business venture which had seemed quite ingenious to Whitey at the time. The venture had embraced the manufacture and sale of police badges in wholesale lots without official sanction.

Whitey had thirty-six dollars in bills and silver amounting to about two dollars and seventy cents when he settled down in his hotel. He had no qualms whatsoever as he prepared to hurl himself against the city editors. He had attacked many a town with weaker financial reserves.

He glanced critically at the afternoon papers of Los Angeles and decided to try the morning publications first, because the pay was generally higher and also because he preferred the odd working hours, being a strange creature at best.

At six o'clock that evening he presented himself at the door leading into the editorial rooms of the *Examiner*. His way was barred by an unfriendly and impertinent boy.

"What's the name of the city editor?" Whitey asked.

"Van Ettisch. Why?"

"I want to see him."

"What about?"

"I'll discuss that with Mr. Van Ettisch."

"If it's a job you're after, he says not to let in any more of these hungry-looking reporters."

"My lad, just such young whelps as you have been trying to keep me out of city rooms from coast to coast. You can't win."

"Them's my orders."

Whitey appeared dismayed, but was not. He departed, walking humbly until he had turned the corner of the hallway and was out of sight. Then he began a thorough search for the back door which instinct and experience told him was there. A whirr of linotypes led him to the composing room. He threaded his way unerringly through it to a door which led to a vast chamber filled with typewriter desks. A number of the desks were occupied by earnest young men, but it was easy for Whitey to pick his way to the throne of the city editor. Van Ettisch looked exactly like a city editor, for one thing, and for another, his desk was in a remote corner, and he sat facing the door.

"Mr. Van Ettisch?" Whitey began, trying to inject dignity, deference and importance into his tone.

"Yes." The reply was neither friendly nor forbidding. It was a bare statement of fact.

Whitey leaped to his recitation. He must get it all out, he knew, before the editor could chill him with the stock reply, "Sorry, but we're all full."

"Mr. Van Ettisch, my name is White. I just got in from Chicago, where I've been doing re-write on the *Herald-Examiner*, and Mr. Duffy Cornell said to look you up and he would recommend me if you want recommendation."

This was untrue. It had been some years since Whitey had worked for that paper, and if Mr. Cornell remembered him at all he certainly would have recommended him as nothing more than an unreliable reporter and a thoroughly bad egg. But Whitey knew that editors do not check up on such things.

"How long since you worked there?" Van Ettisch asked.

"Two months ago."

"Ever work on any other papers?"

"Oh, sure," Whitey rattled off a list of them glibly; not too many, for that would have branded him as a drifter.

"Just do re-write?"

"Oh, no, sir. Assignments, re-write, copy desk. Did make-up down in New Orleans."

This latter was also untrue.

"Married?"

"No, sir."

"Booze hound?"

"Oh, no, sir." Whitey's round face became angelic.

Van Ettisch paused to survey the candidate, after the manner of an expert horse-trader. He saw a stocky, plump man of medium height, with a round, pink, beaming face—a pleasant face, almost always lighted by a smile. His eyes were small and piggy, but they were alert and intelligent. His black hair was parted in the middle and plastered to his head. He was neither well-dressed nor unkempt. In short, he looked typically the reporter.

"Might use you on re-write, temporarily at least," Van Ettisch said. "Can't pay much."

"I don't care about that."

"Fifty a week to start."

"That's fine."

Thus did Theodore Anthony White become a member of the editorial staff of the *Examiner*. He was handed four stories to re-write from the afternoon papers. He acquitted himself satisfactorily, and convinced his employer immediately that he was a man of experience.

Nothing more happened to him until almost nine o'clock. His name was called out, and he scurried to the city desk.

"I've decided to send you on an assignment," Van Ettisch said, handing him a slip of paper on which an address was written. "North Las Palmas Street. That's in Hollywood. Gilbert Vance lives there. You know—the movie actor. We have a tip his wife has left him. If she hasn't, she should. He won't answer the phone, but he's probably there. He'll lie about it, so demand to see Mrs. Vance. If she isn't there call back, and we'll bust the story."

"How do I go? Taxi?"

"Taxi, my eye! Catch a red car on Hill Street marked Gardner Junction. It goes out Hollywood Boulevard. Get off at Las Palmas. You can take a cab from there."

And thus began Whitey's invasion of Hollywood itself.

The surface car pushed slowly through the evening tangle of traffic on Hill Street, darted through the tunnel and turned on Sunset Boulevard. Rows of cheap houses and tawdry shops passed in review. Whitey had heard vaguely that Sunset was a prominent street, and he peered out curiously.

"If this is it, Hollywood's not so hot," he told himself.

He changed his mind gradually. Large apartment buildings, and smart shops and cafés replaced the frame dwellings and boarding houses. He noted by a signpost that the car had now swerved into Hollywood Boulevard.

A few minutes more and he had come upon another business district, the raucous traffic as heavy and disordered as in downtown Los Angeles. Office buildings and theaters came into view upon the real "Broadway" of the city. Flashing signs proclaimed the Music Box, the Vine Street Theater, the Hollywood Playhouse, the Egyptian, the glittering Chinese Theater, the Plaza Hotel, the Roosevelt and El Capitan.

Whitey scrambled to his feet when the conductor shouted, "Las Palmas." A moment later he stood on the pavements of Hollywood Boulevard and surveyed the oddest city in America.

A tremendous uproar was taking place across the street. A truck, bearing a huge generator, was providing power for giant arc-lights which played about the sky and into windows and spectators' eyes. One shop was ablaze with studio "broad" lights. A wheezy tenor, boosted to Gargantuan proportions, was bawling over the radio. Perhaps three hundred persons were milling about the street.

"What are they doing?" Whitey asked another observer. "Making a movie?"

"No. An opening for some beauty shop. A guy can't start a cigar store here any more without raising a row about it."

Whitey found a cab, gave the driver Gilbert Vance's address and was carried away toward his first encounter with a movie star. He did not hear the whirr of a maniacal Destiny's machinery en route.

The cab whined up a badly lighted street. Abruptly, the road bounced against the Hollywood hills and they began to climb. The driver was forced to shift into second gear.

"What a place for a house," Whitey muttered as they began to twist and duck among the hills.

[17]

"Her'y'are," the driver announced, jamming on the brakes without warning. Whitey peered out dubiously and saw only a wooden gate in the darkness. No lights were visible.

"Are you sure this is the place?" he asked.

"You want Gilbert Vance's house, don't you?"

"Yes, but it's all dark."

"You can't see the house from here. Go through that gate and up those stone steps. I oughta know the place. I've carried Vance up to it enough times."

"Well, you better wait for me," said Whitey. He pushed through the gate and began to feel his way around the winding steps, hoping fervently that Vance was not a lover of police dogs. A final turn, after a brief steep climb, brought a flood of light from a large studio window. Whitey could hear a jumble of voices, mingled with a phonograph playing *That's My Weakness Now*.

It was a very odd house, he decided from what he could see of it as he beat the large bronze knocker upon the futuristic half-Chinese, half-Grand Rapids door. His pounding at length brought a highly suspicious Japanese youth who peered out, barely opening the door.

"What you want?"

"I want to see Mr. Vance."

"Not here."

"Nuts; of course he's here. I'm from the *Examiner*."

"Wait."

Whitey quickly slipped his foot in the door to prevent its being locked. After a brief struggle, the servant gave it up and disappeared to carry the message. He returned, followed by a large and rather handsome man, coatless and tieless, his thin, high voice contrasting oddly with his muscular frame.

"Whataya want?"

"Are you Gilbert Vance?"

"Yeah. What of it?"

"My name is White. I'm from the *Examiner* and . . ."

"The hell you are. Where's Jim Mitchell?"

"How do I know? I don't even know Jim Mitchell."

"He's the guy from the *Examiner* that's always around Hollywood."

"Oh, yes," Whitey explained, lying easily. "I remember. I'm a new man on the paper. This is Mitchell's night off."

"Well, what do you want? Let's have it."

"It's this, Mr. Vance. We got a tip down at the office that you and Mrs. Vance are separated, and that she's not living with you any more."

"It's a damned lie."

"Well, that's what we wanted to check up on. Is Mrs. Vance here?"

Vance did not reply for a moment, but studied Whitey carefully. When he did answer, his manner had changed.

"So you're a new man, huh?"

"Yes."

"Been in town long?"

"Poke him in the nose, Gil," came an alcoholic voice from the innards of the house.

Vance ignored the advice.

"I say, you haven't been here long?"

"About six hours."

"I see. Just a minute. I'll bring Mrs. Vance out, and she'll deny that there's any truth in this."

Vance was gone for some moments. He returned with a kittenish blonde, a good many years his junior, whom he led affectionately by the arm.

"Mabel, this is Mr. . . . . at . . ."

"White."

"Yes; Mr. White, of the *Examiner*. He has an absurd report that we have separated. I want you to deny it to his face."

The kittenish blonde giggled and lisped her reply.

"How perfectly ridiculous. Why, I wouldn't think of leaving Mr. Vance."

"You have no intention of separating?"

"Oh, no," they both chorused.

"That's fine. Can I use your telephone?"

"Bust him in the nose, Gil," came the alcoholic voice again.

"Sure, step right in," said Vance.

Whitey followed them into a large and gaudily furnished drawing room, somewhat dishevelled. The blond extra man was playing the piano. His Mexican inamorata was winding the phonograph, by way of providing competition. The leading man, in full evening dress, was asleep on a couch, breathing loudly. Three couples were dancing to the piano. A swarthy man was telling a long and apparently bawdy story to a mixed group. On a pile of cushions in one corner was sprawled a stocky, red-faced and rather morose gentleman with heavy and curiously assorted features. He was quite drunk, obviously, and glared at Whitey who assumed, correctly, that here was the source of the nose-busting advice.

At one end of the large and over-furnished room was a long table, crowded with bottles, tall glasses, ginger ale, seltzer bottles, a bowl of cracked ice and other appurtenances of the bar. On the floor were empty bottles, their straw wrappers strewn indiscriminately about.

"Telephone right here in the hall," said Vance, pointing. "Have a highball?"

As Whitey sat down at the telephone, Vance poured an almost lethal portion of Scotch whiskey into a tall glass, dumped in a chunk of ice, haphazardly added seltzer water, and placed the mixture at Whitey's elbow.

"Mr. Van Ettisch, this is Whitey," the reporter said, when his call eventually reached the city desk. "I'm calling from Vance's house. Yes, both Mr. and Mrs. Vance are here. They deny the separation. What? No, that's the only statement they will make. There's nothing to it. All right, I'll start back right away."

Vance had been listening carefully.

"There won't be anything in the paper about this?" he asked.

"Nope; not a word."

"That's great. Nice of you to fix things up like that. Have another drink?"

"Sure."

He led Whitey back into the center of things. Vance was more than a little intoxicated, Whitey observed, but was concealing it admirably.

"Boys and girls," Vance called, waving his arm like a prize-fight announcer, "want you to meet my old friend, Mr. White, from the *Examiner*."

"Poke him in the nose," came the voice of the man on the floor.

"Now, listen, Joe," Vance said, soothingly. "You lay off, see? This guy is all right, and he just did me a favor. Don't get on one of your fighting jags."

"Never saw a reporter in my life who wasn't a double-crosser," the bellicose guest muttered.

"That's Joe Greet," Vance whispered to Whitey. "A comedy director. He's always talking about fighting, but he's harmless. He hates newspapermen because they sort of jammed him up when he got tight and drove into a street car a little while ago."

Another puissant highball was forced into Whitey's hand.

"Make yourself at home," Vance said. "You don't need to be introduced to anybody. There's the bar, and it's cafeteria style. Just a quiet little family gathering, with everybody friends."

"I'm going back to work as soon as I finish this," Whitey said.

But he was wrong.

Chapter Two

Whitey awakened slowly and reluctantly.

He looked around the room, abstractedly at first, and then more curiously, because it seemed entirely unfamiliar.

He had a taste in his mouth as if someone had just burned an old-fashioned feather bed therein. His head was filled with whirring pistons, and the vague notion came to him that a complete printing press had been installed inside his skull while he slept.

After some moments of staring about the room, he found (a) that he was on a davenport, (b) that he was in someone's living room, (c) that he had removed his trousers and shoes but not his coat before retiring.

The room was not a pretty sight. A broken chair saddened one corner. There were a good many empty bottles on the floor. A chemise dangled from the chandelier. Briefly, it appeared that festivities had taken place there lately.

"This," Whitey told himself, "must be Gilbert Vance's house."

The conclusion did not satisfy him, however, as he continued the inspection. He recalled distinctly that the Vance drawing room had large studio windows toward the west, and there were none here. Moreover, the piano was in the wrong place.

Whitey sat up in some alarm. If not Vance's house, then whose was it? How did he get there? Was the owner aware of his presence? Had they parted on friendly terms? There were no answers to these disturbing questions.

Whitey relaxed with a low groan and tried to piece the evening together. There were large barren gaps in his memory. He remembered arriving at Gilbert Vance's home. He remembered questioning Vance about his wife, drinking several highballs, meeting what seemed to be an extraordinary number of people. He remembered talking intimately with a vivacious blonde, and he remembered banging away triumphantly at the piano for some hours and singing lustily. Then what?

Another thought brought him up with a start. Had he gone back to the *Examiner?* It seemed highly improbable, although he recalled that his employer had ordered him to do so. If that were the case, he reflected, the prospect of his still being a member of the editorial staff of that paper seemed remote indeed. In any event he had telephoned in the story. That was something, and he might be able to explain his non-arrival.

He rubbed his hands reflectively over his face and discovered that his jaw was tender and seemed slightly swollen. Another mystery danced before him. A sore jaw? Then there had been a fight. But where? And what about? And who was his combatant? And how did he fare? He glanced at his knuckles, but found no abrasions. Apparently he had lost whatever skirmish might have taken place.

He lay back and considered the advisability of arising and starting in search of a great deal of cold, cold water. This he did not do, however, partly because he felt incapable of the task and partly because he was vaguely fearful of whom he might encounter if he began to roam about an unfamiliar house, the occupants of which were, so far as he knew, total strangers.

"Good morning," boomed a cheery voice behind him. Whitey's jangling nerves catapulted him from his couch. A beefy Celtic gentleman, with protruding jaw and thick, battered nose, was smiling at him.

"How do you feel?" asked his host.

"I feel," said Whitey, searching for an adequate phrase to describe his distressing condition, "I feel . . . as though I could fly a Zeppelin under a dachshund. I'm just that low."

"I'm none too high myself," his host replied. "I have a taste in my mouth like a bag on a vacuum cleaner."

"Do you think I could promote a glass of water?" Whitey asked. The stranger obligingly fetched it for him, and Whitey gulped it avidly.

"I suggest," the host said, "that you wander into the bath. I've laid out a new toothbrush for you, and a cold shower might add a spark of life. If you don't mind, I'm going to ask you to hurry, because we've got to get started soon."

Whitey mulled over this last remark as he scrubbed

his teeth and stood gratefully under the stinging shower. Get started? Where, for instance? And to recur to a more familiar puzzle, who might this affable gentleman be?

Whitey emerged into the breakfast room eminently presentable. Over a period of years he had acquired the knack of appearing immaculate with whatever materials were at hand. His clothes never seemed the worse for sleeping in them, and with his black hair well parted and sleekly combed he bore no marks of the night before.

A copy of the morning paper was beside his plate. It was the *Times*. He glanced at it casually, but his casual air died abruptly. Prominently displayed he found a headline stating that Gilbert Vance's wife had left him. There was a photograph of Mr. Vance. There was also a photograph of Mrs. Vance, a statuesque brunette.

"Pardon me," said Whitey, gulping quickly and putting down his coffee cup, "is this a picture of Mrs. Vance?"

"It is," said his host, glancing over a bite of toast.

There were a great many things Whitey did not remember about the previous night. One of the things he did recall was that the lady who had been presented to him as Mrs. Vance was a short, plump blonde, and rather young. He laughed heartily.

"What's the trouble?" asked his host.

"Just that the journalistic career of Mr. White has

come to an abrupt conclusion in Los Angeles," Whitey said.

"Why, of course it has," his host commented.

Whitey glanced at him. Why, he asked himself, was this guy always making mysterious cracks like that?

They munched at toast in silence for some time, until Whitey's curiosity got the better of him.

"Pardon me," he began, "but would you mind telling me how I got here last night?"

"Not at all," his host grinned. "I brought you here. You were going pretty good."

"At what time?"

"I think it was about three o'clock."

"From where?"

"From the police station."

"What was I doing in the police station?"

"You were banging on the bars and shouting that they couldn't lock up a man from the *Tribune*."

"What was I in there for?"

"For hitting a policeman."

"Why did I hit a policeman?"

"Well, sir, a number of us were wondering about that. As far as I could determine, you hit him because he asked you to stop throwing ice at the performers."

"Performers?"

"Yes, the performers in the café."

"What café?"

"Don't you remember us going to the Pom-Pom last night?"

"I never heard of the Pom-Pom. What is it?"

"It's a night club in West Hollywood."

"How did we get there?"

"We went there after the fight."

"After the fight? How could we have gone there after the fight when it was there that the fight occurred?"

"Oh, I don't mean the fight with the policeman. I mean the fight at the Pyramid Club."

"Pyramid Club?"

"Yes, the gambling house we were in."

"Oh, yes. So we were in a gambling house?"

"Sure we were. Don't you remember that?"

"I do not."

"You should. You lost three thousand dollars there."

Whitey put down his cup so violently he almost broke his saucer, and stood up in sheer amazement.

"I lost three thousand dollars?"

"Yes, that and what money you had with you."

Whitey searched his pockets rapidly. He could not find a cent.

"Where did I get the three thousand?" he asked.

"You gave them a check."

Whitey's jaw dropped. He sat down and thought this over.

"Oh," he said. "Got a cigarette?" It was the only comment he could think of at the moment.

"If you can't afford to drop three thousand right now," his host suggested, "call Chet Vanderlip at the Bank of Italy and stop payment on the check. Chet's a good guy, even if he is a banker, and he'll watch for it. You can explain to the Marcus brothers you'll settle later."

"No," Whitey smiled, "that's not necessary. It will take care of itself."

At least, Whitey thought, it was cheering to know that someone thought he might have three thousand dollars in a bank, even if it were a bank of which he had never previously heard.

"If you've finished breakfast," his host said, "we'd better be going. It's after nine already."

Whitey rose meekly and followed without protest. He had no idea where they were going, nor for what purpose, but life had been more or less like that ever since he could remember.

The unidentified host's residence seemed to be in a series of bungalow apartments, Whitey noted, as they stepped out into the copyrighted California sunshine. Whitey was led to a garage from which his host extracted a shimmering, impressive roadster, bright green and equipped with all manner of highly polished silver and aluminum decorations.

A traffic signal stopped them at an intersection, and Whitey noticed a signpost that stated they were then at the corner of Franklin and Western avenues.

Whitey broke the silence shortly.

"Getting back to last evening," he began, "aside from losing a mythical three thousand dollars, whom did I fight and what for?"

"Why, as I recall it, you assaulted Lionel Lathingham in the corridor of the gambling house."

"I assaulted Lionel Lathingham, the movie star? What for?"

"The only reason you would offer was that you had seen his latest picture."

Whitey did remember having seen Mr. Lathingham on the screen while waiting for his train in Chicago. It was a pretty bad picture, he recalled. Apparently his mind had cherished it as a secret grudge which had flared up while he was in his cups.

"How did the fight come out?" he asked.

"It didn't last long. I came out of the roulette room just as you hit Lionel in the nose. Then we stopped it. Lionel said you broke his nose, but I doubt if it's really broken. Lionel is always dramatizing things."

A spectacular night, Whitey told himself. He had broken a famous film star's nose, assaulted a policeman, been thrown into and rescued from jail, paid a gambling debt with a rubber check, and wound up the evening in the house of a man whose name he did not know. He churned these details about in his still befuddled mind as he watched the Hollywood scene pass before him.

After driving off what seemed a sheer precipice and encircling a mound of bungalows, they were now climbing a broad, steep highway into the Hollywood hills. Whitey had little taste for scenery. What he wanted was any further news of the night before and information as to his destination. The trip was assuming the proportions of an extended tour.

"Do you mind if I ask one more question?" he began anew. "Just how and under what circumstances did we leave Vance's house last night?"

"It was around midnight," said his host, not glancing away from the highway, and continuing his dizzying speed. "There was quite a row and we decided to go."

"Another row? I suppose I was in that one, too?"

"You were, decidedly."

"Let's have it."

"Well, Vance went into the library and says he found you kissing Peanuts."

"Who is Peanuts?"

"That's his little blonde."

"I wonder if I was kissing her?"

"I don't doubt it. She seemed to be making a play for you."

"Is that right?"

"Yes, she said she adored your playing the piano as you did and insisted upon sitting beside you on the bench."

"Vance was pretty sore, huh?"

"Was he! A good thing he missed you."

"Missed me?"

"Yes, when he threw that bottle. It went through a window."

"Then what?"

"Well, Joe Greet knocked him down and we sat on him and discussed what to do. We decided maybe you two would not get along very well after that. It was then we took you up to the Pyramid Club."

"Who, for instance?"

"Oh, Joe and myself, and his girl Frankie, and Max Wagner, and Scott Pretty, and a few others."

"Who are all those people?"

"Say, you must have been going better than I thought last night if you don't remember anything."

"I never got that way before."

"It must have been that absinthe you were drinking."

"Was I?"

"Yes, straight absinthe, with gin chasers. It's liable to do that."

"I wouldn't doubt it."

There didn't seem to be much more to say. Whitey could think of no more questions and began to watch the road again. They had scaled the hills and were heading down the other side. In a few moments they turned sharply to the right and confronted a vast array of sprawling buildings in a hybrid species of Spanish architecture.

"Here we are," said the mysterious stranger, whirling in at an auto driveway.

"So we are," said Whitey. He thought he could venture that much.

A uniformed gateman swung open the iron portals with a flourish, and the big roadster thundered inside, the driver waving a friendly greeting to the sentinel, who smiled broadly and waved in return.

"Apparently," said Whitey to himself, "we are in a

movie studio. This dump couldn't be anything else."

Indeed, it could not have been anything else. An instant later he saw a sign which proclaimed it to be Colossal Pictures Corporation, Jacob Schmalz, President.

As they whisked through the street inside the studio at a speed which menaced the life and limb of pedestrians, Whitey caught confused glimpses of many people wandering about, actors in make-up, some in strange garb, some in evening dress, fat men in sweaters and knickers, lean men in overalls and Texas hats.

Brakes screeching, the roadster drew up before a red and yellow two-story building. The driver pounced hastily from the car and Whitey, feeling that it was expected of him, did likewise. The mysterious host raced through an open doorway and up a flight of stairs, the pudgy Whitey galloping along behind him. The hallway turned, and the guide flung open the door of a small room and said:

"This place is yours."

"Well," said Whitey.

"Look around the lot if you like. See you at lunch."

The unnamed man thereupon raced down the stairs and was gone. Whitey watched him, blinking in bewilderment.

"You will," he said aloud, "if I'm going to have any lunch."

He surveyed the room. It was furnished with a small desk, two chairs, a microscopic rug, and a wastebasket.

There was one window. The walls were bare except for a large, framed portrait of an elderly, smiling, Jewish gentleman. Beneath the photograph, on a brass plate, were the words:

JACOB SCHMALZ
President, Colossal Pictures

Whitey stared out of the window. It opened into nothing more important than a cement courtyard surrounded, apparently, by more offices exactly like his. He sat down in the chair, put his feet on the desk and stared at the wall for some time.

Then he said:

"Well, I'll be God-damned!"

Chapter Three

Whitey sat alone and almost motionless in his tiny office for some hours.

A person of less philosophical calm might have been tormented by worry. But worry never assailed Whitey. He had been finding himself in odd situations ever since he could remember. He was almost constantly broke, and circumstances had involved him in a great deal of trouble from which he had always emerged successful and triumphant. Equipped with unfailing good humor, an ability to view his woes from the standpoint of an unaffected and slightly amused spectator, and a knack for landing on his feet no matter from what dizzy heights he might be tossed, Whitey never doubted his ability to bring off any emergency.

He wondered about the future, but not with apprehension. His attitude was rather that of the interested reader of a mystery story who hurries through the book only to find out who really killed the District Attorney.

The telephone rang. It was the first communication with the outside world since his host had flung down the stairs. Whitey answered, prepared for any sort of mad message.

"White," said a voice unmistakably his host's, "meet

me in front of the Administration building in five minutes."

The receiver banged in his ear, and Whitey wandered into the hot, midday sun. He had but a vague idea where the Administration building might be, but instinct guided him toward the central wing of the formless mass of structures.

He took up his post there and watched the endless procession of humanity. There were pretty girls, a great many of them. There were a number of masculine faces with the unmistakable stamp of the German and Russian Jew, with dialects to match. There was a constant stream of workmen in overalls.

He had waited but a few moments when his host came upon him.

"Getting acclimated?" he asked, and seized Whitey by the arm. He apparently expected no reply, but dragged his captive through a small gate, across a lawn and into a large and noisy restaurant.

"Some people I want you to meet," he said, and placed Whitey at a round table.

Whitey observed that his host seemed not only popular but a person of no little importance, for almost everyone who came in stopped at his table for a word. Most of them whispered. All of them seemed to have a furtive air. His host graciously introduced them all, so that Whitey was constantly rising, shaking hands perfunctorily with "Mr. Unh-hunh" or "Mr. Yanh-hanh," and then being immediately forgotten.

The chairs at their table filled gradually. Whitey

noticed that his host was choosing the company with some care. There was Mr. Knopfberger, a fat, perspiring German, of pompous and profound mien. There was a small and wizened little man with horn-rimmed glasses and a black moustache, who was glancing about suspiciously as though constantly expecting a process server. His name was Diamond, Whitey learned, and he was, professedly, a writer of scenarios.

There was an enormous, broad-shouldered, beefy man who completely overlapped his chair and almost covered the table when he rested his elbows on it. His most distinguishing feature, Whitey observed, was a ripping, reverberating laugh which rang clearly over the din of the restaurant, and which he apparently could stop and start at will. His name was Tree, and he was introduced to Whitey as "our Scenario Editor."

"Very glad to know you, Mr. White," he said effusively. "Must drop in and see me right away. We'll get started on some things."

Whitey let this pass unchallenged, although he wondered what the things might be.

Lastly, there was an amazingly tall and lean young man, well over six feet, with a hawk-like nose, quick, nervous mannerisms and a seemingly inexhaustible supply of energy, for he was constantly popping out of his chair to button-hole a passer-by. His name was Brood.

"This guy," Whitey told himself, as a matter of instinct, "speaks my language."

There seemed to be no point at which Whitey could

take a hand in the conversation, although his unnamed host and Tree made abortive attempts to include him. They were speaking mostly of personalities with whom Whitey was not familiar, and they frequently laughed immoderately at remarks in which he found no humor.

"You got any hunches for the screen?" Tree asked him, in one of the attempts to engage the newcomer in conversation.

"Not exactly," said Whitey, leaving himself a loophole.

"Well, don't worry. A man like you will get 'em. I know you'll do some splendid things for us."

"Thanks," said Whitey, and borrowed a cigarette from Brood.

"What do you think of Sherwood Anderson?" Tree asked, after another silence.

"I like him," said Whitey.

"So do I. So do I. Marvellous. Marvellous." Tree replied hurriedly. His manner gave Whitey the feeling that Tree would have agreed with any opinion expressed.

"However," Tree went on, "his stuff won't do for pictures."

"I don't think," Whitey replied, "that it bothers him much."

This reply seemed to sadden Tree somewhat, and Whitey was left alone to study the scene about him. It was an enormous room, jammed with tables, every one of them occupied. In addition, there was a constant, boiling group edging and shoving about the cigar counter and soda fountain at the front of the room. The aisles between the tables, too, were filled with the overflow, cruising about from one group of diners to another, slapping acquaintances on the back, holding whispered consultations here and there, shouting across the room and bursting into frequent, loud laughter.

Through this mass, perspiring waitresses were pushing and shoving with loaded trays, and from the kitchen came a subdued rattle of cutlery and heavy crockery. Whitey, whose nerves were none too steady after his riotous evening, felt the desire to throw chairs madly.

Encircling the walls was a row of large framed photographs, more than life-size, with pretty girls and handsome men leering and gaping grotesquely at the diners below. Whitey assumed rightly that they were portraits of the Colossal actors. Over the door was the largest portrait of them all. There beamed the face which Whitey had found on the wall of his office, and under it a placard:

JACOB SCHMALZ
President, Colossal Pictures

Tiring of this gallery, Whitey glanced at the menu. Its cover displayed the same kindly face, with the inevitable accompanying caption.

"I'm beginning to believe," Whitey muttered, "that Jacob Schmalz really is president of Colossal Pictures."

He selected a tentative order from the menu and sat silent for some time, barely listening to the conversation at the table.

A new diversion presented itself. A hush fell over the room—a momentary one. Then came more bedlam than ever. People were springing from their chairs and rushing toward the doors. The men at Whitey's table, attracted by the din, began to peer. His host leaped up and joined the jam at the entrance. Tree, Diamond and Brood followed on his heels, strangely like a football team on the kick-off. Only Knopfberger remained, more gloomy, more profound than ever.

Out of this milling mass emerged, at length, a tiny man, bewildered by all the confusion, but smiling and pushing people from him, repeating over and over again, "Ja, Ja, Ja," with no apparent idea of what he was Ja-ing.

New as he was to this strange land, Whitey had seen too many pictures of the little man not to recognize him as Jacob Schmalz, president of Colossal Pictures Corporation.

Behind him came a sallow youth, no taller than Mr. Schmalz. He, too, was being clawed and pulled and screamed at. He did not respond to any of it but stalked along, silent and important.

"That's Mr. Schmalz, isn't it?" Whitey asked Knopfberger.

"Ja," was the answer.

"Who's the young fellow behind him?" Whitey asked.

"Dot iss his son."

Whitey watched the procession wind along toward a door leading into a private dining room. Schmalz and son eventually made it in safety. The door closed behind them. The pack quieted down, and the individual members started back to their tables.

"Have Mr. Schmalz and his son been away somewhere?" Whitey asked, surprised by the offensive reception.

"Away?" asked Knopfberger. "No. They haff been here for months."

Whitey started to ask what might be the occasion for the excitement. He did not, because he feared that the lugubrious Mr. Knopfberger might burst into tears at any moment. Later he came to find that there was no occasion for it. It was the customary reception given the Schmalzes whenever either emerged from his office.

Brood, Diamond, Tree, and Whitey's host returned to the table, a little out of breath. Whitey himself was out of breath a moment later when his host leaned across the table, in the manner of one making an immensely important announcement, and said:

"I told Mr. Schmalz about you."

Whitey had always been a good poker player.

"Did you indeed?" he commented.

"Yes. He was delighted that I was able to get you."

"That's nice of him."

Whitey's luncheon arrived, and he jabbed at it, thinking as rapidly as his tired brain could function. He came, at last, to a conclusion. This, he told himself, is more than a studio. It's a lunatic asylum as well. The thing for me to do is to keep quiet and see how many cards this guy draws. He evidently thinks I'm a big shot, and I don't see why I shouldn't let him think so.

The meal over, the diners arose.

"Mr. White," his host said, "there's no necessity for you to stay here this afternoon. You probably want to get yourself settled. I just wanted you to meet these boys. Come out in the morning and get together with Tree."

Whitey decided to play a long shot.

"By the way," he said, "I don't happen to have changed my bank accounts yet. Do you suppose I could draw a little money here?"

"Certainly." His host drew a pad of blanks from his pocket, started to write, and then looked up. "How much?"

That was a bad question. Whitey had assumed that he was on salary, but he had no idea what sum it might embrace.

"Oh . . . anything you say."

His host scribbled hastily and handed the slip of paper to Whitey.

"The cashier will fix you up," he said, and hurried off.

Whitey studied the paper intently. It was an order on the cashier of Colossal Pictures for one hundred dollars. His host had signed the name, Henry McGinnis. Under the signature were printed the words, General Manager.

A few moments later Whitey, a hundred dollars in his pocket, stumbled onto the highway and wondered how he might conceivably thread his way from this friendly asylum to the downtown hotel where he had left his bags the day before. The problem solved itself. A beautiful, blonde creature drove past in a racy roadster, jammed on the brakes when she saw him, and stopped with a screech of tires.

"Yooh-hooh, Whitey," she called. "Want a ride?" He did indeed.

"Hello, there," he grinned, and climbed in beside her. "I think I'm going to like Hollywood," he told himself as they sped away.

"I'll bet you don't remember me," smiled the girl as they whirled down the highway toward Hollywood.

"Of course I do," he lied, glibly. "I met you last night at Gilbert Vance's."

This was a reasonable assumption, Whitey decided. He remembered dimly having conversed with a pretty blonde who was not Peanuts Oliver, and this blonde beside him now was very pretty. Her hair was a little too flaxen to be authentic, but it was immensely becoming. Her skin was fair as only those who come from the far north are fair. Her blue eyes seemed to be the innocent eyes of a child. Her figure had made pudgy brokers ogle and wheeze with glee when she had revealed it in New York night clubs.

"I will admit," Whitey went on, "that I don't recall your name."

"I wouldn't wonder," she laughed. "You didn't even recall your own. Mine is Jane Wilson."

"I won't forget it again."

"Are you working out here?"

Whitey believed that he was, and admitted it. Then he asked the same question.

"Just extra work." She sighed. "I can't seem to get a break in pictures."

Whitey puzzled over the seeming incongruity of her doing extra work and driving a handsome and obviously expensive automobile, but discreetly said nothing.

"Do you know of a good place, not too expensive, where I could live in Hollywood?" he asked.

She thought for a moment.

"If you want a nice room," she answered, "I know of a lovely place. It's in a private home. I live there now with two other girls. A middle-aged lady runs it, and I heard her say the other day that she wants a man in the house."

"Now that," Whitey told himself, "sounds like a real spot."

Whitey had a way with women. By the time they reached Hollywood Boulevard she had offered to drive him to the Rosslyn for his bags. He protested; his protestations so nicely modulated that they were overruled.

II

At nine o'clock the next morning, Whitney presented himself at Tree's office, ready for anything. The bulky Scenario Editor greeted him effusively and mapped out a course of action.

"Now what we're doing at present," Tree began, "is searching around for a light comedy story. Sophisticated, gay, yet with its dramatic moments, and a touch of pathos or two, and a chance for some big production scenes and, of course, a lot of rough-and-ready action . . . you know what I mean."

Whitey didn't in the least know. The only story he could think of to fit all these requirements was a complete picturization of, say, the Civil War. But he nodded in polite assent.

"Now, since you're new to picture construction," Tree went on, "I've decided to hold a story conference this morning with some of our more experienced writers."

Half an hour later the conference began. Tree sat at the head of a long table, Whitey at his right, like the guest of honor at a feast. The furtive Diamond was there, seated next to a spectacled but not unattractive young woman who was at some pains to appear intellectual. Her name, it was asserted, was Dixie Devere, which Whitey doubted.

Present also were three gagmen, strange toilers in a strange profession.

There was Jeff Taggart, bulky, awkward, slow-witted, raucous. He wore white socks with low, black shoes, chewed tobacco, and shaved the back of his neck. He had entered the movies as a Keystone Kop. He had never originated—nor forgotten—a comedy situation. It was rumored that he had been a bartender. He denied this with particular vehemence because it was true.

There was Sigmund Wachtel, the permanence of whose position was assured. He was related to Jacob

Schmalz. It was once said of Sigmund that he would have appeared exactly the same with his head turned around, for he had the same bulges in front and behind. This condition prevailed even to his feet, which, like twin ferry-boats, protruded the same distance fore and aft.

There was Johnny Grunwold, who had graduated from Columbia to write the Great American Novel and found himself, eventually, on the Colossal lot re-hashing the worst American gags.

All were introduced gravely to Whitey and shook him by the hand, each murmuring a well-rehearsed speech of welcome.

"Nice people," Whitey thought, "even if they are nuts."

Tree encountered some difficulty in starting his story conference. Dixie Devere launched into a lengthy discourse upon a book she maintained she had read. No one bothered listening. Diamond discussed the purchase of a new car. Taggart and Grunwold talked of the prize-fights at the Hollywood Stadium. Strangers kept popping into the room to exchange pleasantries. Tree managed to achieve comparative quiet at last.

"Now the reason I've called this meeting," he began, "is to start Mr. White on the right trail, so to speak, in writing for the screen. Of course you all know Mr. White's reputation, and the sort of stuff he does.

"We've got to have a farce comedy story for Gilbert Vance right away. The Business Office is in an awful hurry."

"What's the rush?" Grunwold asked. "It'll take a month to get him sober enough to work."

"Now of course, I don't want to hurry you, Mr. White, but you've probably been thinking on some ideas of your own," Tree continued. "If you could just give us something . . ."

"Well," said Whitey, dubiously. "I don't know . . ."

"Of course you understand," Tree broke in, "there's nothing final about this. You know the sort of stuff we want."

"Last night," said Dixie Devere, "I saw that new Richard Dix picture . . ."

"I saw it too," Grunwold commented. "Let's don't make that story any more."

"The main thing is a lotta slap-stick," Taggart murmured confidentially to Whitey. "Pratt falls are always good."

"You gotta have a chase," Wachtel decreed, gutturally.

"Wait! Wait! Don't stop me!" shrieked Dixie Devere suddenly, apparently on the verge of apoplexy. "I've got an idea . . . it's immense . . . terrific . . ."

Whitey awaited this coming thunderbolt with interest.

"Our lead . . . he's a rich man's son . . . a play-boy, see . . . and he meets the girl in a night-club . . ."

"Yeah, I know," Grunwold interrupted. "But she's really a good girl, putting her kid brother through college."

"Nope," said Tree. "Night clubs are out. They been done to death."

"Anyway, where's your chase?" Sigmund asked.

Taggart sprang into action.

"Listen, I got your idea. Great. Lotta possibilities. But instead a' making him a rich playboy, let's make him a real he-man . . . he's a prize-fighter . . ."

"O my God, another prize-fight picture?" cried Grunwold, holding his head. "Why not make him a bartender, Jeff?"

". . . And he meets this dame in a night-club, where these crooked gamblers hang out who wanta fix the fight . . ."

"What fight?" Grunwold asked.

"Why the fight with the champeen of course . . ."

"What's the weight?"

"Don't interrupt me, Grunwold . . . and the champeen's manager is the racketeer what's trying to get this sweet little girl who falls for the lead . . ."

"It's lousy," Diamond said tersely, holding his nose.

"No, Jeff," Tree interrupted, "I don't think it will do. Some companies have made a lotta money with that story, but I'm afraid we can't use it again right now."

"Now, Mr. White, let's hear from you. Any random thoughts that may have come to you will help, and we can work them over."

"Well," said Whitey, "it seems to me . . ."

"Now perhaps we could get something out of this," Tree said. "Let's use the Damon and Pythias idea. We can team Vance up with that new juvenile . . . that sheep-faced ham the Old Man brought back from Europe with him . . . these two guys have been buddies for years, see? Went to school together, and grew up together, see? Then they come to New York, you see, and room together, see? And it doesn't seem as if anyone could ever come between them. . . ."

". . . But then Baby Came," Grunwold murmured, and winked at Whitey.

"Now listen, Johnny," Tree said, turning toward the dissenter reprovingly. "Let's cut out the wise-cracks. We've got to be serious about this. They're yelling for a story."

Grunwold rose and held up his arm.

"Teacher, can I leave the room?" he asked, and without waiting for a reply, walked out into the hall.

It was at this juncture that Whitey observed how dangerous it was for any member of a story conference to leave the room. No sooner had the door closed behind the thirsty dramaturgist, than the others dropped the discussion at hand to pounce upon him.

"That guy," Diamond sang out, "never had a funny idea in his life . . ."

"It beats me," Dixie Devere added. "Always destructive. Never creative. He doesn't know a thing about motivation, or tempo or any of the really finer things of pictures."

"I don't know how he gets by here. He must be somebody's brother," Sigmund Wachtel said. He had heard that expression somewhere. The irony of the phrase, coming from him, did not enter his mind.

"Steals every laugh he ever put in a picture," Taggart accused. "Only thing he's got is a good memory. He's still peddling the gags Chaplin used in his two-reelers."

Thirst quenched, Grunwold returned jauntily to the conference. The cries of the pack died instantly. He was a comrade once more.

This sort of thing went on for hours. It was all very confusing to Whitey. As far as he could determine, the purpose of a story conference seemed to consist of tearing to pieces any idea forwarded. Occasionally the others paused, momentarily, to ask him for a suggestion. He never got beyond "Well, now I . . . ," whereupon one of the other confrères would burst in with a noisy suggestion and bare his throat to the critical fangs of the entire room.

They knocked off for lunch, finally, and Whitey, divining that the same thing would go on during the meal, dodged an invitation to eat with them and slunk away to a hash-house across the street, hoping that temporary solitude might help him collect his mind.

After lunch they were at it again, savage as ever. Changing his tactics, Tree turned the conference into something resembling a Quaker meeting. The various creative minds were sent into a deep silence, thinking hard. To see gagmen think hard is rather a novel sight, Whitey found. They buried their heads in their hands, rested their faces on the table, twisted about in their chairs, ran restless fingers through their hair, and beat upon the wall, intermittently, moaning softly.

At irregular intervals, one of them leaped to his feet, howling like a wounded wolf, and began a series of short, disconnected sentences, sprinkled with oaths and accompanied by wild gestures and grotesque grimaces. It was the accepted method of advancing an idea. Even Grunwold, from habit, did it.

In the midst of each suggestion, Sigmund Wachtel would mutter lugubriously, "Gotta have a chase." Further along, Diamond was sure to say, "It's lousy," and accompany the remark with the inevitable holding of the nose.

Whitey observed that no suggestion was ever completed. Either it was torn to pieces before its creator had told it, or others interrupting seized upon it, twisted it here and there, mangled it horribly and dressed it in such fashion that it was entirely strange to its original creator. In the latter case, a violent, bitter argument was certain to ensue as to whose idea it had been originally. In the first of these battles, so raucous did they become, Whitey expected to see the combatants draw dirks. They always subsided after a time, however, and the late debators seemed as good friends as ever.

Finally Grunwold, by sheer loudness of voice and insolence of manner, managed to offer a fairly intelligible outline of a good, old, standard theme. Just as he was expounding his dramatic climax, Wachtel broke in:

"You gotta have a chase."

"Sigmund," said Grunwald, with patient resignation.

"We're going to have a chase. Don't worry about that any more."

He completed the telling of his tale, described the final scene, held up his hand for silence, and concluded:

"And now, Mr. Diamond, it's your turn to say 'It's lousy,' whereupon all the usual rituals will have been performed."

Late in the afternoon Tree, with his eye on the neighboring golf course, called a recess, announcing that the following day would be similarly spent.

"I think we've got something," he announced. "We'll all sleep on this, and talk it over again tomorrow."

He called Whitey as the group filed from the room.

"You're getting on fine, Mr. White," he said. "You'll get the swing of this in a few days."

"Heaven forbid," Whitey murmured to himself.

III

When Whitey had completed his first, somewhat bewildered week as a member of Colossal's scenario staff, he applied, rather timidly, at the cashier's window for his salary.

"What name?" the clerk asked.

"T. A. White."

A check was flipped across the counter to him. Whitey reeled as he saw the figure. One hundred and fifty dollars! And the hundred dollar advance having been deducted—as Whitey reasoned that it had—his weekly salary amounted to two hundred and fifty dollars a week. He cashed the check quickly, still believing himself in the midst of a pleasant nightmare.

Then came the dawn.

The next morning he found a note upon his desk which said: "See Mr. McGinnis in his office at once."

Whitey was ushered into the presence of the commander-in-chief as soon as he presented himself to the secretary. McGinnis and Brood awaited him. The atmosphere was noticeably tense. McGinnis held a folded newspaper in his hand.

"Mr. White," McGinnis began slowly, "does this, by any chance, happen to be your portrait?"

Whitey glanced at a half-column cut of a thin, sharp-eyed young man, printed beside a column of gossip labelled, *Broadway Banter.*

"Why, no," he said, "it says here that that is Thurston A. White, the wise-cracking columnist."

"It does, indeed," McGinnis said. "Which leads me to believe that you are not Thurston A. White."

Whitey's eyes opened wide.

"Who said I was?" he asked. "Did you think so?"

"You told me so," McGinnis replied without rancour. "You told me so at Gilbert Vance's party."

"Listen, Mr. McGinnis," Whitey said. "I suppose that's why I'm in your scenario department, because you thought I was that New York columnist. Why I've never been in New York.

"I'm awfully sorry, because I didn't know. If you remember that party, you will realize that I hit a movie star, and I didn't recall that; I lost three thousand dollars—theoretically—and I didn't recall that! I slugged a cop, and I didn't recall that. Now how do you suppose I was to remember whether I told you I was Rupert Hughes, or Walter Winchell or Anatole France? I might have, for all I could remember."

McGinnis was silent for a moment. Then he began to laugh, sheepishly, like one who has just undergone a fraternity initiation.

"I'm fired, I suppose," Whitey said.

"Have no doubt of it."

"But listen. I didn't know why you gave me that job. If I had, I'd have tipped you off myself, the next day. I'm nothing but a bum reporter."

Whitey turned to Brood.

"Why don't you give me a job as a press agent in your department?" he asked. "I'll pay back the money I got from the studio."

McGinnis was a good sport. He glanced at Brood. "Can't you fix him up?" he asked.

"I guess so," Brood answered. "Seventy-five a week." Whitey started to reach in his pocket for what remained of his first week's salary.

"Keep your money," McGinnis said, waving his hand. "It's on me. Or rather, it's on Jake Schmalz."

CHAPTER FOUR

DURING Whitey's one week as a celebrity he had settled comfortably into a rather peculiar home life.

Johanna Hubbell had spent an eminently respectable forty-five years in Whittier, California, a holy town. She had come of proper Baptist parents. She had sung in the Baptist choir and, at the age of twenty-three, she had married a proper young Baptist who foreclosed mortgages on week days and passed the collection plate on Sundays.

Johanna, as a matter of fact, was not meant for this. Her plump Baptist body housed the heart and instincts of a pagan. When her husband had been gathered to his fathers, she moved to Hollywood.

Her husband's estate gave her an income of five hundred dollars a month and about thirty thousand dollars in cash. She purchased a pseudo-Spanish hillside home in the midst of Hollywood's residential section with the latter and existed comfortably on the former. She yearned to make up for the dull, lost years in Whittier, with no idea how to go about it. She wanted gayety and song and wassail and mirth. She wanted to Live. Most of all, she wanted youthful companionship, and got it. Her house was too large for Johanna's needs, and she concluded that the best way to surround herself with youth was to rent a portion of her home to younger folk.

Jane Wilson saw her first. Assuming her most proper, maidenly air, Jane peeped at Johanna from her round, innocent eyes and was taken to the expansive Hubbell bosom. Jane paid her rent infrequently, and borrowed it back when she did pay, but she managed to inject a great deal of excitement into Johanna's placid existence. She brought Bobby Arnold into camp on the same basis. Bobby, recognizing it immediately as a happy hunting-ground for a hard working group of blondes, produced Peggy Lewis.

Jane and Peggy and Bobby constituted a trio the like of which had never endangered Hollywood before. All were young. All were blonde. All were predatory. A man with money was not safe within the same block. Among the three, the sum total of knowledge included every conceivable system for extracting money from males while giving nothing in return.

The house became a social center. Rolls-Royces, Packards, Cadillacs and Fords lined the curbing before the house day and night. Their owners came bearing furs, clothes, jewelry and gin. They were fortunate if they had sufficient gasoline in the tank to get them home.

The girls sometimes worked as extras in pictures, but not often, regarding it as a waste of time. The house was the scene of a constant party. The chumps frequently overlapped, and the place would be crowded with them. Jane and Peggy and Bobby handled the guests with the expertness of traffic policemen. Through it all moved the plump, innocent and quiveringly happy figure of Johanna, who marvelled that so many splendid gentlemen came to call and that her roomers were such nice girls.

She knew they were nice girls, for they invariably turned up, some time before morning, to the distress of their escorts, who had been at some pains to arrange that they would not. Johanna was at first a trifle puzzled by the blithe manner in which the girls accepted expensive gifts of clothes and sometimes money, but finally set it down to the harmless custom of a sophisticated age.

Into this battle-ground of the sexes Jane tossed Whitey, who took in the situation at one expert glance, smiled serenely to himself, and turned it into a shambles. Jane originally had catalogued him as an amiable young man with plenty of money who could be separated from it without much effort. She was wrong, and swiftly found it out.

Whitey worked diligently to establish himself in the hearts of all. He ran errands. He was always agreeable. He played Baptist hymns on the piano for Johanna and sang them devoutly. He played bawdy ballads—when Johanna was out of earshot—for Jane and sang them, not so devoutly.

His pleasant smile, fat, rosy cheeks and boyish manner, his unfailing good humor and his ability to accept any mood or mode of conduct which the surroundings of the moment required, won Johanna's heart and made him invaluable to the three blondes of prey. Whitey was not long in becoming the happy Sultan of Hollywood's gaudiest harem. He was precisely the sort that Janes, Peggys and Bobbys have clasped to their bosoms since the beginning of time. They take the toll from their victims. The Whiteys take the toll from them and return it to circulation. It is an economic law.

Whitey roamed about the seraglio, supremely contented. He ate the food and drank the liquor provided by the girls' paying escorts. He filled the house with nondescript friends of his own—newspapermen, bootleggers, press agents, actors, extra men, and other merry fellows. He did one thing that brought him out in sharp relief in Johanna's household. He always paid his rent. And, knowing a good thing when he saw it, he was always careful to keep his major peccadillos away from Johanna's ken.

Looking over the three maidens with practiced eye, Whitey fastened upon Jane as his personal possession, and set out to establish it as a fact. He was hard to resist. Jane could easily elude a more deserving swain who had lavished gifts upon her, wined her, dined her, and made her "temporary" loans.

But Whitey was a different matter. Pouring quarts of liquor down his cast-iron gullet, capering about in light lechery, looking like a little boy and acting like a satyr, he was a problem with which Jane could not cope. Women never attached any importance to being indiscreet with Whitey. The casual manner with which he approached an assignation was disarming. His candidates were always impressed with the belief that there was really no harm in him.

Precisely one week from the time that Whitey became a roomer in Johanna's homestead, he had assumed toward Jane that familiar male smile so akin to that of the tabby who has eaten the canary.

II

Although less remunerative, Whitey found his new duties as a press agent for Colossal Pictures not nearly so troublesome as those of a scenarist with a reputation to maintain. The tasks assigned him were neither difficult nor numerous, and after the years of hectic newspaper work, Whitey felt almost that he was enjoying an extended vacation.

Chief among his duties was the preparation of "press books." A press book is a folder of several pages, newspaper size, which is issued to theaters with every motion picture. It contains suggestions for advertising, synthetic reviews and newspaper publicity stories, in vast quantities and of a deadly level of dullness. Needless to say, the reviews and notices speak highly of the pictures with which they deal.

The owner of the Bijou Dream Theater, of Goshwump, Ohio, for instance, when he rents a picture from Colossal, will find in his press book such items as this:

"Passions of a Prince, the super-production of Colossal Pictures Corporation, directed by that master of the cinema, Heinrich McGinch, and produced by the Napoleon of the screen, Jacob Schmalz, will be the feature attraction at the —————————theater, beginning—————————."

This item, and all similar ones, will go on for paragraphs, extolling the superb cast of players, the heart-gripping drama of the story, the excellence of the direction, the richness of the settings, and the purely philanthropic intent of the producer in bringing such a gem of art within the reach of the masses. The owner of the Bijou Dream Theater fills in the blank spaces with the name of his playhouse and date of engagement and hands it, with his paid advertisement, to the editor of the Goshwump *Star-Eagle*. Without the paid advertisement, the notice has not the remotest chance of seeing print. With it, the editor will probably publish the item without bothering to read it.

Whitey soon was able to write them in his sleep.

There were other duties, too, but not particularly bothersome ones. He roamed about the vast studio, presumably gathering "news" items with which to bombard the daily press. He visited sets where pictures were in course of production. He placated actors who complained that they were not receiving sufficient publicity. He photographed stars with assorted brands of soap and conducted blind-fold tests for magazine advertisements. He was constantly chatting with extra girls and learning their telephone numbers, and cadging drinks at the dressing rooms of the male stars. He often wrote letters and speeches for inarticulate studio executives. He found this a pleasant sport, making it a practice to insert words which he knew the executives could neither define nor pronounce.

He was also called upon to welcome, with feigned

sincerity, the drove of small-fry newspaper correspondents and movie magazine writers who swarmed about the studio, searching, they said, for news, but actually hoping they might talk their way into scenario jobs.

The whole affair was greatly to Whitey's liking. He found a number of hiding places where he was safe from the nervous and bothersome Brood. He enjoyed naps in actors' dressing rooms during the long summer afternoons, or tucked himself away on some cool, dark stage not then in use.

He found, too, an absorbing and fascinating psychological study in the activities of the benign Jacob Schmalz and the army of his relatives which infested the studio. He was to learn there never had been a kindlier nor a more generous figure in the film industry than Jacob Schmalz. In a business manned and operated by rapacious dollar bloodhounds, Schmalz amounted almost to a miracle.

"Papa Jake," he was known in Hollywood; and how he was able to survive in the shark-patrolled waters of Cinema Land was a puzzle no one had yet been able to solve. Yet, not only did he survive, but he amassed a considerable fortune. His studio, conducted along no conventional lines, with a system of mismanagement that only Lewis Carroll, it would seem, could have originated, continued to prosper and add to his fortune.

He filled his payroll with incompetent relatives, and even placed them in positions of importance, yet his studio prospered. He hired and fired General Managers so often that his organization was in a perpetual state of chaos, yet his studio prospered. He squandered tremendous sums on stories no other producer would have considered, yet his studio prospered.

In an industry without a spark of loyalty, where a word of honor is almost an unknown quantity, he was intensely loyal to those in whom he believed, and even fellow producers accepted his word. His cousins and nephews and their children, and their children's children, sought to poison his mind against rivals, brought racial prejudices into play, carried on a deadly campaign of intrigue, pretense, back-biting and fraud—a campaign of which "Papa Jake" was blissfully unaware —yet his studio prospered.

The career of Jacob Schmalz was a living proof of the Biblical assertion that the meek shall inherit the earth.

Through this bedlam and chaos, Whitey moved serenely. He enjoyed it with all the delight of a little boy at the circus. The politics did not concern him because his position was too lowly to be coveted. Always supremely pleasant of disposition, content with his lot, Whitey, after years of roving, seemed to have found a haven. He soon made many friends. He always made friends, wherever he landed, but Hollywood was particularly suited to him.

Henry McGinnis, the reigning ring-master of Colossal, became his closest ally. He was a Scotch-Irishman, literate above his calling, friendly, affable and reasonably honest. He had started his career as an actor, advanced—or descended, as you view it—to writing scenarios, and was abruptly appointed General Manager on one of the sudden impulses for which Jacob Schmalz was celebrated.

McGinnis, amused instead of incensed by Whitey's deception, recognized the cherubic journalist as a civilized man, and came to unburden himself of his private opinions on many an afternoon. He had to talk to someone, and he trusted Whitey.

Brood, Whitey's immediate superior, became a friend, too, and an agreeable companion on those rare occasions in which he achieved a measure of calmness. Tranquillity, however, did not agree with him. He was constantly stirring up the animals with this or that spectacular scheme for quenching "Papa Jake's" insatiable thirst to see his name in print.

Whitey moved about both studio and living quarters, spending his money faster than he earned it, and basking in the warm California sunlight like a well-fed boa constrictor.

Chapter Five

For three months things had been going smoothly for Whitey—too smoothly. Consequently, one morning, when Brood came into the office walking fast, energy in his gait and the gleam of the fanatic in his eye, Whitey watched him suspiciously. He knew Brood had been talking to McGinnis, and he feared trouble.

"Whitey," Brood began, after leading his hireling into his private office, "you are the official manager of a banquet, the biggest banquet Hollywood has ever seen."

Whitey sighed.

"What's it all about?" he asked.

"The banquet is going to be in honor of young Sam. The old man is making him a partner in the business."

"Well, for the love of God, can't 'Papa Jake' take Sam into the business without giving him a banquet?" Whitey asked.

" 'Papa Jake' is not giving it. The employees of Colossal are giving it as a spontaneous testimonial to the popularity of young Sam."

"Like hell they are!" Whitey protested. "You and McGinnis cooked this up to red-apple the old man."

Brood eyed him defiantly.

"Whether you like it or not," he observed archly,

"you're in it. McGinnis and I have decided you're going to run it. So you'll do it and like it."

Whitey resignedly gave a mournful ear to the details.

Nothing on earth can equal the spectacle of a Hollywood banquet, and Brood was ambitiously preparing to outdo all previous efforts. There were to be more guests, and they were to be more celebrated, than in any affair of its kind. There were to be more and longer speeches, and a bigger and better dinner. The largest dining room at the Ambassador Hotel was engaged, and invitations were tendered all the celebrities and near-celebrities of Hollywood.

The expenses were to be defrayed by charging the guests ten dollars a plate. In addition, the employees were to show their esteem for Sam by donating a tenth of their weekly salary to buy him a watch. Sam did not need a watch. He already had seven. The employees did need the money. Nevertheless, the employees bought Sam a watch.

Do not imagine that the celebrities of Hollywood turned an unresponsive ear to Brood's imitation-engraved invitation to pay ten dollars for the privilege of watching Sam Schmalz eat. Hollywood operates on the Golden Rule basis of "You come to my banquet and I'll come to yours." Moreover, there is not a star, nor a director—not even a producer, however powerful—who is certain that some day he may not want a job with Colossal Pictures Corporation. Colossal is at the end of the cinema line, but the Hollywood skids run fast.

The return mail brought acceptances and checks by

the scores. Names that have rung around the world, names that have been identified with the biggest pictures and the biggest scandals, names attached to faces that are nightly flashed on screens in Moscow and Buenos Aires and New York and Singapore were placed on the list of "guests" at the banquet in honor of Sam Schmalz.

All this was acutely painful to Whitey. It caused him no end of trouble, for one thing, and for another, he resented young Sam Schmalz with a vigor which seemed highly incongruous in one of so placid and friendly a nature. Samuel Schmalz was not as offensive as Whitey believed. No one could have been. He had never been given an opportunity to become anything but a spoiled and arrogant son of a wealthy man. He had never been to school. His education consisted of what bits of information a dismayed tutor could beat into his head while following him around the studio.

The big lot at Colossal had been his nursery, his playground, and the limits of his world. He had grown up there, surrounded by his father's soothsayers and yes-men. He had been coddled and petted by sycophants, used as a political pawn by scheming relatives, flattered by job seekers, and smiled upon by the pretty girls. He had never been denied anything he wanted. He had never had to rely upon himself. He had never been told the truth. Small wonder, now that he had reached a point bordering on man's estate, that he was sometimes generous, more often cruel, intolerant, arrogant and unreasonable. He was a boy who had never had a chance.

Whitey did not realize that young Sam was thought-less instead of vicious, and, consequently, bestowed upon him a dislike worthy of a better cause. Whitey watched him strutting about the lot, hiring and firing his elders, inserting his fingers into many pies, tearing down the labored efforts of skilled workers with the whims of immaturity, and Whitey marvelled.

"They actually treat him," he said, "as though he were a grown man."

Despite his views on the banquet and its honor guest, however, plans for the event went ahead like the in-exorable march of time. A famous author was brow-beaten into acting as toastmaster. A song writer prepared a ballad about Sam. Broadway wits and Holly-wood gagmen prepared, for the program, sketches and bits designed at once to tickle Sam's risibilities and flatter his little ego. A two-reel film depicting his life was rushed through production at the studio.

As the date of the banquet approached, Whitey found himself in a maelstrom of inner politics. He was be-sieged by nephews and cousins and hangers-on. He was cajoled and abused by dukes and barons of the Schmalz dynasty. Even the most obscure relatives insisted on sitting at the speaker's table, right next to Sam. And if each one were not there, it meant Whitey's job. After a few days of this, Whitey ran in despair to McGinnis.

"It's a mathematical impossibility to put more than

twenty people at Sam's table," he wailed, "and he has more second-cousins than that!"

"Tell 'em to go and find a good, big lake," McGinnis counselled, unperturbed.

"Yes, and if I do, they'll make me jump in it," Whitey argued. "You know very well any one of those feeble-minded cousins can cost me my job by saying ten words to Sam or the old man. They'll do it, too, if I don't put 'em all up there."

"Listen to me, Whitey," McGinnis said, soothingly. "I've been officer of the day in this dump for a year now. That's longer than anyone else ever lasted. The old man thinks I'm great, even if I am a Gentile. I'll arrange the seating at this banquet, and I'll make 'em like it. You quit worrying about those Yid relatives."

The day of the banquet found Whitey with an excellent chance of losing his mind. The acceptance list exceeded five hundred, and Whitey found he must somehow contrive to jam additional tables into the room. Young Sam insisted on seeing the program, and when it was reluctantly shown him, demanded almost impossible changes. "Papa Jake's" secretary telephoned every five minutes to add another old friend to the list. Relatives, whose existence even McGinnis had never suspected, were dropping off every train. A long lost cousin was coming by plane.

Like a man watching kettles boil in two distant spots, Whitey raced hurriedly from studio to hotel and back. He must prepare the place cards. He must see that the fifteen hundred dollar watch was brought from the

jewelers. He must arrange for the delivery of four
cases of Scotch whiskey to the little barroom behind
the banquet hall. He must talk to a knot of indignant
cousins. He must explain to Siegfried Deer, an old
schoolmate of "Papa Jake," why he would not be permitted to make a speech in his vaudeville dialect. He
must sober up Gilbert Vance sufficiently to have him at
the banquet. He must explain to young Sam why the
evening's program could not be broadcast over the
radio. (Modest thought!) He must seize a thousand
loose ends and tie them together before the famous of
filmdom began pouring into the Ambassador.

At five o'clock Whitey sighed with relief and wiped
his brow. Things seemed to be coming through. The
tables were ready. The decorations were in place. The
fifteen hundred dollar watch was in his pocket. He
arranged the place cards at last in the order that Mc-
Ginnis had devised to conform with the intricacies of
the Colossal caste system.

Then, Whitey did a dangerous thing. He opened a
bottle of the banquet Scotch and took a drink. One
drink led to a second. The second, to a third. Whitey
was on his way.

Tucking the bottle into his pocket, Whitey leaped
into a cab and dashed home to don his rented evening
clothes. By the time he had jerked his tie into place,
the last of the Scotch had rattled down his capacious
throat, and it was time to start for the scene of the
orgy. Just tight enough to be in top form, Whitey
hurried to the banquet hall and found it in wild con-

fusion. During his absence, an army of cousins had sneaked into the hall and rearranged the place cards to suit their own desires. Friends had been separated. Prominent guests had been shunted far down the line. Russians who spoke no English were placed beside Greeks who spoke no Russian.

Whitey found McGinnis and Brood, and they leaped frantically to the task of straightening out the mess, while the guests collected and began to have at the Scotch. Only half an hour late, McGinnis, Brood and Whitey flung open the doors and waited for the complaints as the diners filed in. There were plenty. Young Sam was in a towering rage because they were late. The relatives were collectively indignant because their work had been undone. Actors cried to the heavens that they would leave unless given positions of more prominence. At last a measure of order was established. McGinnis, Brood and Whitey, soothing, explaining, threatening and apologizing, herded them into chairs. It almost would have passed for a civilized gathering.

The three Gentile workers in the vineyard surveyed the room. They sighed with mingled exhaustion and relief. Then they retired to the bar.

"Heaven help me," McGinnis sighed, clutching a highball, "I swore I'd quit before I'd go through another one of these banquets. But here I am."

"Yep," said Brood, "here *we* are. It's not as bad as the last one. Remember when we forgot to save a place for the old man's brother?"

"Do I?" McGinnis replied. "And Sam got so sore

because one of the speakers referred to him as a boy?
I'll swear I'm going to spank that kid some day!"

"Do you have these often?" Whitey asked.

"On the slightest provocation," McGinnis replied.
"The old man eats 'em up."

"Well," he said, "I've got to go in and sit down. I'm
supposed to make a speech." He took another one,
quick.

"We'd better all go in," said Brood.

Whitey slipped another bottle into his pocket and
followed them unobtrusively back to the banquet hall.

It was quite an affair. Charlie Chaplin was there,
extremely bored and wondering how soon he could de-
cently get away. Jack Gilbert was there, too. Why,
he knew not. Almost all of "Papa Jake's" fellow producers attended, among them Joseph M. Schenck, Louis
B. Mayer, with his two lieutenants, Irving Thalberg and
Harry Rapf, Carl Laemmle and his son, Jesse Lasky, a
quorum of the Warner brothers, Sol Wurtzel, Winfield
Sheehan, and B. P. Schulberg.

Present, too, were Richard Barthelmess, Glenn Tryon,
Reginald Denny, Jack Mulhall, Edmund Lowe, Norman
Kerry, Lloyd Hughes, Conrad Nagel, Monte Blue,
Frank Lloyd, Lewis Milestone, Alfred Werker, Richard
Wallace, Fred Newmeyer, Harold Lloyd, William
Seiter, Fred Niblo, Ernst Lubitsch, Cecil de Mille and
brother, William, Sid Grauman, and scores of lesser
actors, directors, writers and hangers-on in the film
industry. Some of them came because the Schmalzes
had attended their banquets. Some of them came out

of a sense of duty. Some of them came because they revered old "Papa Jake." Some of them came because they wanted jobs.

John Barrymore, as was his custom, wired regrets.

Everyone was reasonably sober, not because they wanted to be but because it is impolitic to be in one's cups publicly in Hollywood. The town is too small.

An expensive orchestra played loudly to drown out the din of so many actors and producers at food, and Whitey continued to marvel that such a collection of real celebrities could be gathered for such an insignificant event.

Incidentally, he did not neglect his Scotch.

II

Speeches had been made. Songs had been sung. Sketches had been enacted. Yawns had been stifled. It was late at night, and everyone wanted to go home. But the supreme moment, the *pièce de résistance*, had yet to arrive.

"Papa Jake" and young Sam had listened with every evidence of enjoyment to enough flattery, adulation and praise to turn the most hardened stomach. McGinnis, nerved to the ordeal by several covert visits to the bar, had made his speech and given Sam his fifteen hundred dollar watch.

With a blare of trumpets, the toastmaster introduced "Papa Jake." The kindly, little old man arose feebly to his feet.

"I am overwhelm by this occasion," he began, in a

quavering voice. "It iss splendid. I t'enk you all for coming to honor me und my boy.

"Now, I haff great pleasure to announce that my son, Samuel, has learn about the business and now deserves the honor I am about to place mit him. Not only haff I decided to make him a partner, but he iss also to be General Manager of my studio."

"Papa Jake" sat down amid raucous applause. There were a few startled faces. Chief among them was McGinnis.

"So Sam is going to be the boss," he muttered. "A hell of a fine way to break it to me."

". . . and a little child shall lead them," came a slightly alcoholic voice from a group of actors.

Young Sam was on his feet now and seemed to be addressing himself to McGinnis. As from a long distance, the dethroned General Manager heard him saying:

"At this time I wish to deliver the thanks of my father and myself to one who has been prominent in our service for the past year. I refer, of course, to Henry McGinnis, our General Manager for that time. He has been an invaluable and tireless worker, and to him goes a great deal of the credit for our past success.

"In honor of his retirement, and as an expression of our thanks, I present him with this gold fountain pen and pencil. On it is inscribed: 'To Henry McGinnis, with the best wishes of Jacob and Samuel Schmalz.'"

Sam showed his teeth in a leering smile, handed the package to McGinnis and sat down. McGinnis fingered the gift uncertainly. He could not make up his mind whether to thank the Schmalzes briefly and drop the incident, or to arise and hurl the gift at his late employers.

The necessity for making a decision was removed. Whitey had arisen, and was pounding on the table with the now empty bottle. He swayed magnificently, and his face gleamed with a satanic smile.

"I am undecided," he began, leering about him, "how to start this speech. The customary 'Gentlemen' would hardly do."

He paused to let this observation sink in. All hands were too amazed to interfere. Whitey lurched, steadied himself with his chair, and continued:

"In case you don't know, I'm going to make a speech for Henry McGinnis. After a year of successful work, he has just been disgracefully fired in public, and his services rewarded by a fountain pen you can duplicate in any drug store.

"I will close my remarks with this advice to Mr. McGinnis. A man who is badly treated in a film studio is no more entitled to sympathy than a man who is beaten up in a whorehouse. No gentleman should be caught in either place."

Whitey bowed and tossed the bottle to the floor. The silence was oppressive. Young Sam started to his feet and thought better of it. Whitey shoved back his chair and strode majestically for the door. Six hundred pairs of eyes followed him. Just as he was lurching through the exit, McGinnis arose.

"Wait a minute, Whitey," he called. "I'm going with you."

The gold fountain pen and pencil remained by his plate on the table.

CHAPTER SIX

THE ensuing party lasted for days.

The morning after the banquet found Whitey once more on Henry McGinnis' davenport. He remembered vaguely that they had launched out from the Ambassador, leaving a shocked and bewildered gathering behind, hooking three bottles of Scotch en route.

Whisper a secret to a trusted friend in the fastnesses of the Hollywood hills and, three minutes later, total strangers will be discussing it in Culver City. When Whitey and McGinnis dropped into the Brown Derby for a sandwich and a bottle of ginger ale, they found that most of the customers already present had heard of the climax of Sam Schmalz' banquet. Whitey was the hero of the evening. All Hollywood had been yearning to insult Sam for years. Whitey was the first to jeopardize his standing in the film industry by so doing. He pointed out modestly that he had no standing, and thus could jeopardize none.

McGinnis remained in something of a daze, his mood wavering between amusement and belligerency. Their table was the center of activity. Actors, directors and writers came to shake the hand of the man who had called Sam Schmalz out of name.

The next morning Whitey and McGinnis, feeling exceptionally low, washed down their bacon and eggs with Scotch. By noon they had purchased another case. By three o'clock they were at Johanna's, surrounded by Whitey's harem.

It did not take long for Hollywood to ferret out the party. By nightfall the house was overflowing with people, gin bottles, seltzer bottles, Scotch bottles, actors, cracked ice and Johanna. Joe Greet arrived, and, wisely observing that the demand for femininity was greater than the supply, telephoned for the entire chorus of a musical show. The chorus arrived in a fleet of yellow cabs, accompanied by four chorus men. The chorus men were kicked down the hill, and the cab drivers were brought in to join the party in lieu of paying the fares.

Whitey weaved gaily through the assemblage, like the master of ceremonies at a night club. He made surreptitious engagements with half the chorus, cautiously hid out three bottles of Scotch against the morrow, sang and played *The Gay Caballero* (uncensored version), borrowed twenty dollars from McGinnis when he found a psychological moment in which to do so, slept under the piano for half an hour and arose, completely refreshed, to become, once more, the party's most hilarious member.

Gilbert Vance and Peanuts arrived. Max Wagner, the most famous extra man in Hollywood, sang Mexican folk songs in a throaty baritone for an hour before he discovered, to his intense horror, that Johanna spoke Spanish perfectly. McGinnis became heavily amorous toward Johanna, which both delighted and frightened the hostess. Her Baptist morality was left undefiled, however, for after a brief attack upon its citadels, McGinnis fell into a deep coma from which he could not be aroused for hours.

The house emptied itself gradually. Gilbert Vance found that Joe Greet had taken his automobile, and retaliated by driving off an abandoned taxicab, the owner of which had departed with the last consignment of chorus girls.

Johanna at length found herself alone in a house littered with debris and blue with cigarette smoke. Only McGinnis remained, snoring thickly.

"I wonder," she said to herself, "what has become of Whitey and the girls."

She began a tour of inspection and came finally to Whitey's room. Poking her head into the darkened chamber, she saw someone in bed.

"Whitey," she asked, "have you seen anything of the girls?"

"No ma'am," said Whitey, unctuously. "Not a thing."

Johanna heard a giggle and snapped on the light. Whitey's round and slightly embarrassed face gleamed above the blankets. Under them, Johanna saw two other wriggling forms. Chemises and filmy garments were draped upon the furniture.

Whitey, Peggy and Jane moved the next morning, amid a deep silence. Johanna placed her home on sale.

II

The junction of Wilcox and Cahuenga avenues forms the apex of a triangle—unconsciously phallic—of which Hollywood boulevard is the base. The section contains innumerable apartment houses devoted to the three Hollywood G's—girls, gin and gynecology.

Starting from the Warner Brothers' Theater, where Hollywood rakes take their posts to wait for the dancers from the prologues, this tiny section of a city within a city sweeps upward to a smashing crescendo at the Major Apartment-Hotel.

When Hollywood was the peaceful village of Colegrove—named after Senator Cornelius Cole, who lived to be more than a hundred, but never saw anything like this—the triangular section once harbored the country estate of Paul De Longpre, a painter of flowers. Now it is devoted to gilders of lilies.

The triangle is Hollywood boiled to its very essence. Homesteads of old residents rub shoulders with the harems of producers' women.

Between these streets one can find actors, authors, artists, acrobats and astrologers, coon-shouters, chorus girls, confidence men, comedians, camera-crankers, Christian Scientists, and call-houses, directors, gagmen, song writers, sadists, psalm singers, soothsayers, and sycophants, press agents, pugilists, policemen, perverts, pickpockets, panhandlers, pimps, playwrights, prostitutes, and parsons and playgirls (both unfrocked), bootleggers, bandits, bookmakers and Babbitts, remittance men, radio announcers and realtors, Jews, Gentiles, Mohammedans and Rosicrucians, all living like Mormons, manicurists, mannikins, misanthropes, misogynists and masochists, women of all sexes and men of none.

The Major Apartment-Hotel had the cream of the collection. Into it moved Whitey and Jane, to add the finishing touch. The Major consisted of three floors above the ground and was familiarly known as the Riding Academy. The management divided the tenants into three classes and segregated them by floors.

The second floor was devoted to what were jestingly known as the Respectables, and the third to those who were gay but reasonably quiet. The top floor was designated as the Violent Ward. Guests were kept under scrutiny at all times and were moved about like chessmen. It did not take Whitey long to achieve the top floor.

No such collection of tenants has ever been seen in any hostelry save Matteawan.

There was Fanya Pausdrovnavitch, a Serbian, who kept a baby python in her room, and dipped batiks and snuff. There was Bob Carey, self-confessedly a gagman, whose friends got him jobs so he could pay back what he had borrowed. He always celebrated his jobs before he began them, and consequently was never able to arrive for the first day's work.

There was Fanchon Dubarois, a langorous vampire of the screen, whose reputed Latin ancestry was somewhat belied by the fact that her father was a Pullman porter. There was Marguerite Fish, a sheep-faced character actress, who was at once a Christian Scientist, a numerologist and a nymphomaniac.

There was Hank Strauss, a lean, aesthetic soul, who held revival meetings in the winter and dealt blackjack at Tia Juana in the summer. There was Elmer Thistlewaite, whose only visible means of support was a trained goose, which he rented for use in pictures.

There were three greasy gentlemen from Brooklyn who claimed European titles of nobility and did no work. There was another man whose father really had been a duke, but who claimed no title and sold automobiles for a living.

There was Jerry Straubel, a gloomy, gin-soaked intellectual, who conducted a salon on the top floor, and was at perfect liberty to coin and circulate his bitter epigrams on the film industry because he was not obliged to earn his living therein. There was Johnny Rocco, a dapper young Sicilian, whose profession of bootlegging had won for him a larger list of acquaintances in Hollywood than any one save, perhaps, Jim Mitchell of the *Examiner*.

On the third floor was a man who did not drink and had never been known to have an assignation with either man or woman. He was perfectly normal. Consequently, he was regarded with suspicion by all.

III

Jane Wilson, before she met Whitey, had never given her heart—not the remotest little corner of it—to anyone. A girl from up-state New York, Jane had started her rather remarkable career in the chorus of a Broadway show at the age of sixteen. Next season found her dancing in one of the more dubious Manhattan night clubs. She had been an apt pupil of the world's wisest school. Her motto was: Never give a broker an even break.

At the age of eighteen she had climaxed an all-night party by marrying a personable young man whose father really was a millionaire. The bridegroom had neglected to tell her, however, that his parent was no longer speaking to him. It took Jane fifteen days to discover that her husband was not only penniless but jobless, and fifteen minutes more to leave his bed and board.

He had developed, while in his cups, the annoying trait of breaking in upon her at night clubs and apartments and spotting her charming face with black eyes and bruised cheek bones. Wearying of this, and hoping for happier hunting grounds in the far west, Jane had cried transportation from a sympathetic admirer and left New York even more quietly than she had arrived.

Whitey had her number from the first meeting.

Something about his contradictory personality, his twisted sense of humor, and his nonchalant distaste for taking life seriously, fascinated her dangerously.

Her two years in New York and her year in Hollywood had not yet placed visible marks upon her. Men found her voluptuously innocent air completely devastating. Her personality was almost as contradictory as that of her consort. She could be greedy, avaricious, grasping and deceitful. She could be generous, friendly, helpful and kind. She would wheedle expensive gifts from rich companions, or walk ten blocks to save cab-fare for some moonstruck clerk with whom she happened to spend an evening.

Whitey took her money and her favors indiscriminately, drank her liquor, pawned her jewelry, often interfered with the pursuit of her calling, and generally managed to keep her on the border-line of hysteria. She adored him, coddled him, and not infrequently hated him. One thing she could never do was stay away from him.

Often his prankish cruelties and infidelities threw her into spasms of rage in which she beat ineffectively with her tiny fists on his round head, or screamed and hurled perfume bottles and dishes at him. Whitey, at such times, would protect himself in the clinches, dodge the bottles, and smile benignly. The tantrum over, she would creep repentantly into his fat lap once more.

"Damn you," she howled one day when she found he had held open house with four bottles of cognac an admirer had given her, "Damn you! I hate you! You treat me just like I do those butter-and-egg men . . . that's my racket, and you pull it on me."

"There, there," Whitey cooed, "Whom the Lord loveth he chasteneth."

IV

After his spectacular resignation from Colossal, Whitey made no particular effort to find employment.

He saw no economic reason for it. Jane took care of the rent. They had engaged a single room and bath for Whitey, and a kitchenette apartment for Jane, not as a concession to convention but to give Jane more elbow room for dealing with the trade.

Just at this time she had come upon a business man —the proprietor of a wholesale drug store in downtown Los Angeles—who was credulous even beyond his class. He really believed Whitey was her cousin and he financed Jane in a course of voice culture, at a price that would have trained an entire opera company. In return for this, he was privileged, sometimes, to hold Jane's hand and to buy dinners and gin for Whitey.

With his final week's salary from Colossal, Whitey had a little capital which he husbanded with a shrewdness surprising in one so profligate. For some weeks after they had joined the curious colony at the Major, his program did not vary much. He arose at noon and cadged breakfast from Jane. By midafternoon he was ready to go calling on the various tenants, all of whom he knew intimately after the first week.

He established credit with Johnny Rocco, the Sicilian bootlegger. He learned to avoid Carey except for those rare occasions when the cinema humorist was in funds. He drank many an afternoon away with Straubel, the gloomy Schopenhauer of the Major. He played pinochle with the three greasy noblemen from Brooklyn. He made friends with the baby python and developed a superficial taste for Science and numerology that he might have access to Marguerite Fish's third weakness.

By dusk he was always comfortably potted and in a mood for anything.

Jane invariably had an engagement for the evening to dine or dance or attend the theater, or all three, and Whitey was a free agent until early in the morning. It was his theory that once adequately tight, something always turned up. And he seemed to be right.

"What'll we do this evening?" Joe Greet asked one afternoon when the liquid level of the first bottle began to sink.

Whitey's reply stated his entire philosophy on the matter.

"I don't know," he said. "Let's take a few drinks and find out."

His attitude toward Jane was expansive and tolerant, a great deal more so than hers toward him, for she was intensely jealous, which he privately regarded as exquisite irony. He never gave the slightest concern to her actions when they were apart, which they were, frequently, from dusk until after midnight. His attitude was that she might be cheating on him, but for the life of him he could not determine when she was doing it. He could see no reason, consequently, why she should criticize him for what peccadillos life might offer during her absence.

During this brief but highly diverting period of his career in Hollywood, Whitey became a familiar figure in the movie colony, particularly to that section bounded by Wilcox and Cahuenga. His list of addresses and phone numbers became prodigious. He roamed in and out of apartment houses and bungalows drinking, playing, and singing like a modern troubador, inviting himself to parties, staying for dinner and ofttimes for the subsequent breakfast, engaging in frequent, amiable seduction of those sweethearts and wives left unguarded during working hours, and constituting a one-man scourge to the peace, quiet, and morality of the neighborhood.

At this time he made two particularly close friends, both of whom proved to be a considerable influence upon him. They were Joe Greet and Grace Harper.

Joe, who had started the acquaintance by advising a mass attack on Whitey when they first met at Gilbert Vance's party, ended by becoming his confidant and constant companion.

No stranger character ever entered Hollywood than Joe. At the age of sixteen he emerged cautiously from a box-car in the Southern Pacific yards, a screen-struck, gawky lad. He had become an extra man and a double in dangerous scenes. By some strange process of reasoning, a producer had tried to make a comedy star of him and even filmed a number of one-reel comedies in the attempt. The comedies were frightful, even for one-reel comedies, and Joe was fired. He starved for months, lurking about the studio of his late employment to rifle his fan mail of stamps and quarters which the morbidly curious had sent with requests for his photograph. Even the dog and horse stars in Hollywood get fan mail, but Joe's became less and less as more and more of his comedies were shown. Hunger at last drove him to take a job running a projection machine in the studio where he had been a star.

Bad actor as he was, Joe had a strange sense of humor and a distinct knack of putting it on the screen. Some years later found him a comedy director, half-genius and half-lunatic. He became fat and mature, shrewd and intelligent, in a mad sort of way. He brooded much on the dark ways of the universe. He read heavy volumes, selecting them helter-skelter, and changed his viewpoints radically with every new discovery. He was always falling heavily in and out of love and as constantly in and out of jobs. He received three hundred dollars a week when he worked, and lived on a grand scale in a large apartment at the Major. When he was out of work, he crept into a dingy furnished room and waited, uncomplaining, for another job. All in all, he made a splendid running mate for Whitey.

Grace Harper was a dark and rather attractive girl whose visible means of support, working as an extra in pictures, seemed oddly matched with her smart roadster and expensive apartment. Whitey met her while visiting the set where Joe was directing a comedy. In seven minutes he had learned her name, address, telephone number, peculiarities, and vulnerable points of approach.

"Go ahead," Joe told Whitey, when the first conversation was over, "have your fun. Only it can't be done."

"What can't be done?" Whitey asked.

"Grace."

"Five gets you ten it can," said Whitey confidently.

The current price of gin in Hollywood was two dollars a bottle. Whitey bought two bottles with the bet he won from Joe.

Never had Whitey found a more convenient arrangement. From midnight until noon his time belonged to Jane. Three evenings a week he averaged with Grace. It came to be tacitly understood between them that Tuesday and Friday always found her with an engagement. Whitey was too tactful to ask with whom she might have those engagements. He trusted his journalistic abilities to find an answer to that question in due time.

Since Grace Harper never used her roadster on either Tuesday or Friday, it became the custom for him to borrow it on those evenings. Driving Grace's car home to Jane, after a pleasantly riotous brawl elsewhere one evening, Whitey sighed contentedly.

"Who said a man can't eat his cake and have it, too?" he asked himself oracularly. Then he added: "Thank God for broad-minded women!"

Chapter Seven

After a blissful month of this, Whitey did, for him, a surprising thing. He started to work.

At ten o'clock one morning the telephone jarred him from deep slumber.

"Whitey," said a familiar voice, "this is McGinnis."

"What are you doing up in the middle of the night?" Whitey complained sleepily.

"I'm a working man," McGinnis said, "and I'll make one of you. Do you want a job?"

"I can't see any future in work, myself," Whitey observed, "but it seems to be fashionable. What's it all about?"

"A job that's made for you. I'm now Production Manager for an outfit making pictures with Mme. Rethea Clore."

"That old battle-axe can't make pictures, can she?"

"Not herself. From her books. You know the stuff she writes—you're just the kind that would read it."

"What am I supposed to do?"

"Publicity for the old dame. She's as crazy as— well, she's the craziest author I ever knew—I can't go any stronger than that. You're the only press agent I know who could get along with her. Come on over."

An hour later, Whitey presented himself at Mc-

Ginnis' office in one of Hollywood's rental studios. His pink face glistened, and his black hair was glued neatly to his head.

"Now listen, you little gargoyle," McGinnis said, leading him down a hallway, "play your cards well and you're set for life. She dotes on young punks like you. Don't be surprised at anything she says. And, above all, don't wisecrack her. She's nine hundred years old. She has three million dollars and no sense of humor, but she's as smart as an auctioneer. Be profound."

They were ushered into a surprising office. The walls were of a ghastly green. The windows had been recut into irregular jagged triangles. A large tiger-skin had been thrown over the dark, sinisterly red rug.

Behind a semi-circular oaken desk sat Rethea Clore. She matched the office! Rethea Clore was said to be part Russian, part French and part Cockney, and looked it. Her age Whitey guessed to be fifty. He was twenty years too low, but she might easily have passed for thirty-five. Her hair was a dark, unnatural red. Her eyes were the color of crème de menthe. Her features were sharp. Her mouth drew a long, tight line across her face. Her gleaming white teeth suggested fangs. She was dressed in a long, severe garment of black, and she wore many large emeralds to match her eyes.

Rethea Clore clutched the edges of her unusual desk and leaned forward, regarding Whitey searchingly as a hungry lioness peers through the bars at a fat child.

"Madame Clore," McGinnis began, "this is Mr. White."

The searching scrutiny continued for some time.

"Your name," she said "is wrong. You are not White. It does not suit you. Your name should suggest color—passion—crimson. You are dangerous."

Whitey did not change expression. He thought rapidly, but the only answer he could find was wholly inadequate.

"Perhaps you are right," he gurgled.

"I am always right," she said. "You are a tiger man."

McGinnis knew his stuff.

"Your searching analysis of character intrigues me, Madame Clore," he said. "How do you class me?"

Mme. Clore moved her gaze as an electrician would focus a spotlight.

"You," she said slowly, "are bovine."

McGinnis grinned. Whitey turned and bowed to him.

"Leave me alone with Mr. White," Mme. Clore ordered. McGinnis nodded and started for the door when the telephone on her desk called the authoress' attention momentarily. As she answered it, McGinnis whispered to Whitey:

"I think she likes you. 'Yes' her all over the joint and in a week you'll be wearing a tiger skin."

Mme. Clore turned again to Whitey, who met her stare unflinchingly.

"You have soul—the soul of an artist," she declared. "I can feel it. We will do wonderful things together."

"I hope so," observed Whitey, trying to be fervent, while he said to himself, "that's the old oil."

"Hope! One of the greatest things in the world," she discoursed. "Genius is the only greater thing. I have both."

"I'm sure of it," Whitey confirmed her.

"You have read my book, *The Tigress?*" she asked, switching the conversation's trend abruptly.

He was too practiced a liar for her.

"Three times," he said. "It is splendid."

"Splendid? Splendid is a pale word. *The Tigress* is the greatest book ever written in English. Millions of copies have been sold—are being sold."

"Really?" Whitey asked, observing mentally that she could outdo him on any sort of praise he might venture.

"Millions. *The Tigress* is the love story of all time. Into it I poured all my intense soul—my feeling—my power—my genius—my sense of Love. . . . Love! *Love!* What a divine thing it is! Not carnal passion, but a pure and holy flame . . . a white heat of feeling . . ."

"I have always felt that way, too," Whitey said, thinking smugly of both Jane and Grace.

"*The Tigress* will be ranked by succeeding generations with the Bible. It will be remembered when all other fiction but the works of Shakespeare is forgotten."

Whitey was tempted to reply, "the hell you say," but did not. The swift thought came that McGinnis

had unloosed a maniac upon him. Not daring to comment one way or the other on Mme. Clore's rather lib-
eral predictions, he sought refuge in asking permission
to smoke.

"If you like," she said, waving a bejeweled hand in
regal disregard.

Whitey, the soul of generosity, offered her a cigarette
from a crushed paper package.

"I do not smoke," she said. "The thought of women
smoking is abhorrent to me."

They talked for an hour, Whitey feinting cautiously,
but keeping a glove over his chin at all times. The conversation revolved about Mme. Clore. She reiterated
the fact that *The Tigress* was the greatest of all fic-
tional creations; that it was a story of pure and holy
love, despite some jealous critics who had commented
that it was a tale for and by the mind of a chamber-
maid; that Mme. Clore detested smoking in women, or
drinking in either men or women; that necking was
equally as abhorrent because it "frittered away the
holy passion," by which she seemed to set great store;
that she was in reality a titled Englishwoman who chose
to conceal her identity for her art; that she never read
modern works, save her own; that she was an authority
on virtually everything; that she was an intimate of the
rich and famous in every land; that she was a familiar
figure in all the European courts (royal, not police);
that, although she had never attempted motion pictures
before, she was about to demonstrate her all embracing
genius by making the screen version of *The Tigress*

the most artistic and commercially successful film production in history.

Whitey staggered out, somewhat dazed, and sought counsel with McGinnis. Seeing that he needed a drink, McGinnis supplied one, and then explained the situation.

"I've got you on the payroll at a hundred a week," he said. "It's more than you're worth, but, what the hell, it's not my money.

"The old dame has a fortune, I guess. That pornographic book of hers really has sold into the millions, and she's written some others. She seems to have a lot of drag with the public, for reasons unknown to me."

"Does she really believe all that parsley about her book?" Whitey asked.

"Does she believe it? Sure she believes it. You mean that stuff about Shakespeare and the Bible? I thought she was clowning when she first pulled that on me, and it almost cost me my job."

"What am I supposed to do?" Whitey asked. "Follow her around and let her practice those theories of the divine passion on me?"

"That," said McGinnis, "is something that will have to work itself out. Just now she seems to have a blond young Limey in her wake. If you can muscle him out, that's up to you. It doesn't interest me, because I'm too old for that sort of thing."

"Are you the head boss of this outfit?" Whitey asked.

"No. I'm only the production manager. Moe Fishbein got her first, and he's taking her plenty. I think she's putting up all the dough. I never heard of Moe doing any pitching."

"Well," said Whitey, rising to depart, "give me another drink and I'll try it."

II

For the first time in his life, Whitey saw his name lettered on the door of an office. It wasn't much of an office—a cubbyhole barely large enough to contain a small desk and two chairs. To Whitey, who had been accustomed to the haphazard use of any typewriter in the midst of a noisy city room, or to bending his nose over a copy desk, bumping elbows with his fellows, it was magnificent.

He settled into this tiny sanctuary comfortably, prepared to collect his one hundred dollars a week with a minimum of effort. He did not reckon, however, with the difficulties of dealing with three separate and conflicting dervishes of energy and misdirected enthusiasms —Rethea Clore, McGinnis and Moe Fishbein.

Fishbein was a tall and almost completely bald Polish Jew. His broken English effectively concealed a shrewdness and cunning which had guided him profitably through a lifetime in the theatrical business. He was constantly edging into ventures where someone else advanced the money. He had been in almost all the major film companies. All of them eventually had paid him large sums to get out before he stole the film out of the cameras. He produced an idea a second, some of them not bad. His conception of efficiency was to keep every employee in a lather of apprehension and fear. He combined an insatiable taste for personal publicity with an exaggerated opinion of its value. Thus he was a constant distress to the procession of press agents who filed through his employ. He goaded McGinnis, who, in self-defense, goaded Whitey, who fled to the bosom of Rethea Clore.

Whitey was forced to spend some hours every day in consultation with the authoress. The conferences were devoted to monologues upon the magnificence of her writings and diatribes against anyone who opposed her on any matter.

McGinnis and Fishbein did offer some opposition to her more bizarre theories on the manufacture of motion pictures. Even though her money was at stake, both men had a standing of a sort to maintain within the industry and could not afford to be connected with a production too conspiciously unsuccessful. They persuaded her, at length, that it would be best to engage an experienced director instead of making the picture herself. It was only after a mighty series of battles that they dissuaded her from giving the leading role in the picture to the blond and totally inexperienced young Englishman in her train.

A disinterested designer was finally foisted upon her to create the settings. Mme. Clore screamed loudly that she was the supreme authority upon such things, and could do it much better herself. This so annoyed the capable young artist engaged for the task that he secretly inserted into the settings a host of almost undisguised phallic symbols, which would have driven Mme. Clore into hysterics had she ever heard of such things.

Whitey heard all these arguments enacted twice, once in deadly earnest by Mme. Clore, and once in a rough burlesque by McGinnis. He heard from Mme. Clore, also, lengthy and repetitious denunciations of Hollywood, with particular reference to the oafish stupidity of film producers, the barbaric crassness of the entire cinema industry, and the vulgarity of Americans in general.

For one who had written so prurient a novel, Mme. Clore was a constant marvel to Whitey. He could not determine whether her professed prudery on almost every subject was the result of a pose or of senility. He listened to her patiently, day after day, and often wondered just how unbalanced she really was. He observed, beneath her irrational bombast and spectacular conceit, a shrewdness and cunning not to be discounted. She was a bit balmy, no doubt, but not to the extent that her conversation might indicate. Many of her loudest conceits were to attract attention. Many of her poses were studied to develop "personality." Her tantrums were turned on and off to suit her convenience. Her confidences were lavished upon every member of the troupe in order to gain allies and create tale-bearers.

III

Mme. Clore, too, inspired no doubt by the leering Fishbein, began to hunger for greater attention in the public prints. One fine morning she tossed a particularly alarming bomb under the placid Whitey.

"Mr. White," she began, after summoning him to her lair, "I have something most important for you to do."

Whitey was accustomed to such advance pother over trivialities, and asked for details calmly enough.

"I wish to have a reception for the press of Hollywood," she said. "You are to arrange it."

Whitey had seen receptions for the press of Hollywood, and recoiled in horror.

"Really, Madame Clore," he said, "I'd advise against that . . ."

"I have decided," she interrupted, firmly.

"But have you met all these mangy press representatives in Hollywood?" he asked. "Some of them are pretty terrible, and you can't ask one without asking them all."

"How many will that be?"

"About fifty or seventy-five, all together. They're jealous as cats, and if you leave one out, you've made an enemy for life."

"We will have them all," said Madame Clore regally. "What kind of a party?"

Mme. Clore struck an effective pose, and thought hard.

"I have it . . . a tea. And chamber music. I know some very splendid Russian musicians. They will provide music."

"And you're going to serve tea?"

"Certainly."

"I'm sorry, Madame Clore. . . . you understand that I'm thinking of your best interests, and the interests of the picture . . . but nobody ever served tea at a Hollywood tea. Especially at a party for the press."

"What are you suggesting?"

"I'm suggesting about five cases of Scotch—maybe six."

"You know my attitude toward drink."

"I do. I know the attitude of the press toward it, too. They're a bunch of human vats. Now, Madame Clore, I presume you are doing this only to help exploit your picture. I know these people. If you serve them tea and try to make them listen to Russian music, they'll stamp out in a body, and abuse you all over Hollywood . . . and all over their publications."

Mme. Clore was horrified, so she said, and announced that she had met many charming journalists. She could not believe the American press was so abased.

"Why you yourself, Mr. White," she said, firing an almost unanswerably diplomatic broadside, "were lately of the press."

"That's true," Whitey countered, "but most of these people are not. Most of them are bums that couldn't hold a job on a newspaper. Some of them are all right, but the rest are a lot of moochers. A Hollywood party to them means a riot, at which someone else supplies the riotous materials."

So it was decided that Whitey should stage a reception for the press at the Beverly Hills home Mme. Clore had engaged. Chamber music was to constitute the entertainment. Tea was to be served.

Moaning piteously, Whitey ran to McGinnis, from whom he received no comfort.

"If the old dame wants to serve 'em tea or dog biscuits, it's not off your hide. You're getting a yard a week for the softest touch outside of being President. What do you care if they crab the Madame's shindig?"

"You don't know these pirates," Whitey wailed. "They'll walk out on us, and they'll ride Mme. Clore from now on. I went to one of these things when I was at Colossal. The liquor didn't arrive for an hour, and I thought they'd pull the walls down."

Whitey even appealed to Fishbein, whom he generally avoided diligently. This desperate effort was useless. Fishbein had staged too many quarrels with his angel already, and foresaw many others in the future. He could not afford to cross her in this because, as he philosophically told himself, it wasn't old man Fishbein's son they'd be burying. Even as he refused intervention, he prepared to toss Whitey to the wolves if the press reception went awry.

Whitey prepared for the event with grave misgivings. He did copper his own bets as best he could. He delivered the invitations personally, by telephone, and to each prospective guest he made it clear that the party was to be strictly non-alcoholic, and that in the event of their attendance they would listen to Russian music and like it. Nobody believed him.

Early on the afternoon of the reception, dressed in his new blue suit—shaven, shined, shorn and sober— Whitey waited in the drawing room of Mme. Clore's temporary home, highly apprehensive.

Mme. Clore, queerly but impressively gowned, eyes greener, hair redder than ever, stalked imperiously about and did some refined gloating on Whitey's behalf.

"I fear," she began, with that peculiarly insolent manner she always assumed when trying to be flippant, "I fear, Mr. White, that you were unduly timorous about our little afternoon."

Whitey said nothing, but peered out of the windows nervously, biting his nails. Again and again he tried to assume the careless abandon which had seen him through so many years.

"This old girl," he told himself, "must have the Indian sign on me."

They began to come—a gurgling, gossiping, thirsty crew. Whitey's heart turned to paste. It was worse than he had anticipated. He received them at the door and presented them to Mme. Clore. With horrified eyes he watched them peering about the spacious rooms, searching for the bar. All had taken Whitey's invitation lightly. The combination of Hollywood's playboy and the exotic authoress did not go with tea and concerts, they reasoned, and flocked forth gaily as to a jamboree. There must have been sixty of them, as oddly assorted a menagerie as one could have gathered from all the seven seas.

There was Lucille Jettifer, the terror of them all, because of the power attached to her position as editor of a leading film publication. A plump, middle-aged woman in flapper garb, her tired, whining voice expressed a life-long petulance. She was constantly expecting to be offended, and inwardly preparing revenge on the printed page.

There was Jennie Queen, also middle-aged, but dowdy, giggling and smirking, exchanging the latest and bluest Hollywood gossip. She was a prurient spinster, virginal of necessity, spending all her waking hours in an actively reciprocated hatred of Lucille Jettifer.

There was Basil Kingsford, a pale young man with a British accent too thick to be plausible, and a manner so offensive that Whitey had always suspected him of being a relative of Sam Schmalz.

There was Gladys Parkins, enormous of girth and weighing a good twenty stone, soggily unattractive, possessed of the delusion that all males were pursuing her with immoral intent and the fear that something would deter them. She wrote monthly articles on the *Love Confessions of the Film Stars* for one of the more vapid magazines.

There was Wilhelmina McKittredge and her lugubrious husband, Jimmy. Hollywood was wont to say they were perfectly matched, as neither could possibly have trapped any other mate. She had long since been granted all Hollywood non-stop conversational prizes, winning hands down despite false teeth. He was the official heavy drinker of the press. Both were intensely jealous.

There was Beatrice Raftery, semi-officially known as the Iron Horse. She was taller than Gladys Parkins, but about the same shape, red-faced, breathless and eternally agog. She bore the title of editor and wore a robe of intellectualism some sizes too large for her.

There was Bill Kelley, small, timid, ineffectual and unimportant, who would have crawled from a hospital cot to attend a press function.

There was Captain Arthur Johnson, a former British army officer and a gay old dog, who came to all such parties hoping for good Irish whiskey.

There was Minnie Hebner, two inches too tall for Singer's Midgets, who changed her hair and religion twice a year. She babbled in baby talk and was an expert at feeling hurt.

There was Bobby DeSales, a sleek young man whose connection with Lucille Jettifer's publication, it had been rumored, was a trifle more than that of an employee, and whose frequent breakfasts with Lucille somewhat substantiated the rumor.

There was Herman Jones, publisher and editor of the *Hollywood Weekly*, who had never been seen in public without a roll of the magazines under his arm, which he gave away like handbills. He had managed to break into the *American Mercury's* "Americana" column more frequently than any other one writer.

There was Johnny Moon, a youth of twenty, all black hair and teeth, who had elbowed his way into a side job as scenario writer by limitless praise in print of the studio officials on whom he had fastened.

There was a sneering, shifty-eyed representative of an "inside" theatrical publication, looking for and manufacturing evil; there was a representative of an obscure Swedish film publication, who worked mornings in a delicatessen; there was a representative of an equally obscure German film publication, who badgered his countrymen in the studios to get him extra work; there was a representative of an even more obscure French film publication, who also had the agency for a hand laundry; there were daily newspaper reporters covering Hollywood, present frankly and self-confessedly for a drink; there were space writers for eastern newspapers and the foreign press; there were several ringers who had heard of the party and eased themselves in.

There was also present Virginia Morris, a writer for the movie magazines. She was distinguished from her sisters by being both attractive and congenial. She worked at the trade because it was easier than being a stenographer.

Through this gabbling mob weaved Whitey, diplomatic and fearful, shaking hands, breathing apologies, soothing ruffled egos, shunting off too malignant pests, trying to keep Mme. Clore from being trampled to death.

There were high-spots. Five magazine writers

(three female) tried to interest Mme. Clore in their original screen stories. Four writers (two female) demanded that they be engaged, on the spot, to write the scenario for *The Tigress*. Gladys Parkins accused Johnny Moon of making improper advances to her, and he laughed so derisively that she was more indignant than if he had. Lucille Jettifer and Jennie Queen sneered sweet barbs. Wilhelmina McKittredge cornered Mme. Clore for a disastrous ten minutes and proved, for all time, that her supremacy at uninterrupted conversation was international.

The rakish ex-army officer from Britain pranced about the younger women goatishly, pinching their legs, and eyeing Mme. Clore speculatively. Izzy Jamieson, from the Ghetto, operating under the lifelong belief that he was a wit, told stories in a Jewish dialect to the discomfiture of those who were unable to elude him.

Beatrice Raftery came upon Gladys Parkins, denounced her for having stolen an idea from her, and started to flounce out. She was overhauled and placated by the perspiring Whitey.

Bill Kelley was apprehended by Whitey surreptitiously placing a long-distance call for New York at Mme. Clore's expense.

Minnie Hebner, announcing herself as insulted because Mme. Clore's greeting had not been sufficiently effusive, drew up to her full height of four feet, three inches, and lisped:

"I will not thtay where I'm not wanted."

Resisting an impulse to spank her, Whitey assured her that no insult was intended and fetched her back to Mme. Clore, who was somewhat bewildered by this time. Jimmy McKittredge, the press lush, began to chant:

"Where's the liquor? Where's the liquor? Where's the liquor? Where's the liquor? . . ."

The others took it up, most of the men, and even some of the women.

Whitey hustled to Mme. Clore in a panic.

"Let's start this music," he whispered, "before they tear the place to pieces."

"They do seem a bit peculiar," said Mme. Clore, and signalled the musicians to take their places, while Whitey managed to cram the unruly guests into the folding chairs which had been provided.

They were almost quiet during the first half of the opening number. Mme. Clore sat stiffly in her chair, while Whitey, standing at the rear of the room, watched with terror for what he knew was coming, and whispered with the sympathetic Jim Mitchell, of the *Examiner*.

"Watch that gang of wolves, Jim," Whitey said. "They're going to start throwing those chairs in a minute."

"Yep," said Jim. "Our glorious press. Aren't they beauts? Every time I come to one of these I wonder why anybody ever uses that line, 'I used to be a news-paperman myself'."

Before the first selection had ended, a wave of whispering began. It grew to undisguised conversation and

[106]

swelled to a babble. The music paused. No one missed it. Mme. Clore, furious, swept down upon Whitey.

"Mr. White," she said, "you were right. This is impossible. Tell these people to leave."

"You can't do that, Madame Clore," he argued. "It would ruin us."

"What do you suggest?"

"The only way to save it is to send for some liquor and let these Indians drink and fight."

Mme. Clore considered this and looked at Mitchell. They were as opposite as the poles, but even in her wrath she could recognize a gentleman.

"And what do you think?" she asked him.

"I'd do what Whitey says, Madame Clore," he said, apologetically. "It's a sad state of affairs, but you can't afford to offend these people. I hope you won't hold this against me, too."

"Of course not." She turned to Whitey. "Send for your liquor. I will not stay. Nor will my friends, the musicians. You may phone me at the Ambassador when the orgy is over."

She started away, Whitey trotting at her heels.

"Please, Madame Clore," he whined. "Don't think I wanted to do this."

She was able to smile.

"I understand," she said, and went on. At a wave of her hand the disconcerted musicians followed. When she had gone, Whitey stood on a chair and whooped for attention.

"Ladies and gentlemen," he cried, "we have called off

the music because it was lousy. The bootlegger is on his way. It looks like a party."

IV

It was a party.

Offered an extra ten dollars if he made it in fifteen minutes, Johnny Rocco arrived with six cases of Scotch and tried to stay for the party. It was too rough for him, and he left shortly. Jim Mitchell sprang into the breach and hurried away for a Chevrolet-load of ginger ale. Whitey frightened the servants into assisting in the distribution of drinks.

The reception to the press, after one false start, was under way.

They rolled back the rugs and danced to radio music. Whitey, game to the last, was the partner, alternately, of Beatrice Raftery, who towered above him, wheezing as she thundered about, and Minnie Hebner, who nestled her head comfortably just above his umbilicus.

Jimmy McKittredge fastened himself firmly to a bottle of Scotch on a settee, wisely choosing a haven from which he would not have far to fall.

Gladys Parkins captured Mitchell and took twenty minutes to insinuate that Jack Gilbert had hinted at an assignation during a recent interview.

Johnny Moon amused himself by throwing empty ginger ale bottles at the chandelier. Captain Arthur Johnson sneaked upstairs with the second maid.

After Mitchell had eluded her, Gladys Parkins became desperately ill. The ever solicitous Herman Jones sacrificed his precious stack of *Hollywood Weeklies* as a pillow and stood by to wipe off her face at stated intervals. The next day she accused him of lecherous conduct.

Basil Kingsford fell down a flight of stairs and broke his arm. Later he sued Mme. Clore for damages.

Lucille Jettifer and Jennie Queen became embroiled in an argument which reached its climax when Jennie sank two talons in Lucille's hair and Bobby DeSales knocked Jennie flat.

A general brawl might have followed, save for Whitey, who stepped into the rôle of bouncer and restored peace by brandishing a heavy curtain rod about him.

Izzy Jamieson borrowed ten dollars from the butler.

At seven o'clock they succeeded in clearing the house. Whitey kicked Jimmy McKittredge down the steps, hard, and with Mitchell's help managed to drag Beatrice Raftery, unconscious, to her car.

Whitey stood at the door and searched the guests for filched bottles, finding about two to every three departing journalists.

Then, with Mitchell, he stood sadly to survey the wreckage.

A beautiful Chinese urn had been smashed. A chair had been hurled through a studio window. Someone had danced on the polished floor with hobnails. There were nine burns from abandoned cigarettes in the expensive rug. A drink had been spilled in the grand piano. Someone had left a lighted cigar on a mahogany side table. An entire bottle of ginger ale had been prankishly poured on a beautiful chair upholstered in brocaded silk. An arm had been chipped from a bit of statuary Mme. Clore had brought from Italy. A moustache had been pencilled on the lip of her late husband's oil portrait. Seven glasses were broken. Three spoons were missing. The second maid had been seduced. The cook had quit.

The press had been entertained.

CHAPTER EIGHT

DINING alone that night in Henry's, and speculating upon the possibility of his remaining in the employ of Mme. Clore after she had viewed the havoc caused by the press reception, Whitey met the most beautiful girl in Hollywood.

He found her a welcome relief, wearied as he was by the events of the day, and sated for the moment with both Jane and Grace. She was a supremely attractive, thoroughly normal, thoroughly moral young woman whom one might have encountered in any civilized city or village. She would sell you a cup of coffee for a nickel, fetch you a sandwich, or repel your advances with a manner she might have acquired at Wellesley, but which actually sprang from the public schools of Newton, Iowa.

Her name was Dorothy Irving. She had come to Hollywood because her portrait had inadvertently been entered in a beauty contest and because, later, when she was adjudged the winner, her parents had unwisely permitted her to accept transportation expenses and a six months' contract to appear in the movies as a reward for being the most attractive maiden in Iowa.

In Hollywood she remained both attractive and a maiden, which accounted for her eventual employment as a waitress. Contrary to popular belief, employment as a waitress is a badge of virtue rather than an indication of its lack, particularly when the example is as attractive as Dorothy Irving. She had stepped off the train about a year before, knowing as little about the movies as she did about the religious customs of the Phoenicians. She had been bewildered by the greetings of a press agent and a battery of cameramen who had no film in their cameras.

She had been whisked to the film factory which had staged the beauty contest. She had been photographed, interviewed, frightened, and assigned to a tiny cubicle of a dressing room. She had been ogled and pawed by assistant directors, press agents, cameramen, and minor studio executives. She had been shoved about in extra crowds, herded into mobs with other similarly bewildered contest winners, and eventually, she had been more or less forgotten.

The engaging young fellow who had staged the contest and had plucked her from her Iowa home might have advised and guided her wisely. Unfortunately, he had long since been discharged and had dropped from sight, forgetting completely the girls he had uprooted from their native heaths.

That Dorothy had been completely ignored during her six months in the studio is not quite true. She had been eyed covetously by more than one studio employee. She had repulsed their advances with naïve shrewdness, and most of them had turned to other more ductile contest winners.

Israel Hoffberger, one of the over-lords of the studio where she was employed, however, had at once more cunning and more persistence than the others. When the six months' period was over, and no attempt had been made to give the girls any sort of real opportunity to display possible talent, he summoned the disappointed Dorothy to his office and delivered himself of a particularly specious harangue.

"Miss Irving," he began, in his most authoritative and businesslike manner, "your six months' contract, as you know, has expired. By the terms of our agreement, we will advance the return transportation expenses to all the contest winners who care to go home."

He paused significantly, while Dorothy waited, not knowing what to expect.

She said, finally:

"I suppose the only thing for me to do is to go home."

"That, of course," he answered, "is entirely up to you. Personally, I should dislike to see you go back. You are young and unusually attractive. I have seen some of the rushes in which you appear and you have an exceptionally fine photographic personality."

He paused again, to let this sink in.

"What do you advise, Mr. Hoffberger?" she asked.

"I hate to advise you, one way or the other. However if I were in your place, I'd stick it out. You probably have saved a little money. We'll give you your transportation in cash, which will be about a hundred dollars. That should enable you to live for a while. Now, I can't promise you anything, you understand, but I'm interested in your future, and I'll do all I can to help you. I've already spoken to two or three directors on the lot about you."

Mr. Hoffberger was making one of the most familiar and oft-repeated speeches ever heard in Hollywood. How was Dorothy to know that?

She decided to stay. Most of the other girls—with two of whom she had shared an apartment—went home. Dorothy watched them leave rather wistfully. Helen King, twenty-year-old flapper from Chicago, and wise beyond her years, had also decided to remain. The two girls kept the old apartment.

Save for a few days' extra work, the jobs never developed. Mr. Hoffberger displayed a great deal of conversational interest and advanced many reasons why the projected "better parts" had not materialized. Dorothy's savings dwindled rapidly. Helen was generous enough and permitted her to remain in the apartment, but Dorothy was a proud little soul.

Helen had a way of getting on, mostly through the good offices of an assistant director who managed to keep her almost constantly employed as an extra. The assistant sometimes got Dorothy a day's work, too. This ceased after a time. The assistant had a friend, a cameraman. Dorothy's attitude toward the cameraman was precisely what it had been toward the others. Boys of Dorothy's acquaintance in Newton, Iowa, had not expected an immediate delivery of body and soul in return for a seventy-five cent meal. So Dorothy came to refuse the meals proffered her.

After her money was entirely gone, Dorothy remained in the apartment for another month. Helen paid the rent and kept the kitchen stocked with food. But Helen, who wanted a career on the screen and knew how to get it, became extremely exasperated with her room-mate. Hoffberger continued to telephone, once or twice a week, to inquire solicitously after Dorothy's welfare. It was after one of these calls that Helen revealed her private opinions.

"Why act so stand-offish with Hoffberger?" she demanded. "He's one of the biggest men in Hollywood."

"What do you expect me to do?" Dorothy asked mildly.

"Do? I think you could be civil to him. He's taking an interest in you. I wish he would in me. Why don't you go out to the studio and see him? You haven't been there for a month."

Dorothy went, finally. The interview started smoothly enough, but its ending was highly unsatisfactory to both participants. Hoffberger inquired after her welfare, expressed deep sorrow that he had been unable to place her in any good rôles, and ended with an offer of financial assistance and perhaps the use of living quarters in an apartment house which he owned.

Dorothy applied for work in Henry's that same day and got it.

All this, Dorothy told Whitey that evening. The dinner rush was over. Things were quiet. She felt that she must talk to someone, and Whitey was a person who inspired confidence. He listened to the recital with growing indignation and resentment. His code of personal ethics was a variable, moth-eaten thing. He had repeatedly flouted all ten of the commandments except the one about worshipping graven images, and he could never see any fun in that. But for all this, Whitey had the normal amount of sportsmanship in him. And Dorothy was such a tiny antagonist to be pitted against the system which Hoffberger symbolized. It wasn't a fair fight.

It was obvious that Dorothy was precisely the type who would never accept the Hoffbergers. Yet her large, brown eyes, her friendly, innocent face, her trim little figure, and the charm of her smile might have won her many followers on the screen. A number of girls have made a success with less. As she told him her story, Whitey admired the absence of rancour, the independence of spirit, and the calm philosophy of the attractive little creature.

"Couldn't you continue to do extra work?" he asked.

"I suppose so," she said. "I didn't want to—very much. Men like Hoffberger were always around me. Why is it they all act that way toward me? Do I look like a bad girl?"

"You don't," Whitey answered. "I think that's what's the matter. There are plenty of girls in Hollywood, tough ones. Hoffberger and those other crocodiles are tired of them."

"I don't hold it against Mr. Hoffberger," she said.

"I suppose he thought when I accepted his advice about staying that I realized what he meant."

"Probably," he said. "Still, Hoffberger is pretty much of a rat. He wasn't sure what you thought, and the town is full of girls who would jump at the chance of sleeping with him."

"I suppose I'm old-fashioned and silly," she said. "It might have been a big chance. But it isn't the way I want a chance. You can't really buy success in pictures that way, can you?"

"It wouldn't seem so. But a lot of girls have—some of the biggest stars."

"Yes, there's Helen. I don't think she's so awfully attractive, but she has a contract with K.F.C."

"Did the assistant get it for her?"

"No. She doesn't see him any more. I believe it was the Production Manager."

"You don't live with her now?"

"No. The Production Manager objected to her living with other girls."

She brought him pie, which he attacked thoughtfully, and after disposing of another customer who had been attempting to attract her attention for some time, Dorothy returned.

"You know," Whitey said, "I'm not a moral person. But I think you were right about Hoffberger. He wouldn't have been much help. It would have been someone else after him. Once you start, there's no stopping place. There are a lot of girls who get along in pictures without that."

"I've always thought so," she said. "But I've given up any idea of pictures now. Directors come in here, sometimes, and ask me to come out for screen tests. I've never done it."

"I don't see why you should give up the idea of pictures. There are a lot of nice people here, people who are really intelligent and civilized. And it's the greatest career in the world, if you hit. Look at all the broken-down blondes making big money. Christ, it would be fun to put you over in pictures and then laugh at Hoffberger! Maybe I'll try it."

She looked at him silently, with what was more than a casual glance. He caught it. He had finished dinner by this time, and arose.

"Listen," he said, replying to her look, "I'm not a Hoffberger. I'm not of any importance in the studios and never will be. I'm not trying to kid anybody about that. But I've been a newspaperman, and that's a lot smarter racket than this business. Look at the newspapermen who have knocked them over in it—Monta Bell, Mike Boylan, Julian Johnson, George Marion, Luther Reed, Joe Jackson, Jimmy Gruen, Tom Reed, Randy Bartlett—it's full of 'em. I'm going to work this town like a police beat. There's not much difference."

He paused again.

"When do you get off work?"

"Half an hour."

"If I meet you in half an hour will you let me drive you home?"

[118]

"Yes."

In street attire, at that time, wrapped in her inexpensive but becoming coat, Dorothy drew as many eyes as though she had been a screen star when she stepped from the curb to the seat beside Whitey in the new roadster on which he had made the first payment.

"Like to go for a drive before I take you home?" he asked.

"I'd love it."

They wound slowly out Sunset boulevard and through the glittering mansions of Beverly Hills. It was a soft warm night. On a little rise in the highway they paused to watch the twinkling lights of Los Angeles shame the stars.

"Who knows?" he said expansively. "We might both be high-hatting them out here some day. It's the biggest roulette game in the world."

"Somehow," she said cheerfully, "I think your chances are better than mine."

"Somehow," he replied, "I don't agree with you. I'm notning but a big bluff. You're a real diamond in a pawnshop window. All you've got to do is try. You've got to fight and elbow and hit low in the clinches and lie and make promises you won't keep. I'll do that all right; but I haven't the energy to keep it up. Lord, it would be wonderful to lick this town through you. You just be yourself. I'll be your manager and do the dirty work."

At eleven o'clock he delivered her to the home where she dwelt in a furnished room. In many ways it had been the pleasantest evening either had spent in Hollywood. He was the first man she had met in the town who had not made overtures to her. She was the first girl in town he had not made overtures to. As he drove toward the Major, he felt particularly benign.

"I suppose I'm crazy," he told himself. "If I try to put anyone over, it should be Jane. But, what the hell! Jane could take care of herself in a forecastle."

Chapter Nine

DOROTHY IRVING remained in his thoughts, and he turned over in his mind many schemes to find her a chance on the screen.

Meanwhile, however, Mme. Clore occupied most of his time and energy. Contrary to his expectations, he had not lost his job because of the party for the press. Mme. Clore, with the temporary calmness which sometimes overtakes irrational folk, paid for the wreckage and said nothing, except to chide him occasionally for having sprung from so raucous a profession.

Plans for the epic picturization of the book which was to rank with Shakespeare were forging ahead. Albert Blynn, a smooth-talking, shifty-eyed but rather personable individual, had been engaged as director. He had been a leading man before dissipation left its traces too heavily on his features. Blynn had been selected by Fishbein, principally because the producer secretly had him under personal contract and was charging Mme. Clore an extra thousand dollars a week for his services. Moreover, Fishbein felt that he could depend upon his own hireling to keep his temper reasonably in check while dealing with the flaming authoress.

The selection of the players was no small task. Mme. Clore had instantly agreed that Sonia Varon, the exotic foreign beauty, was the only choice for the feminine lead. She still wailed to the heavens whenever anyone save her young Briton was mentioned for the opposite rôle, however.

Dozens of the more prominent leading men of Hollywood were rejected for the part. Others, more prosperous and independent, who might have been acceptable, snorted openly at the prospect of appearing in a rôle so artificial and vapid, with the added disadvantage of having Mme. Clore always under foot.

Whitey was harassed by cross-fire. Fishbein raged at him constantly, and Mme. Clore made impossible demands. McGinnis, with his own troubles in dealing with these two cantankerous patrons of the cinema, could do little to help him. Blynn, wrapped in a mantle of conceit so vast that it sometimes concealed even his general ignorance, took an instant dislike to Whitey, who returned the disaffection with vigor.

Whitey found himself pulled and hauled from all sides. Minor employees of the troupe were constantly badgering him to influence Mme. Clore this way or that, as it became general knowledge that she had considerable confidence in him. None of these things were calculated to improve his disposition nor help his peace of mind.

This prologue of bickering continued for weeks.

Players finally were engaged. Settings were built, conforming to Mme. Clore's bizarre ideas but with what restraint the art director could manage. A day was finally fixed when the first twirl was to be given the camera crank.

Mme. Clore, worn out by weeks of quarreling, went to Santa Barbara to rest for the battles to come.

McGinnis, given momentary freedom, departed in the opposite direction—for Tia Juana.

Fishbein had weightier matters before him than harassing Whitey, and Blynn, whom Whitey treated with lofty disdain, was unable to bother him.

Consequently, when the exodus to Santa Barbara and Tia Juana started, on a Friday afternoon, Whitey sneaked away early from the studio. Jane was dancing with the voice culturist at the Ambassador. Whitey induced a bellboy to admit him to Jane's apartment where he found, to his delight, six bottles of champagne which some willing victim had contributed.

Champagne and gin do not make a judicious mixture. By eight o'clock that evening, Whitey found himself in a mood for hilarity, but with no accomplices. Joe Greet was working all night at his comedy studio. Jim Mitchell was at home, and refused to leave the bosom of his family. Straubel had retired early and would not answer the door. Whitey even rapped on the door of Bob Carey, but the official sponger of the Major had found victims elsewhere.

Returning to his room, Whitey sat on the bed and searched his mind for possible play-fellows. He heard a typewriter clattering in the adjoining room, and considered inviting the stranger—who had moved in a few days before—to his party.

The necessity for a decision was removed, however. The typewriter was silenced. Whitey could hear his neighbor moving about. Then there came a rap on the door.

It was the new tenant, a tall, pale and passively good-looking young man of about thirty. He appeared somewhat haggard, and dark circles rimmed his eyes.

"Wonder if I could borrow your bottle-opener?" he asked.

Whitey supplied it, and the visitor invited him to have a highball. The invitation was gladly accepted, and both went to the stranger's room.

"My name," the newcomer said, applying the opener to a bottle of ginger ale, "is Carson—Frank Carson ——"

"Oh, yes," said Whitey, "you're . . ."

"I'll finish it for you," Carson interrupted. "I'm Louise Bagshaw's husband. Damn it, I wish I weren't."

"Sorry," Whitey said. "My name's White, Theodore Anthony White, known familiarly as Whitey."

"Oh, yes. I've heard of you. You're the guy that busted up Sam Schmalz's banquet. I wish I'd been there to see it. Don't mind recalling my famous wife. I'm used to it."

"I should think you'd be glad of it—to be married to such a beautiful girl as that."

"Yes? Well, I was glad of it, once."

Carson poured two drinks, and filled the glasses with ice and ginger ale. Whitey noticed that his hand trembled as he held the glasses.

"God! I'm all shot to pieces," Carson said. "I've been going for days."

"I've heard your typewriter a lot lately," Whitey said. "I supposed you were working."

"Yes, I've been working—trying to—between drinks."

He stared moodily out the window at the steady procession of traffic on Cahuenga Avenue.

"What's the use? I'll never be a writer, or anything else. Star's husband—that's all I am."

"I wish I was one," Whitey commented.

"Yes, you'd like it. For about a week. I stood it— Christ! I stood it for years."

"Are you separated?"

"You're damned right we are. I walked out last Friday night. Walked out of a Beverly Hills house as big as a mausoleum, and about as home-like, to a room and bath in this dump. I'll sleep in the gutter, too, before I'll go back. Star's husband!"

Whitey guessed that his host was full of liquor, and that it was forcing him to talk against his will.

"That's tough," Whitey said.

"I'll say it's tough. If I wasn't in love with the beautiful little tramp I could laugh it off. But what are you going to do when you love 'em and can't have 'em . . . because you're not handsome enough to be a matinee idol, or fatheaded enough to be a director."

"Well, that's Hollywood."

"Hollywood! That's just what it is. I wish I'd never seen the place, or heard of it. I'd like to plant a bomb under Mulholland Dam and wash the lousy town into San Pedro Bay."

"Ahhh!" he went on. "What are my troubles to you? I don't want to bore you, but Christ! I've got to talk to somebody. I'll go nuts in here by myself all the time."

"You're not boring me," Whitey said. "Go ahead and talk."

"I'm raving, I guess. Pour me another drink, will you?"

He handed his empty glass to Whitey.

"I'm going to tell you about it, whether you like it or not."

Carson was silent as Whitey mixed him a highball.

"I haven't got a friend in this town, or anywhere else, now, I guess. Nobody gives a damn about me. Nobody thinks of me as anything but a legalized pimp, whose status is somewhere between the butler and the Pekinese. He hasn't as much authority as the butler, and he isn't permitted the familiarity of the dog. I wonder I didn't walk out long ago."

Whitey could find no appropriate comment, and kept silent.

"I should have known better than to come to this town. Dumb, that's all I was. That kike Baumgarten did it. I oughta stick a knife in him. Still, he wasn't to blame. I guess he thought he was giving us a break."

"What did Baumgarten do?" Whitey asked.

"He came through Duluth one day, damn him, and he

[126]

saw a picture of Louise. Why the hell couldn't he have stayed out of that town? I had a nice little business there. We had been married two years, and were happy as hell. I had the prettiest wife in the city, and she was crazy about me. Nice little home, almost paid for, making plenty of money . . . for us . . . then.

"Baumgarten saw her picture in a photographer's window and fell for it. She'd had it taken as a surprise to give me on my birthday, too, if you want to mix a little irony in it.

"He looked her up through the photographer, and that evening he came out to the house. Told her she was the perfect screen type, and he'd give her a contract if she'd come to Hollywood. She'd never even thought of getting in the movies till that fat Jew came along.

"I tried to talk her out of it. All our friends were in Duluth. My God! We were sitting on top of the world. But I couldn't budge her. Baumgarten was a fast talking guy, and she got a thrill out of how important he was. Important! The four-flusher! He isn't even a big shot in this mining camp.

"I don't believe Baumgarten wanted her in the movies. He was planning to make her with all his chatter, and when he found she had a husband he had to go through with it.

"Well, we fell for it. I couldn't stand it to say 'No,' when she wanted to go so badly. I was too crazy about her to deny her anything. We sold the business, we sold the car, and out we came, like a couple of yaps.

"On the way out I began to think about what would happen if she began to make a lot of money like those stars were supposed to make. But what the hell could I do?

"They put her on salary at seventy-five dollars a week for six months. We had to live on it. The railroad fare out here and buying her a lot of clothes and getting settled took all our money but about two thousand, and we dribbled that away.

"I tried to find work, but the best I could do was a job as some punk clerk at about thirty-five dollars a week. I never learned any business. My father left me the store—it was a shoe store—and I didn't have the capital to start one out here.

"I did take a job as a clerk in a shoe store down on the Boulevard one day, but she made me quit. Said it would make her ridiculous. A picture actress having a husband clerking in a shoe store! Ridiculous! My God, what's more ridiculous than making faces at a movie camera?

"We lived in a single apartment down on Gower street and just managed to get by on her salary. It was terrible. I didn't have a thing to do. She was at the studio all day. I moped around the place—used to drive her to work in the morning in the Ford we bought —then bum around, take in the ball game, or go swimming until it was time to pick her up. She'd work nights, too, a lot, and sometimes I'd hardly see her for three or four days.

"I wanted to do extra work, but she put the bum on

that, too. Said it would be as bad for her appearance as having me clerk in a shoe store.

"I had two strikes on me all the time, and it took me years to figure it out."

Carson poured himself another drink—a stiff one.

"One thing I would never do, by God! I never would hang about the set like some of these lapdogs.

"Well, things went on like that for a while, and then she got a break. Jack Sylvester kind of liked her and gave her the lead in *Manicurist*. It was a rotten picture but the boobs went for it. It only cost about sixty thousand to make and they cleaned up.

"Everything broke lucky for her. Some smart agent wiggled her out of her contract and she signed a new one, believe it or not, for twenty-five hundred dollars a week, with the salary sliding up to five thousand dollars a week in five years. All that dough for a cute little dame that didn't know how to act, and never will!

"Right away she began to change. Hollywood got her. Wednesday luncheon at the Montmartre. A lot of big parties with these four-flushers, running around to beach clubs, and the Mayfair, and to other stars' homes, and all that stuff!

"We had to move into a house big enough for twenty people, and hire more up-stage servants than the King of England has. That house was what finished me.

"You'd never think she was the same kid I'd married. She was as sweet as they come, then. Never took a drink, didn't smoke, and thought I was the greatest guy in the world. Modest and quiet and refined.

"Before that mansion came along, it was what *we* were doing. Then it was what *she* was doing. She'd always said before that as soon as we made enough we'd beat it somewhere and live in a civilized burg. Nuts! You couldn't drag her out of Hollywood.

"From the time we moved in there it was like living with a Duchess—and being a page-boy. She bought a Rolls-Royce and a million dollars worth of clothes. The house was always full of punks. They didn't like me. I didn't like them any better. We all knew it, too.

"They were wise-cracking behind my back. I could feel it. I caught that faggoty ham, Bill Holmes, passing a fly crack about 'Mr. Bagshaw' one day. I fixed him up perfect. He couldn't work for a month, until they scraped his nose out of his left ear.

"She got to riding me, too. Not in any tangible way —just dirty little digs. It was supposed to be kidding, but it was kidding on the level. Sly remarks about money—how it must be great to be a gentleman of leisure. Gentleman of leisure, my eye! I'd have run a filling station, or been a motorman.

"I asked her to lend me the money to start a business of some kind. She gave me five thousand bucks. It wasn't enough for a shoe store, so I opened a little restaurant—under another name, so as not to embarrass her with her swell friends. It flopped, of course. I didn't know how to run one.

"After that, nothing I said or did was worth a damn. She treated me like I was an amiable half-wit she had to put up with."

Carson paused again and reached for the bottle. It was empty. He hurled it through the window.

"Let's call a bootlegger. No, I can't. I haven't got but three or four bucks, and Rocco won't give me any more credit."

"I've got a drink in my room," Whitey said, and fetched a fresh bottle of gin, while Carson paced about the tiny room.

"It's a wonder that five thousand bucks didn't finish me," he went on, "but I stuck it out. I was so crazy in love with her that I couldn't bear to leave.

"She got more and more high-hat. She even started to develop an English accent, but I kidded her out of that. She took French lessons, too. French lessons in Hollywood! My sweet Moses! If she'd studied Hebrew, it might have been some use to her.

"I got burned up at something one day and told her I'd walk out and leave her if she wanted to be free. She talked me out of it. I thought she was still in love with me. She wasn't. I was a convenient guy to have around. Nice for errands.

"I got to dodging some of those damn parties she was always going to. They bored me stiff, and I despised the people. I was always invited. Sure, because I had to be. They'd say, 'Bring Frank along, too—and your husband, of course.'

"It got so that when I didn't go, they quit asking me, just assuming I wouldn't go. I got to drinking a lot, too. Christ! What else was there to do? I wouldn't see her for a week at a time, except maybe to pass her in the hall. She'd go out to the studio in the morning, come back about six, get dressed, and beat it out somewhere. Generally, I didn't even know where. If she had people at the house, I'd go somewhere else, unless it was a small party and I half-way liked some of the people.

"It wasn't all those other people's fault. I couldn't blame them for what they thought of me. I looked like a lazy, good-for-nothing bum, sponging off my wife. Never had anything to say; drunk half the time. I couldn't go around explaining to everybody.

"What a spot! I was the lonesomest guy in Hollywood. Nothing to do. Three cars in the garage for me to drive. A hell of a big house on a five acre estate. So many servants around they got in your hair. Plenty of money—if I asked her for it. A basement full of Scotch.

"And what the hell could I do with it all? The only friends I had were her friends, and they were no friends at all. I could have found some good guys in Hollywood—fellows like you. How could I meet 'em? And then what? If I'd taken them out to the house she'd have called the cops."

Carson paused to refill the glasses.

"What's the use of talking like this? I could rave all week. There was some stuff in *Variety*, in that *Inside Dope on the Movies* column. It didn't use any names, but it hinted plenty that there was something doing between Louise and Sylvester. One of these yes-guys that was always around the house showed it to me. The little rat! He pretended it meant somebody else. He knew who it meant, all right. And he knew I knew.

"I guess I knew it was true long before, but I wouldn't admit it to myself. But there it was in print, and all Hollywood snickering at me. It was in the afternoon that I saw it, and I began to get drunk. Every drink made me madder. I was going to show it to Louise when she came home, and I fully intended to beat hell out of her.

"About six o'clock she phoned the cook she had to work late and wouldn't be home to dinner. That made me plenty sore. I'd been thinking up things to say to her for hours, and I was so full of them I thought I'd explode.

"I didn't eat a bite. I told the butler to jump in the lake and kept on drinking until about ten o'clock that night. I was on a fighting jag, if you ever saw one. I went out and got the roadster and drove to the studio.

"It was all dark. No lights or anything. I asked the night gateman if the Sylvester company was working, and he said they'd quit at five o'clock that afternoon.

"I drove to Sylvester's apartment. There was one of those little tradesmen's openings in the door. I shoved on it till the catch gave way, and then I could just reach down and open the door from the inside.

"They were there, all right—half dressed. Boy, were they surprised! I had a bottle in my hand and I guess they thought I was going to kill them both. I must have looked like a ghost.

"I'll hand it to Sylvester. He's only a little guy, but he took it standing up. She was scared to death. Sylvester said, 'Well, Frank, here we are. It's my fault. What do you want to do?'

"I didn't know. I stood there a minute, and then I told Louise to put on her clothes, and she went to do it. I said to Sylvester. 'You're a dirty rat, but I guess you've done just what everybody else in this town would have done.'

"He said, 'I know I am. It's my fault. Don't blame Louise.' I guess I should have popped him, at that. Only I couldn't very well. He had too much nerve. Just stood there and wouldn't defend himself.

"Louise came out and we drove home together. She'd got over being scared of me. I guess she saw I wasn't going to do anything. Cold! She was as cold as a producer's heart—as hard as an anvil. She said, 'You've got a hell of a nerve, busting in on me like that.' Can you tie that? I said, 'I suppose my position in the matter has nothing to do with it.'

"She said, 'You've known what your position has been for a long time, and you've accepted it. I've given you a better house than you've ever had, a car, and lots of money. You seemed to be satisfied. I don't see why you should do this now.'

"It dawned on me, then, that this had been going on for a long time, and she thought I knew it and was putting up with it. I felt like crying. I guess I did, a little. I asked, 'Sylvester is not the first one, then?' She laughed at me. 'You poor boob,' she said, 'are you trying to make me think you didn't know it?'

"We were at home by this time. I got out of the car and left it in the driveway. I had about twenty bucks in my pocket. It was her money and I offered it to her. She laughed, and wouldn't take it, so I threw it on the porch.

"I had to go somewhere, so I went around to the servants' quarters and borrowed twenty-five dollars from the nigger chauffeur. He was the only good guy on the place. I wired my brother in Minneapolis next day and paid him back. And here I am."

He paused for a long time.

"What have you been writing?" Whitey asked.

"A scenario—trying to. What's the use? I'm no writer. I can't even spell any more. And I couldn't sell it if it was good. The producers would see my name on it and say: 'It's no good. He can't do anything. He's nothing but a star's husband.' "

They sat in silence for a long time, Carson shivered.

"God!" he said. "I feel terrible. I've got to stop drinking or I'll have the D.T.'s. I've got to get some sleep. Be a good guy, will you, and ask the boy to bring me some veronal, or something?"

Whitey brought him some sleeping tablets, tucked him into bed and brought him a glass of water.

"I'm going out for a while," Whitey said, "but I'll be back pretty soon. If you want anything just pound on the wall."

"Christ, what a town!" Whitey remarked to himself, back in his own room. "Blackmail, adultery, kept women, dipsomaniacs, liars, and pimps!"

Deeply as Carson's tale had moved him, Whitey was never able to keep a serious mood long, and, moreover, he had consumed not a little gin during the recital.

He pawed through his constantly growing list of telephone numbers, and spun the dial unceasingly. Bobby Willis—previous engagement. Helen—not at home. Jeanne—ill. Marianne—husband home. Pearle —not speaking to him.

He even telephoned Dorothy Irving; why, he did not know, for the unswerving propriety of his conduct with her did not match his intentions for the evening. Happily, she was working the late shift again.

He called three rooms at random at the Studio Club. Two were blanks, and on the third call his ear was jarred by the receiver being violently banged on the hook. He had completely forgotten that he had left Lois standing on the corner of Sunset and Western while he launched forth to more alluring fields.

He proposed an engagement with the night switchboard operator at the Major. It had been tried before and only a tinkling laugh met his suggestion.

Then he thought of Grace. It was Friday, the evening of Grace's heavy date. What was a heavy date to Whitey, money in his pocket, a new roadster to do his bidding, full of gin, champagne, and self-confidence? It was after ten o'clock when he drew up, somewhat haphazardly, before the bungalow court in which Grace lived. An imposing sedan stood in front of the place. It meant nothing to Whitey.

One dim light burned in Grace's apartment, and that not in the living room. Whitey battered noisily at the door. No answer.. He pounded again, arousing the neighbors for some distance around. The door was opened a tiny crack at last.

"What is it?" whispered Grace.

Whitey, standing in the dark, was struck by a sudden inspiration.

"Hollywood police," he boomed, and edged his toe into the crack in the door. She did not recognize him.

"Just a minute, and I'll let you in," she said in terror, and turned to switch on the light. Whitey stepped in, grinning like a satyr, just in time to see a small figure, shirt-tail flying, whisk furtively through the kitchen and out the back door.

Grace's voice trembled with indignation as she saw Whitey. Tears of anger were near the surface.

"Whitey, Whitey!" she said. "Why would you come here tonight?"

"Why shouldn't I?" he protested, open-face in his innocence. "Can't a man call on an old friend?"

"I told you never to come here on Friday. You've ruined it all."

"Ruined what all?" he asked.

"Everything!"

"Who was the little squirt running out of the back door?"

"None of your damn business!"

Whitey quite composedly wound the phonograph and set the needle.

"Want a drink?" he asked, and pulled the last bottle of Jane's champagne from one pocket and a bottle of gin from another.

Grace whirled about, furious. She eyed the champagne covetously, but decided to denounce him anyway.

"Whitey, you little rat, get out of here!" she screamed. "I'll never let you in my apartment again."

"Now, now," he soothed, "you're all unstrung. Don't say ill-considered things like that."

She followed him, chattering in feminine, futile wrath into the kitchen.

"You chiselling, dirty little pimp!" she snapped. "Ruining the best thing I ever had—borrowing my car —running around with other women in it ——"

Whitey pulled the wrapping from the champagne bottle and dexterously removed the cork.

"I don't see," he commented, pouring a glassful of the sparkling beverage, "why you should take on so because a pal comes over to give you some Mumm's. I've been here before and you've never objected."

He handed her the champagne and measured out three fingers of gin for himself.

"It's not me," she said, calming a little as she sipped the wine. "I like you, Whitey. But I've got a daddy, and you know it."

"I don't see why he should be so timid about it," Whitey argued. "He's not the only daddy in Hollywood. I'd like to have given him a drink. After all,

I'm indebted to him for some pleasant evenings here."

"He's probably going over Cahuenga Pass now, the way he got started," she giggled, almost completely coaxed from her savage mood. "He's scared to death he'll get his name in the papers."

Whitey said nothing to this, but digested it thoroughly. A man afraid to get his name in the papers might be valuable, somehow, he thought. He decided to learn the man's identity, feeling that such information never came amiss.

He stayed for almost an hour, playing the phonograph, stretching out languidly on the davenport, drinking at intervals, and ignoring her abortive attempts to get him out. She was rather apprehensive, but she could not be very harsh with him. His boyish audacity, coupled with the champagne, prevented that. Whitey was not as languid as he looked. He had chosen a spot nearest the windows opening on the street, reasoning that the departed guest, once he had overcome his initial fright, would hardly abandon his expensive car. At length, Whitey heard the door of the automobile closed quietly. He arose to depart.

"I won't stay where I'm not welcome," he said.

Grace followed him to the door.

"You're a darling, Whitey," she said. "I should be mad at you, but I can't. Give me a ring tomorrow."

Whitey kissed her with hasty fervency and departed. His theory had been correct. The owner of the car was standing on the sidewalk, a thin, sallow, little man, hat pulled far down over his face. He had reasoned, as Whitey thought he would, that the visitor was not of the police.

As the stranger saw Whitey, surely not a sinister figure, lurch a shade unsteadily from the doorway, the little man started to brush past him. Whitey was tight, but his brain was functioning. He paused, pretended to reel into the little figure, peered into his face, and recognized him instantly.

"Why, Mr. Hoffberger," he said, and placed a gently restraining hand on his arm, "so glad to meet you. I've seen your name and picture in the papers so many times, and heard a lot about you."

Hoffberger tried to wriggle from his grasp, but could not.

"Have a drink?" Whitey asked, and pulled the almost empty gin bottle from his pocket.

"No," said Hoffberger gruffly, and pulled away to proceed on into the apartment.

"Don't get sore about it," Whitey called placatingly, then went to his car.

A hundred half-finished thoughts swarmed through his buzzing mind as he sped up the street into Sunset boulevard, and he laughed uproariously. So Israel Hoffberger was paying the rent for Grace Harper! An intriguing discovery, and Whitey wondered what might be done with it. Nothing for the present, but a valuable bit of information to file away in his chubby head.

Israel Hoffberger! The man who had induced Dorothy Irving to stay in Hollywood, and then had done nothing for her. The most feared man of any studio official. Still in his twenties, he had forced himself into a highly important position in the industry. He had personally supervised and produced scores of big pictures. He had elbowed other officials of his studio out of power. He spent hundreds of thousands of dollars on snap decisions, ordered directors about with imperial authority, kept famous writers waiting hours to see him, made or killed stars with a word, ruled thousands of employees by fear and broke those who stood up against him. Truly an opponent worthy of Whitey's steel.

Israel Hoffberger!

Chapter Ten

THE dreary task of filming the passionate tale of *The Tigress* began the next Monday morning, and immediately developed into a combination debating marathon, hog-calling contest and battle royal. Mme. Clore managed to sound the keynote of the entire affair early on that first morning when she spied in makeup and costume for the first time, Romaine Randolph, the personable young man who had been engaged, over her protests, to play the lead in the picture.

The authoress apparently had planned her scene with care. When Randolph came upon the set she stared at him with horror in her eyes, screamed, and covered her face with her hands. All this was done in the presence of Fishbein, McGinnis, Blynn, Sonia Varon, Whitey, and upwards of a hundred extras, carpenters and electricians. It was calculated to embarrass Randolph to the utmost.

The actor heard the scream, glared venomously at Mme. Clore, then turned abruptly and stalked off the set. It took Whitey and McGinnis two hours to induce him to return. Randolph paced nervously about the tiny dressing room asigned to him, his handsome visage scowling in fury.

"I won't do it," he repeated again and again. "I

tell you, I won't do it. I knew she didn't want me in this part, but I never thought she'd pull a scene like that. You can find another boy."

They continued to plead and argue with the enraged Thespian.

"I'll get a job driving a hack first," he said. "I'll be God-damned if I'll take any more off that old harridan, contract or no contract."

"Please, Randy," McGinnis soothed, "you'll put me in an awful hole. You were the only leading man all hands could agree on."

"It doesn't look like I was agreed on," Randolph stormed. "I wouldn't go back there and give her a chance to play another gag like that for twice the money I'm getting. This will be a horrible picture, anyway."

"My Lord," groaned McGinnis. "I've never dealt with so much temperament in all my life."

Randolph whirled about to answer this.

"You've known me a long time, Mac," he said. "Have I ever pulled any temperament on anybody before? No. Well, I'm not doing it now. I'm just a good journeyman actor, and I know my trade. I didn't ask for this part. Fishbein ragged me for a week to take it. The old bandit cried on my shoulder and even asked me to cut my salary. Now I walk out on the set and she screams like I'd tried to poison all her grandchildren."

But they prevailed upon him to return and try it once more. Fishbein extracted from Mme. Clore a promise that she would unleash no more tantrums. Randolph insisted, as the price of his return, that the authoress was never to address any remark of any nature to or about him.

Mme. Clore, frustrated in her attempts to rag the actor, settled upon Blynn and within two days was able to keep him in a perpetual blind fury. No item was too small to escape her. She questioned every order, objected to every scene, remonstrated at every movement.

"No person of gentle birth would do a thing like that," was her inevitable criticism of every action suggested by Blynn to the players.

The seventeenth time this statement was made, Blynn replied, "No person of gentle birth would belly-ache so God-damned much, either."

It took some hours to repair this breach.

The director could match her in arrogance, and was fully as unreasonable, but he lacked her gift for invective and polemics. Consequently, he contented himself with prowling about the set and ridiculing her to delighted electricians and property boys.

The beautiful and tempestuous Sonia Varon, jealous equally of Randolph and Blynn, and never willing to surrender the spotlight in the smallest particular, tried to edge into this guerrilla warfare with her own bursts of temperament. The others were so far beyond her that she could find no foothold in the quarrels at all. Consequently, she turned to abusing the minor workers on the set, and became the arch-enemy of the assistant director, the cameraman and the harried, lisping costume designer, none of whom could please her in any way.

Randolph, protected by his armed truce, began to derive a species of lugubrious amusement from his connection with the picture. Whitey spent most of his time on the set, for it was the best show in town, and Randolph adopted him immediately as his confidant. The actor amused himself by lolling in his canvas chair and burlesquing the entire matter in a half-audible whisper.

Thus was Art led along its rocky road.

II

From the roaring temperaments of Rethea Clore, Blynn and Sonia Varon, from his pleasant but rather fatiguing surreptitious visits to Grace, and from the frequent outbursts of Jane, Whitey often fled to the companionship of Dorothy Irving for occasional moments of peace and quiet.

When she was not working and he could sneak away from the cinematic battlefield, they often motored to Santa Monica to spend the warm afternoons on the beach. Or, when her evenings were free, they enjoyed quiet and sober visits to the theater. Whitey was always immensely pleased with himself during these infrequently spasms of good behavior.

Her combination of naïve innocence and independence delighted him anew whenever they were together, and the confidence and trust she placed in him filled Whitey with a strange variety of paternal interest which was ordinarily quite foreign to him.

During this period of his Hollywood career, Whitey became a firm friend of Romaine Randolph and consequently experienced a decided change in his attitude toward actors. Hitherto he had regarded them as a minor blight on Hollywood which had to be endured because they were, after all, useful. Now he came to realize that Randolph typified the better class of his profession and that there was, distinctly, a better class.

Whitey informed Randolph of his changed views one day when they were closeted in the actor's dressing room with a jug of home-made kümmel which Randolph had fetched with him to the studio under the theory that he could never foretell when a snake might bite him.

"Sure," Randolph expounded, "there are good actors. Some of them are almost human. It's the fatheaded ones that give the trade a bad name."

It was one of Randolph's practices never to refer to his occupation save as a trade.

"Actors," he went on, "are like ministers. Only the bad ones get in the headlines. There are some good ministers, too, but you only hear about the ones that run away with the choir girls."

"I've always disliked actors as a class," Whitey said. "I never really knew one until I came to Hollywood."

"I'll grant you," Randolph said, "that it's no profession for a grown man. But, what the hell! there's money in it. All actors don't kid themselves about being 'artists.' You may be damn sure I don't. My God, the things I've done in the name of acting. Tent shows, medicine shows, carnivals, tank-town vaudeville. I played in a Tom Show when I was seventeen and did sleight-of-hand tricks and sold boxes of candy—a prize in each and every package—between the acts.

"I starved to death in New York two winters trying to be a juvenile . . . used to cook in an all-night lunch wagon nights and bum around the booking agents day-times.

"A leading man I knew told me he'd made two hundred dollars a week in Hollywood and ran out because he was afraid they'd pinch him for grand larceny. I'd never made that much money in my life, except for two weeks when I ran a lottery up in Wyoming. But I knew I could do anything he could, so I borrowed the fare and came out here.

"That was ten years ago. I met a guy who used to be the heavy and take tickets in a tent show I was in. He was a director and he gave me a job. In six months I was making three hundred a week and working most of the time. I felt like a pickpocket every time they paid me. There were such a lot of actors better than I'll ever be back on Broadway borrowing dimes for breakfast.

"I'm still not a good actor, but I've got a home and two cars all paid for and a wife who thinks I'm a riot. I've got fifty thousand bucks in bonds, and if they ever get onto me I can still cook a good hamburger steak."

He paused and glared at Whitey.

"You're too damned good a listener," he said. "Here I am, denying I'm as bad as these other hams, and I do a monologue about myself."

"It's the softest racket I ever ran into," Whitey said. "I'm making twice as much as I ever got on a newspaper, doing half the work and getting nine times the laughs."

"Laughs?" Randolph cried. "The town is full of 'em! Take it seriously and it'll drive you nuts. Look at Blynn. He thinks he's an artist. He's out there now, raving and swearing with that looney author when he might as well be taking it easy and thinking how much he's overpaid.

"Guys like Blynn are what make this picture business a burden. There are some good guys directing pictures, too, but it's the ones like Blynn who make their racket ridiculous.

"The same way with the producers. Some of them are intelligent, and some of them are honest. And the Jews aren't the worst. I had a contract with an Irishman once, and I swore I'd never work for a Gentile again as long as I lived."

"Some producers are all right," Whitey agreed. "Old Jake Schmalz would give you the shirt off his back."

"Sure he would," Randolph said, "but Hoffberger would snatch yours off if you didn't watch him. He's as crooked as a snake—and looks like one. Yet the guy he works for, old Aaron Michaels, would do anything for you."

"I'd like to find some way to hook into the real

money," Whitey said. "I'm just a piker compared to you and guys like Blynn."

"Be a scenario writer," Randolph advised. "You don't have to be good. Beat on the table and shout about the premise and the theme and the plot motivation. It doesn't make any difference what you do, the director will hash it up anyway."

"I tried that once," Whitey said, recalling his week at Colossal. "The story conferences lick me. I never could finish a sentence."

"You have to start as a train announcer," Randolph said.

"I'd like to be famous," Whitey declared. "It must be great to ride around and have people point you out. It goes over great with the women."

Randolph poured himself another drink.

"Fame?" he said. "What does anybody want to be famous for in Hollywood? What does it get you?"

He strode about the dressing room like a Hamlet delivering his soliloquy.

"Fame, my eye! They name a sandwich after you, maybe, in a café on the Boulevard.

"They put your name in the ads of the *World Premieres*. You see your mug on billboards, and your name in electric lights. What of it? If you're single, chances are you're supposed to be engaged to Clara Bow. You get stuck on a beach house in Malibu. You're posted on the delinquent list at the Writers' Club—you find all the famous names there.

"Reporters come out and pry into your business.

Every week or so they start a rumor that you've split up with your wife. If you're single and a dame ditches you, they print that, too. Sweet of them, isn't it?

"Press agents write stuff you never see and sign your name to it. Then these wise-cracking columnists pick it up and prove how dumb you are.

"You're famous then, see? You're making twice as much money as the President. Then what happens?

"You make a payment down on a Rolls-Royce. You eat lunch at the Montmartre so a lot of yaps can stare at you. You get on the sucker list of all the racketeers in town. These trade paper guys come out and sell you advertising you don't want. Goggle-eyed dames from the fan magazines want to write your Love Confessions. You can't turn 'em down, so you make a boob out of yourself in print.

"You pay too much dough for everything, because everybody puts up their prices when they see a movie star coming.

"You build a house as big as a Carnegie Library— but without the books. You hire a press agent to make you look foolish and a business manager to gyp you.

"You think you're too important to have your name in the telephone book. You take it out, and then your friends can't find you.

"You pick up an English accent and try to hide the fact that you were born in Johnson Gap, Arkansas.

"The gossipers tear you to pieces. They'll say you're up-stage, that you can't read and write, that your wife is cheating on you, that you're having an affair with your leading woman, that you're a Greek, or a hop-head, or a pansy, and God knows what; they'll say you're a genius, or a dipsomaniac, or both; they'll say you earn seventeen thousand dollars a week and haven't a dime, or that you won't spend a penny; they'll say your folks are in the poorhouse and you won't help 'em.

"Hollywood fame! You'll have it then.

"Now what? You get so God-damned important you can't have any fun. You wither and die and they give you one of these Sons-and-Daughters-of-I-will-arise Hollywood funerals, so everybody you knew can get a lot of free publicity weeping at the bier. Then the District Attorney horns in on some of the headlines and starts a lot of rumors that you were bumped off or you had some horrible disease.

"That's Hollywood fame! Thank God, I'm just a ham leading man."

Randolph had punctuated this grandiose bit of oratory with frequent attacks on the vicious kümmel. Having finished both, he slid into a large chair and went placidly to sleep.

III

Whitey walked rather uncertainly to the set, wondering if Randolph would be needed in any more scenes that day, and, if so, what possibility there might be of his performing them. He sneered at Blynn, smiled at Sonia Varon, speculating mildly on what manner she might receive amorous advances, then caught a glimpse of another group. It consisted of three persons. One was Mme. Clore, the second was Fishbein, and the third was Israel Hoffberger, who was paying a visit to the set.

Whitey tried to duck away without being seen, but Mme. Clore summoned him and courteously introduced him to the visiting executive. Hoffberger looked at him long and searchingly as they shook hands.

"I believe," he said, with great unction, "that I have met Mr. White somewhere before."

The tone and the look on his sinister face left no doubt in Whitey's mind that the little man had recognized him from the encounter at Grace's apartment. He grinned, somewhat sheepishly, and excused himself a moment later.

Fishbein and Hoffberger had been bosom friends for many years. Therefore, Whitey was not surprised, next morning, to learn that his employment with the Rethea Clore unit had ended abruptly.

CHAPTER ELEVEN

Upon his abrupt discharge from the job with Rethea Clore, Whitey found himself with about three hundred dollars and no very good prospect of future employment in Hollywood. Israel Hoffberger was one of the most powerful figures in the film industry. Whitey reasoned that if Hoffberger could have him discharged from one position, he probably could do so from every other if he chose. Consequently, assuming that he could do nothing further to injure his chances in Hollywood, inasmuch as there seemed to be no more chances, Whitey set about to devise some means of making his enemy acutely uncomfortable.

At first thought, the possibility of his ever being able to confound a man of such wealth and position seemed remote indeed. But with all the nonchalance of a penniless police reporter before whom mayors and police chiefs tremble, Whitey attacked the problem as best he could.

The only conceivable opening, Whitey decided, was through Hoffberger's clandestine affair with Grace Harper. In order to make the most of it, and for personal reasons as well, he spent a great deal of time with the friendly, dark-eyed extra girl. The next few weeks were happy ones for Whitey, who never worried about his economic status until his last penny was gone. He made a payment on the roadster from his savings, which assured him of transportation for another month.

It was midsummer again and his program was a simple and satisfactory one. He spent his afternoons swimming at Santa Monica, his evenings with Grace or in roistering with the merry blades of the Major, and his nights with Jane.

And one evening he found an opening in his silent, one-man campaign against Israel Hoffberger. Whitey went to Grace's apartment laden with gin, and after several highballs, they decided to dine in state at the Plantation, out on Washington boulevard. While Grace was dressing, Whitey prowled about her apartment abstractedly. Her handbag was on the dining table. He went through it, more out of curiosity than with any notion of petty thievery. And there he found it—a check made out to Grace and signed by Israel Hoffberger, obviously for the coming month's rent.

"The poor, dumb sap!" he chortled. "Making it out in her name."

He pocketed it and replaced the bag just as Grace emerged from her boudoir.

The check buried deep in his pocket, Whitey was not a highly entertaining companion for Grace that evening. He was searching for some plan of action that might embroil Hoffberger in a great deal of embarrassment and trouble. On first consideration, there seemed to be nothing in particular he could do about it. Hoffberger was a bachelor, and the code of Hollywood toward mistresses was broad and expansive. Whitey puzzled over the rooming-house ordinance, but gave it up as impractical. For one thing, that ancient morality law could hardly be applied to apartments, and for another, he shrank from any action that would embarrass Grace.

"Anyway," he told himself, as they drove homeward late that night, "I have documentary evidence that the handsome Mr. Hoffberger is eating off his knife with an extra girl. That's something."

Grace never solved the mystery of the check's disappearance. She vaguely suspected Whitey when she first missed it and informed her patron that it was gone. The check was never presented to the bank for payment, however, and they assumed it had been lost.

Hoffberger gave her another.

II

Whitey made a few desultory efforts to find employment in the studios, but the blank reception which greeted him everywhere indicated that Hoffberger had dropped a warning word to his fellow producers. Things are done that way in the studios of Hollywood. Many an employee suddenly has found himself against a brick wall. Often he is unable to find out what mighty personage he has offended.

Whitey attempted to do some fiction writing in a half-hearted sort of way. He was too lazy to follow through any difficult campaign of work, and a single rejection slip was enough to discourage him for months. In one burst of energy he did devote several days to preparing an outline of an original screen story based on an incident he had witnessed in Chicago. He called the story *Gun Man*, and thought it not bad, himself. Having finished it, however, he had no idea how to market it, and the various scenario editors to whom he mailed it, returned the manuscript with dizzying rapidity.

His improvident and careless manner of living caused a rapid decline in his hoard of savings. Jane, who had fallen out with the voice culturist, was proving a rather expensive luxury, too, and he considered making an attempt to find work on one of the Los Angeles papers.

One morning he read an item in *The Examiner* which seemed to offer him a golden opportunity. It was an announcement of the engagement of Israel Hoffberger and Ruth Michaels, the daughter of Aaron Michaels.

Whitey mulled this over for many an hour.

Aaron Michaels was president and ruling head of the vast film corporation which employed Hoffberger in the capacity of supervising executive. Michaels was one of the most distinguished ornaments of the picture industry. He was a dignified and cultured gentleman who commanded respect and admiration in every circle he entered. His business career and his private life were both spotless, and his reputation for honesty and integrity was unassailable. In the most peculiar, and often the shadiest industry of all time, he stood head and shoulders above his associates.

But the quality about him which interested Whitey most, from the standpoint of Hoffberger, was his religion. Michaels was a devout, orthodox Jew, proud of his creed and faithful to every tenet of it. He was a home-loving man whose greatest pride was in his family, and his daughter Ruth was the chief concern of his life. She had been sheltered from the world, educated in the religion of her fathers, and zealously guarded from any contact with the more sordid side of the industry in which her father was a leader.

After reading the announcement of the engagement, Whitey stretched out on his bed, smoked many cigarettes, and stared hard at the ceiling as he contemplated a course of action. Would Hoffberger dare have his employer know that he had been supporting a mistress while he was courting Miss Michaels? Whitey, knowing Michaels' reputation, was fairly certain that the producer was ignorant of it.

Whitey, too, was aware how much the alliance would mean to Hoffberger. It would assure him of a permanent place in the industry, which means as much to a supervisor as it does to an office boy. And it would give him, eventually, a tremendous share in one of the largest and richest organizations in the world. But what to do with this tangled bit of information?

The only tangible evidence Whitey had was the check, and any move on his part would be blackmail of the baldest sort. This did not alarm Whitey much. He had a profound contempt for the police. His journalistic career had included a fairly comprehensive record of bribery, minor blackmail, graft, forgery, and a few odd jobs of house-breaking. Moral scruples were unknown to him.

He thought of Dorothy Irving and bounced to his feet in glee. Here, he reflected, might be an opportunity to get his protégée her chance upon the screen and at the same time bring considerable uneasiness to the man who had done a bad turn for both of them. How to do it was another matter. Hoffberger was notorious as one of the most unapproachable of the Hollywood studio barons, and he would not be likely to welcome an interview with the man who had disturbed his amours.

Whitey had broken in on senators and governors with gay unconcern, however, and he felt utterly confident that he could somehow contrive a meeting. He considered several methods. He might apply at the studio representing himself as a reporter from one of the downtown papers, but that meant a preliminary scrutiny from the press department of the studio. He thought of writing Hoffberger a letter, hinting at the importance of such an interview, but rejected it immediately because it would give his victim documentary evidence of his activities. He studied Hoffberger's habits as best he could, trying to find an unguarded moment in the executive's busy schedule.

One evening chance arranged the meeting, after Whitey had been unable to do so. Dancing at the Roosevelt with Jane, Whitey stumbled into Hoffberger, in the wash-room of the hotel. There was no one else in the room at the moment. Whitey had no thought of finding his man here, but leaped at the opportunity avidly.

"Mr. Hoffberger," he said, pleasantly enough, "can I talk to you for five minutes seriously, on a matter of business?"

Hoffberger recognized Whitey and scowled.

"I have nothing to talk to you about," he said shortly, and turned away.

"No," Whitey answered, "you haven't. But I have something to talk to you about, and you'll want to hear it."

Something in Whitey's tone made Hoffberger wary.

"Well, what is it? I haven't all night. I'm dining with some friends."

"Let's do it some other time, then," Whitey proposed. "It can wait a few days. I really need a little time. I know," he paused significantly, "you'll be glad to hear me."

Hoffberger jerked a paper towel from the holder and rubbed his hands, thinking fast. He couldn't imagine what Whitey might have in his mind, except, perhaps, something in connection with the episode at Grace's apartment. But his electric brain told him to tread softly.

"Come out to the studio," he said.

"Can't I see you at home? You're so busy at the studio, and this is very important."

That might be better, Hoffberger reflected. If there were any trouble in the air, it would be better to keep this man away from the office. He gave Whitey his address, set the meeting for the following night, and left without another word. He was far from easy in his mind. He feared reporters, and this smooth-talking, sharp-eyed, young man made him unusually apprehensive.

III

Whitey was taking a desperate chance and knew it. His scheme might easily embroil him in the law, but he decided to risk it. He gave the check to Joe Greet so that it could not be found on him if Hoffberger chose to invite police to the interview.

Next evening, at the appointed hour, he rapped at the door of the impressive house where Hoffberger lived with his family. Previously, he had made careful survey of the neighbourhood for several blocks, and saw no police cars or evidence of a trap.

Hoffberger, most decidedly, was not cordial.

This mysterious interview had been on his mind all day, and the more he dwelt on it, the more uneasy he became. Instinct told him this surely was connected with Grace, and he had thought of questioning her about it, but decided against it.

"I'll give you just ten minutes," Hoffberger said, as he led Whitey into the library. "Why I'm doing this I don't know."

Whitey had peered about the house carefully as he entered, and was fairly certain there were no listeners.

"Do you remember Dorothy Irving?" he began.

"Dorothy Irving? Yes. What about her?"

"She came to Hollywood, you know, on a beauty contest staged by your company. You induced her to stay. She is now working as a waitress in Henry's. All I want to do is to ask you to give her another chance on the screen."

Hoffberger snorted in contempt.

"Is that what you came here for? Is that why you persuaded me to break an important business appointment?"

He started toward the door, raging.

"Wait a minute, Mr. Hoffberger," Whitey continued. "That isn't all. Miss Irving deserves a chance. She didn't get a real one before. I know she'll make good. You're the man to give her that chance."

"This sounds like a cheap, amateurish attempt at blackmail," Hoffberger stormed. "I've had no connection with Miss Irving at all, except that I was an official in the studio where she came as a contest winner. We lived up to every agreement we made. I don't owe her a thing."

"Very well," said Whitey calmly, "I'll concede that. You don't owe her a thing, except that she'd be back home where she belongs if you hadn't persuaded her to stay."

"I did nothing of the sort."

"All right. We'll not argue about that. There is just one thing more. I've decided to have a chat with Aaron Michaels—a long, personal visit."

Hoffberger's outward calmness effectively concealed

the sudden, vague terror this innocent remark brought him.

"A talk about what?"

Whitey smiled benignly.

"A talk about you and Grace Harper."

Hoffberger had played in poker games where thousands were at stake. He did not change expression.

"Do you know what I'm going to do?" he asked. "I'm going to phone the Hollywood police and have you arrested for attempted blackmail."

He reached for the telephone.

"That'll be fine," Whitey said. "Before you do, just consider what you're going to tell them. Have I tried to blackmail you? All I came for—if you call the police—was to ask for a job. You haven't a thing on me."

Hoffberger did not make the call.

"You haven't a thing on me, either. What do you know about Grace Harper and me?"

"I caught you in her apartment. I've seen you there other times when you didn't know I was watching, and I know you are paying the rent."

"You can't prove it."

"That's something Mr. Michaels can decide. He'll love the idea that you were keeping a mistress while you were engaged to his daughter, won't he! You're a model boy, all right. So he thinks. You don't drink and you don't smoke. But here's one place where you've stubbed your toe."

"He won't believe it—your word against mine—a cheap, drunken press agent!"

Whitey grew stern.

"Listen to this, you little kike," he said, dangerously calm. "Another crack like that and I'll not only queer you with Michaels, but I'll break that smug little pan of yours, too. He doesn't have to take my word for it. I've got proof—on paper—that you can't explain away.

"And here's something else," he continued. "You're going through with this and you're not going to make any trouble for Grace or Miss Irving, either. Neither of them knows anything about this. They never will know it, unless you tell them.

"You can call this blackmail if you want. I'm not getting a dime out of it. All I'm doing is to help a nice kid that you tried to buy and couldn't.

"Make up your mind right now whether Dorothy Irving gets her contract or I pay a visit to Michaels."

Hoffberger sat down before his desk and was silent for a long time. He could not believe that he had left a trail behind him, but instinct told him that Whitey was dangerous.

"Let's have your proof," he said at last.

"You'll get your proof when I see Dorothy Irving's signed contract for a year."

"You're bluffing. I won't do a thing."

"What do you think old man Michaels would say if he saw your personal check made out to Grace Harper?"

Hoffberger remembered the lost check with a start. He inwardly abused himself for not having broken with Grace sooner, as he had intended.

"Another thing," Whitey continued. "You might be able to explain this check away, but suppose Michaels asked to see your cancelled checks for the last year or so. You keep them and he'll know it."

Why not? Hoffberger asked himself. A year's contract for Dorothy Irving would be easy to arrange, and if he could get the check away from Whitey, it would prevent any possible slip-up in his lucrative marriage plans.

"How can I do this?" he asked.

"It's simple. Go into Henry's tomorrow evening. Dorothy will be working there, thanks to you. Make an appointment with her. I'll bring her out to the studio and we'll sign the contract. I don't intend to hold you up. I just want to get this girl a chance. After the contract is signed I'll tear up the check. But I want it understood that she's to be given a real chance—not forgotten."

"I couldn't trust you to tear it up."

"You'll have to trust me," Whitey decreed. "You're a trusting soul, anyway, handing out personal checks like that. It'll be a lesson to you."

IV

Four days later, the dramatic pages of the Los Angeles newspapers announced that Israel Hoffberger had made another of his sensational screen discoveries and had signed Dorothy Irving to a year's contract.

Mr. Hoffberger was none too happy as he read these items, but he was consoled by the comforting knowledge that the vagrant check was nothing now but a pile of ashes. Whitey, of course, had photographed the check as a matter of precaution. But Hoffberger did not know it.

Dorothy was joyous but bewildered, Whitey exuberant, as they drove away from the studio, her contract for a year safe in his possession.

"I don't understand," she said, "why Mr. Hoffberger should do this now."

"Oh," said Whitey, loftily, "he's not such a bad guy, after all. I told him about you and he decided maybe he hadn't treated you right. Anyway, he's in love, and a man always feels benign when he's in love."

Whitey drove back to the Major feeling as happy as though he had found a million dollars in cash on the pavement.

"Old man White," he sang to himself, "just going about the world scattering sunshine and doing good everywhere!"

He had triumphed over his arch-enemy, indulged in some visible gloating, and launched his protégée upon what might prove a successful screen career.

True, less than twenty dollars remained of his savings, and he was no nearer employment than he had been before the Hoffberger incident, but the world seemed an eminently satisfactory place.

CHAPTER TWELVE

MONDAY dawned as a raw October day. Summer was through. So, apparently, was Whitey in the picture business.

His rent had been unpaid for two weeks. The finance company had seized his roadster for failure to make payments. Joe Greet had been fired from his job as comedy director largely because he had joined Whitey in a three-day spree to celebrate the victory over Hoff-berger. McGinnis was out of town on a long location trip. Whitey owed various sums to almost every tenant of the Major. Checks he had strewn about were bouncing with a dull, sickening thud on everyone who had been so injudicious as to cash them. Rocco had shut off his credit.

He might have borrowed from Romaine Randolph, but hesitated to do so because he was aware of the im-positions constantly being placed on prominent actors.

Worst of all, he had fallen out with Jane. In his cups he had been unable to refrain from boasting of his feat in getting Dorothy Irving her contract. Jane, upon learning of it, had flown into a furious tantrum —for which she could hardly be blamed—because Whitey had not given her the opportunity.

The celebration of his triumph left him with a raw

taste in his mouth and nerves jangling like a burglar alarm. He drank pitchers of ice water and berated himself for his various follies.

"What a chump," he groaned to himself. "Throwing my money around as if I had millions . . . quarreling with producers and getting myself barred from studios . . ."

He sat in his tiny room, this morning, for some hours. Formless fears and vague apprehensions beset him on all sides. He had the feeling that unknown horrors would pounce upon him if he left his sanctuary. He even resolved to quit drinking.

Hunger drove him to the lobby at last. He determined to find some kind soul who might buy him breakfast and stake him to carfare. He had not a dime, nor an overcoat, and the chill wind from the Pacific did nothing to restore his calm. He hoped to sneak out of the lobby undetected by the management, but the desk clerk called his name just as he was sidling through the door.

"Some mail for you," the clerk called, almost civilly, and handed Whitey several envelopes. They promised nothing of interest. A bill for his rent, included among his letters, depressed him first. There was also a bill from a florist and a threatening note from the proprietor of a cabaret who had taken an entirely worthless check in payment for a large and expensive dinner party. There was an invitation to attend an opening at the Cathay Circle Theater, providing he sent ten dollars for tickets.

Then he found it. A thin letter from the K.F.C. Studio caught his eye. He almost threw it away, assuming it to be an advertisement.

Inside he found a short, courteous note from Paul Bannon, an official of the studio. It informed him that his screen story, *Gun Man*, had been passed on favorably and accepted, and that if he would call at the studio to sign the necessary papers, agreements and releases, a check for five thousand dollars would be given to him.

Whitey stared at the letter for some moments in dumb amazement. It was utterly impossible, he told himself, for he had never sent his story to K.F.C. at all. It was some one's vicious practical joke, he decided. Then he saw a likely explanation. Jane had had a copy of the story, and Paul Bannon had been squiring her about, to his own financial loss. Apparently she had exerted her professional wiles to induce him to accept the story.

The shock was too great for Whitey to map out a course of action for some time. After turning the letter over and over in his hand, and reading it again and again, he made his first move. It was to find the manager of the Major.

"Mr. Fletcher," he said, when that cold-eyed boniface had granted him an audience. "How'd you like to have me pay my bill."

Fletcher eyed him with intense suspicion.

"What's the gag?" he asked. "Have you really got the money?"

"Have I got it!" Whitey shouted, and brandished the letter triumphantly. "Look at that. Drive me over to the studio and I'll pay you what I owe you. I haven't a penny outside of this."

An hour later, after Whitey had interviewed the pompous Scenario Editor of the K.F.C. Studio, signed innumerable documents and clutched a check for five thousand dollars, he stood on Hollywood Boulevard in front of the Bank of Italy. He had paid his rent. In his pocket he caressed a roll of bills amounting to slightly less than a thousand dollars. In another pocket was a bright, new bankbook, with the single entry of four thousand dollars on the first page.

Gone were all recollections of the early morning remorse. The sun was shining again. There were so many things Whitey wanted to do that he could find no starting point. After staring into the busy traffic at Highland Avenue and the Boulevard for some moments, he summoned a taxicab and ordered the driver to proceed down Hollywood Boulevard.

"Anybody that doesn't like this life is crazy," he told the driver, who looked at Whitey carefully and wondered if he were sufficiently far gone to roll.

The cab continued through the center of Hollywood until Van Ness Avenue had been passed. The street gave Whitey an inspiration.

"Turn down here," he ordered, "and go to Lucey's on Melrose. It's right next to the Lasky studio."

At Lucey's, Hollywood's foremost speakeasy, Whitey drank a cup of coffee, two Martinis and a synthetic absinthe frappé.   Occasionally he laughed aloud in sheer exuberance, to the intense surprise of the startled Italian waiter, who shook his head and muttered, "This Hollywood—what a place."

From Lucey's he telephoned Joe Greet and told him to stand by.   Then he re-entered the waiting cab and drove to Schwab's, on the Boulevard.   There he rapidly selected three suits, a dozen shirts, six gaudy ties, an assortment of silk underwear, two suits of purple pajamas, three pairs of shoes, and a stick.   He had no hat, but didn't notice it.   He offered the tailor an extra ten if one of the suits were ready that afternoon.

He also phoned Johnny Rocco.   Joe Greet and Rocco were waiting in his room when he returned to the Major, the latter with three cases of Scotch and the firm intention of taking them back unless cash payment developed.   Whitey ordered a dozen seltzer bottles, a case of ginger ale and a bathtub full of ice.   Then he began to call his creditors, while Joe and Rocco alternately served him drinks.

By three o'clock that afternoon he owed not a cent in the world except, of course, for various forgotten debts in Chicago, New Orleans, Denver, Seattle, Kansas City and other ports where his journalistic bark had touched.

Whitey held open house, and all the Major swarmed to his room.   Came Fanya Pausdrovnavitch, who was induced to leave her baby python behind, and the gloomy Straubel, and Marguerite Fish, and—naturally—Bob Carey, and the voluptuous Fanchon Dubarois, who immediately began to cast about for some means of dipping into Whitey's roll, and the three greasy gentlemen from Brooklyn. Even the normal man on the third floor came up to watch the fun.

Whitey paid the hotel bills of both Joe Greet and Frank Carson, and dragged the latter protestingly to the party.

Jane Wilson came, too, with the polite and affable Paul Bannon in tow. The executive had already apprised her of the purchase of *Gun Man*. The news immediately erased her indignation at Whitey, as he was fairly certain it would.

Bannon grinned as he shook hands with Whitey.

"So you're Whitey?" he said. "I've heard a lot about you?"

"Heard about me?" asked Whitey, in surprise. "From whom?"

"From everybody," Bannon answered. "You're as famous in Hollywood as Aimee Semple McPherson, or Peter the Hermit. I was present during your spectacular speech at the Sam Schmalz banquet for one thing. I think it ranks with the Gettysburg address."

Whitey liked him instantly. No more charming soul had ever set foot in Hollywood. Bannon was a cultured, dapper little cosmopolite, of Jewish birth, who was known in New York and Paris and Vienna as widely as he was in Hollywood. Why he had ever elected to waste his various talents on the film industry Whitey could never learn.

No thought of the morrow disturbed Whitey. The

sum of five thousand dollars was so vast that he could not see beyond it. He was Hollywood's playboy. With Jane and Joe Greet and Frank Carson and the amused Bannon, who could never have imagined Whitey, the jubilant author sailed about Hollywood like a conquering hero.

He acquired the first evening dress of his career. With his string of camp-followers he upset the dignity of the Biltmore supper room, was twice ejected from the Roosevelt, invaded the Cocoanut Grove, took over La Boheme for an entire evening, hired a fleet of cabs to take his party to Santa Monica for a midnight swim in the chilly Pacific, and visited the gaudy Pom-Pom on the return trip. He hunted up strange speakeasies and fancy bordellos in downtown Los Angeles, and roamed in and out of the castles of the cinema great.

Hollywood was his.

It was Paul Bannon who gave Whitey his first glimpse of a Beverly Hills party. Whitey insisted that Frank Carson be included. For days he had tried to shake the husband of Louise Bagshaw from his despondency, but was successful only for brief intervals.

"I can't go," Carson protested. "I don't feel like it, and besides I haven't any decent clothes."

"I'll buy you a Tuxedo," Whitey argued, but Carson would not be persuaded.

"Besides," he said, "I might meet Louise. She's sure to be there. I couldn't stand that."

"That's just why I want you to go," Whitey an-

[172]

swered. "Put up your chin and show her you're not licked."

Carson could not be moved, and the evening of the gaudy affair found Whitey, Jane and Bannon reluctantly leaving him behind.

They came from miles around to the vast pink palace inhabited by Sonia Varon and her consort of the dubious, European title. Only about half of those who arrived had been invited. This did not cramp the party, however. It is customary to prepare for a certain amount of overflow.

McGinnis was there, back from location, unwillingly escorting the radiant Rethea Clore, who peered at Whitey somewhat coolly.

Fishbein was there, too, with his pretty wife, some twenty years his junior. So was Romaine Randolph, and Gilbert Vance, with Peanuts, of course, and Lucille Jettifer, with the inevitable Bobby DeSales, and the be-moustached screen hero, Gerald Normandy, whose capacity for both alcohol and lechery had become a Hollywood legend, and Louise Bagshaw, with Jack Sylvester, who had been her constant public companion since Carson had stormed away. There was Tom Reilly, the belligerent pugilist-novelist, who remained aloof in a corner, drinking prodigiously and snarling at the passing film stars. With him was Jack Jarnegan, the famous Irish director. Present too was Israel Hoffberger, with his fiancée, Ruth Michaels. Hoffberger refused to return Whitey's pleasant greeting.

There were assorted actors, playwrights, scenario

writers, directors, producers, novelists, actresses and artists of dubious abilities. There was a smattering of the European nobility which infests Hollywood, whose titles, somehow, seem to condone their conduct. There were unpedigreed Hollywood blondes, and Hollywood gigolos, never together, of course. There were song writers, and several stage stars, and a tennis champion and a publisher, and a middle-weight prizefighter, and the profligate son of one of the nation's richest men, and a writer for a national magazine who was later to lampoon them all in print.

There were servants under-foot. There was a buffet supper large enough to feed the Belgian army. There was synthetic champagne, made the week before in Boyle Heights, but the wary avoided it for the gin, un-blushingly synthetic but reasonably safe.

There was Whitey, too, of course.

Eminently presentable, well tailored, just drunk enough to be irresistible, his eyes always on the alert for adventure and seduction, Whitey circled about the enormous mansion, a beast of prey, ready for anything.

There was dancing to the music of what almost amounted to a symphony orchestra. There was swim-ming in the huge pool of black and yellow tile. There was a card room where the producers gathered for pinochle and poker. There was a luxurious projection room where *The Tigress* just completed, was to be shown later. There was a spacious garden and many secluded nooks for the luring of willing females.

There was a buzz of conversation, punctuated by

laughter. So steady and persistent was it that Whitey was reminded of the Cubs' Park in Chicago just before a World Series game.

Friends and strangers wandered in and out, bidden and unbidden, mingling with easy, small-town familiarity. The same people had attended the same parties, in the same circle of mansions, had danced with the same partners, delivered the same witticisms, drunk the same drinks and slept with the same females for many a year.

And the talk? They discussed pictures, and yachts, and pictures, and women, and pictures, and men, and pictures, and each other—out of earshot—and pictures, and divers other subjects, including pictures.

"I'd like you to come out to the studio and see my picture," Whitey heard one director say, quite seriously. "I want you to get those Lubitsch touches of mine . . ."

A quaint situation presented itself when Gerald Normandy found himself seated upon a spacious divan with one former wife, one former mistress, and his flame of the moment. The three fell to comparing notes on him, discussing peculiarities, traits and intimate mannerisms. He bowed himself away, graciously remarking that he did not care to be a restraining influence on the conversation.

Whitey saw a sad, dark little man, obviously Continental, wandering dispiritedly through the crowd, and was told that it was the royal husband of Sonia Varon.

"Ah," Whitey commented "the egg that laid the Golden Goose."

With Romaine Randolph he joined a hilarious group of actors who were discussing, as usual, the film industry.

"He means well? And in the picture business? Don't kid me!"

". . . I don't know what his name is, but he certainly cuts a lovely throat."

"He's no actor. He couldn't play an old man well, if he was a hundred years old . . ."

". . . You know what they call the Producers' Association now? 'The Seven That Should Be Hanged' . . ."

"Louise Bagshaw told me she's going to have an appendicitis operation."

". . . What? Another one? She's had that appendix removed four times this year."

"She probably meant Hollywood appendicitis . . ."

"Didja hear the new answer to 'Who was the lady I saw you with last night? . . . 'That's no lady . . . that girl's in pictures'."

"Y' know, I just figured out why actors squander their money on yachts. It's so they can get away where the casting directors can't phone 'em. After two years at Colossal, I've decided to get a rowboat, put a sail on it, and start out to sea with a good off-shore wind. And when a man-eating shark comes up and shows his teeth, I'm going to laugh at him, and say, 'You can't scare

me, you little runt; I've worked for Sam Schmalz.' Then
I'll go overboard . . ."

Whitey contrived to elbow Hoffberger into a corner
where the producer could not, with decency, elude him.

"How's my protégée, Dorothy Irving, getting
along?" He asked, innocently.

"Very well," said Hoffberger. "I think she'll be a hit
on the screen."

"I'm convinced of it, too," Whitey answered. "That's
why I . . . prevailed . . . upon you to give her a
chance."

"What is your intense interest in the lady?" Hoffberger asked, with a vicious smile.

"Purely altruistic," Whitey replied, and returned the
smile. "I'd like to see a nice girl get along in pictures
just for the novelty of it. I'm the only man in the
world who ever pimped for a virgin."

Whitey managed an introduction to Louise Bagshaw.
He wanted to see for himself just what it was about
her that had made Frank Carson yearn for her so
futilely. She surprised him, for he could discover no
great amount of physical charm, and no mentality
whatsoever.

"I'm a friend of your husband," Whitey was indiscreet enough to say.

She simpered.

"And how is dear Frank?" she asked. He observed
that her assumed British accent had been restored since
Carson's restraining influence had departed.

"He's . . . all right," he returned. "He lives in the apartment next to me."

"Frank is a dear boy," she said. "I was frightfully fond of him, but we were just incompatible . . . We artists, you know . . . Just impossible to get along. I hope he does well."

"He says he's looking for a job in a shoe store," Whitey replied, bluntly.

"Oh dear," she sighed, then added quickly. "Give him my love, won't you, Mr. White? I shall never forget him."

She ended the conversation abruptly. Whitey, a moment later, saw her flit across the floor to dance with Sylvester.

For want of something better to do, Whitey entered into a long discourse with Lucille Jettifer, who had become somewhat expansive in her cups. He discussed the higher reaches of journalism with a platitudinous depth which surprised even himself, agreed with her upon the importance of film critics and the quality of her magazine, held her hand tentatively, and decided that if he could oust Bobby DeSales from his position of lap-dog, temporarily, he could probably benefit by her patronage. Apparently, he concluded, this would not be difficult to do. In fact he was launching preliminary overtures with that in mind when a servant summoned him to the telephone.

"Whitey," said a voice, "this is Joe Greet. I've got some bad news. Frank Carson just killed himself up here at the Major. He left a note for you."

"I'll be right up there," Whitey said, and raced back to the ballroom to tell Jane of his departure. En route, he came upon Louise Bagshaw and Sylvester, dancing, and broke in upon them.

"You may be interested to know," he said, rather thickly, "that Frank Carson has just shot himself."

"Oh, dear!" Louise clutched her throat. Sylvester looked extremely uncomfortable.

"Where is he?" the director asked.

"At the Major Hotel, on Cahuenga."

"I'll go there right away," Louise said.

"That's fine," Whitey clicked through his teeth as he started away. "A pity you didn't go there yesterday. He might be alive yet."

CHAPTER THIRTEEN

LOUISE BAGSHAW tried to conceal from the press the real reason for her husband's suicide. Whitey forestalled this through Jim Mitchell and his other friends among the reporters, and the sob stories that appeared throughout the land did neither Miss Bagshaw nor Jack Sylvester a great deal of good. Whitey felt the most he could do for the unhappy Carson was to reveal what had prompted him to end his life.

Miss Bagshaw, weeping copiously for the benefit of the news photographers, and staging daily collapses whenever members of the press were present, tried to take charge of the funeral and give her late husband a gaudy, Hollywood burial.

But Carson's note to Whitey said:

"Good-bye, Whitey. You're the only friend I've got. Please make them ship my body back to my brother in Minneapolis. I wouldn't rest easy if they buried me here. I hope you get a better break with life than I did."

Whitey, after a great deal of bickering, managed to carry out Carson's request, and refused to let Miss Bagshaw contribute a cent toward the expenses. She wept and pleaded. Her tawdry little heart had been touched, not so much by the tragic suicide as by the realization that she had caused it. She attempted to conceal her own feeling of guilt by a display of dramatics.

"Frank was my husband," she howled at Whitey. "I'll bury him here and pay for it myself."

"You'll do nothing of the sort," Whitey said. "I'm going to do what he asked, and I'm going to pay for it. You threw down a good guy when you had him. Now that it's too late, you're trying to cover up what a rotten wife you've been."

"Look here," Sylvester put in, "you can't talk that way to Miss Bagshaw."

Whitey smiled at him savagely.

"I *am* talking that way to Miss Bagshaw," he said, with great emphasis. "And furthermore, Mr. Sylvester, the more you keep out of this the better. You've got a hell of a nerve coming around here at all. You speak out of turn again, and I'll smear you all over the end of Hollywood."

"You don't realize how dear Frank was to me," Miss Bagshaw said, trying to inject a sob into her voice.

"I realize it perfectly," Whitey said. "That's just why I intend to take this into my own hands. I never saw anything so ghoulish in my life, as you two hanging around here after he's dead. You broke his heart, both of you; and now that he's killed himself, the only thing it means to you is a chance for a lot of publicity at the funeral.

"You're a couple of important people in this mining camp," he continued. "That's what Frank called it. But one thing you can't stand is notoriety. You've had some already, but if you don't keep out of this you're going to get a lot more. I'm an expert on notoriety."

Whitey won the argument, as he had a way of doing. He paid the undertaker and the expense of sending the body east. He wrote as diplomatic a letter as he could compose to Carson's brother. He made all the arrangements, gathered together the pitifully few possessions Carson could call his own, and managed to conduct the entire affair in scrupulously good taste.

II

The afternoon that they were to ship the earthly remains of Frank Carson to his brother in Minneapolis, a little group gathered in the undertaking parlors.

Louise Bagshaw was not present. Neither was Jack Sylvester. Neither were any of those who had once been guests in the mansion Frank once regarded as home. Neither were any other of the cinema great who had called him friend and ridiculed him behind his back.

Whitey was there. So were Jane, and McGinnis, and Joe Greet, and Jim Mitchell, and Bob Carey, and the night bellboy from the Major, and Johnny Rocco.

The negro chauffeur who had loaned Frank twenty-five dollars could not come because he had to drive his mistress to a tea that afternoon. He sent flowers instead.

There was no ceremony. The group stood about awkwardly, feeling that some observance of the occasion should be made. But no one knew what to do. The people who had befriended him when his old circle of acquaintances had turned him away, took a last look at the husband of Louise Bagshaw before they crated the coffin. An expression of peace was on his face. He might almost have been asleep, dreaming of the girl he had known in Duluth.

"He was a good guy," said Whitey.

"Yes," said Joe Greet, "a good, square guy sitting in a game where the cards were stacked."

"God-damn!" said Johnny Rocco. "Think of a dame trading him for Jack Sylvester, and figuring she had come out ahead!"

Jane Wilson wept a little, and Rocco, a sentimental Latin, did too. McGinnis swore softly, and said nothing.

"Did Carson owe you any money?" Whitey asked Rocco.

"Not a cent," Rocco lied, and continued. "Who's paying the expenses back to Minneapolis?"

"I am."

"Only half," said Rocco. "The other half is mine."

When the express company truck came for the box, they all returned silently to the Major. Jane wondered how any member of her sex could be as cruel as Louise Bagshaw. Rocco wondered if Carson would have liked him to bump off Jack Sylvester. Whitey wondered if a prolonged spree would make him forget the events of the past few days.

Frank Carson would have approved of the circumstances surrounding his departure from Hollywood.

Chapter Fourteen

Lucille Jettifer, apparently recalling with pleasure Whitey's tentative advances at Sonia Varon's party, invited Whitey and Jane to be her guests at the world premiere of a new picture at the Cathay Circle Theater.

A lengthy and bibulous dinner preceded the theater party. No one goes to the first night of a movie in Hollywood before nine o'clock, and the more wary ones not until nine-thirty, even though the events are uniformly scheduled to begin at half-past eight. The lateness is a result of itself. Hollywood has learned by experience that no premiere ever starts on time, and consequently no one ever arrives at the appointed hour. Thus, the festivities begin later and later on every succeeding occasion. Where this will end, no one knows.

It was the usual blatant, raucous, befuddling opening night of which Hollywood alone is capable. Giant spotlights pawed the sky and glared into the eyes of spectators. Thousands of gaping movie fans jammed the streets to see the stars come in. So great was the jam, indeed, that it was with great difficulty the stars could come in at all. Hawkers rented boxes and folding chairs to gapers. Hordes of uniformed police, who

[184]

should have been pursuing bandits, kept the on-lookers
in line.

A giant voice amplifier, operated from the roof,
announced the arrival of every celebrity. The announce-
ments were not always correct, but they satisfied. Edmund Lowe was introduced as Reginald Denny. Pauline
Frederick was mistaken for Joan Crawford. Irving
Thalberg was somewhat astonished to hear that he was
Charlie Chaplin.

Lucille Jettifer, sweeping grandly through the lobby
in a startling red evening gown, was announced of
course, and bowed and smirked to the watchers, who
had no idea of her identity or occupation, but were sure
that Jane Wilson and the handsome Bobby DeSales
must be celebrities.

The audience of stars and near-stars, celebrities and
near-celebrities, assembled at last in the theater. It
might have been Old Home Week. Friends greeted
friends, wandered up and down the aisles, retired to
the smoking room for last-minute nips at flasks, and
chatted noisily during the projection of the news-reel
and comedy.

Whitey, befuddled by seventeen highballs before dinner and almost as many after, basked in the clammy
warmth of the crowded theater and wondered how soon
the liquor would wear off and the hang-over set in.

The feature picture, for the first showing of which
all these famous folk had gathered so ostentatiously,
began at last. Whitey tried to find out what it was
about, but gave up after the first reel. It was a war

picture, as far as he could ascertain, for there seemed to be a prodigious number of scenes of marching men and weeping wives, and the drummer was working himself into a lather by hammering upon his instruments to produce martial noises.

Whitey was pretty certain there was a Red Cross nurse wandering through it, and a French girl, and an overly handsome leading man who had never mastered a military salute. The scenes in No Man's Land distressed him somewhat because of the frequent, blinding flashes on the screen, and he yearned more heartily for the Armistice than he had ever done during his service in France.

The last thing he remembered was being scowled at for suddenly applauding the death of a pompous character actor, in the uniform of a Roxy doorman, who had just spoken the title:

"We do not make war on women."

Then he slumped forward quietly in his seat, put his head on Lucille Jettifer's muscular shoulder, and went to sleep.

He must have slept through the remainder of the picture, for when he regained semi-consciousness, the lights in the pit were turned on, and the audience was applauding vigorously, probably because the picture had drawn to a close at last.

Still half asleep, he saw upon the stage a dapper man in full evening dress who seemed to be making a speech. It was probably Fred Niblo, he told himself, because Fred Niblo made most of the speeches in Hollywood, although it might have been Conrad Nagel, or Charlie Murray, or even Al Jolson.

Then Jane was shaking him by the shoulders and he sat up with a start to find that the aisles were jammed with sweating drama-lovers crowding for the exits.

His brain was still somewhat numb when he found himself in the crowded lobby, shaking hands with a tall, plump gentleman whose name he did not hear.

"How'd you like the picture?" Whitey heard him ask, and feeling that some reply was necessary, said:

"The stench of it almost kept me awake."

He was told later that the unnamed man had directed the picture.

Lucille, Jane, Bobby and Whitey crowded into Lucille's limousine, and were being whisked away, he knew not where. He found a flask in the side-pocket of the car and drank deeply, hoping fervently that it would not turn out to be automobile polish, then went off into another doze.

They drew up before what seemed to be a palatial private home, some time later, and Whitey filed in behind the others obediently, trusting that whoever might be the host would permit him to take a nap before joining whatever party was on foot.

Hardly had he entered, however, until he was wide awake again. The party had barely set foot in the hall when Whitey found himself cut off from the herd and edged into a small, private office, where two polite Greeks confronted him.

"You're Theodore Anthony White, aren't you?" asked one, courteously.

"Yes," said Whitey, his befuddled brain still working on only a few cylinders, but warning him, intuitively, of danger. He glanced about him swiftly and realized, to his horror, that he was once more in the Pyramid Gambling Club.

One of the Greeks produced an oblong slip of paper.

"A little matter of a check you gave us here," said the spokesman for the gamblers.

"What about it?" Whitey asked, blinking, and cursing himself as an idiot for having come.

"It's marked, 'No Account In This Bank,' you see," the gambler said. "We didn't say anything about it before, but you happen to have the money now, and we'll appreciate a settlement."

Whitey sensed that rough treatment lay behind those soft and courteous words. He grinned.

"You win," he said. "I'll give you another check— a good one."

He was seated at the desk, a blank check and fountain pen appearing before him. Whitey filled in the check, blotted it carefully, and handed it over.

"Let me advise," said the elder Greek, "that you do not stop payment on this."

"I won't," Whitey assured him. "You can bank on that. But how did you happen to know that I had the money?"

"That," said the gambler, "is a very important part of operating a gambling house in Hollywood. I know, for instance, that you worked at Colossal, and after that for Moe Fishbein. I also know that you live at the Major Hotel, that you recently sold a scenario, and that you have, at this moment, three thousand three hundred and forty-five dollars and sixty-six cents in the bank, unless you have written a check since three o'clock this afternoon."

"You don't run a detective bureau on the side, do you?" Whitey asked.

"It almost amounts to that," the Greek replied. "In view of the successful transaction of our business, let me suggest some wine."

He summoned a waiter, who scurried back with a quart of excellent champagne and glasses.

"You see," said Whitey's gracious host, pouring, "we get bad checks here all the time. We'll take checks from almost anyone. They may be good, we reason, and inasmuch as all the money stays in the house, we lose nothing in actual cash. Eventually, we collect on most of them, as we have on yours."

"Quite a system," said Whitey. "Would you mind telling me how it works?"

"Why, no. A few dollars a week paid to one or two tellers in all the leading Hollywood banks gets us the financial status of everyone who gives rubber checks here."

"What if I hadn't come back?" Whitey asked.

"We'd have waited till you did. Almost everyone in Hollywood comes up here, eventually. We've been running gambling houses in this town for years. There isn't another such institution in Hollywood that is honest and that the movie people can trust. We run a square game and everybody knows it. That means a great deal. Consequently, we expect to be paid."

The Greek arose.

"If you'll pardon me, Mr. White, I must run along. Finish your wine."

He paused as he was going out the door.

"I might say, Mr. White, that your credit here is unlimited—to the sum of three hundred and forty-five dollars and sixty-six cents and what money you have in pocket."

II

At three o'clock that morning, Whitey lurched from the Pyramid Club with seventeen dollars in cash and a bank balance of five dollars and sixty-six cents. In all his career he had never seen a man deal blackjack as fast as the sharp-eyed dealer he had encountered.

His evening had not been entirely in vain, however. He had successfully eluded Jane and Bobby, and the lady who accompanied him from the Pyramid Club was Lucille Jettifer.

Chapter Fifteen

BEAUTIFUL as they may have been in theory, Whitey's plans went completely awry from the moment he stepped into the Pyramid Club.

He did not remember coming home from Lucille Jettifer's bungalow, although it was evident that he must have done so, for he awakened in his own room about noon. True, he had beaten a path to the fat and fluttering heart of Lucille. In so doing, however, he had cast Jane into a violent and jealous temper from which he could not withdraw her.

"Ditching me there," she screamed at him, when he called at her apartment, "and going off with that fat old mamma."

"Ditching you, nothing," he argued, trying to be soothing. "There were men all around you. All I did was drive Lucille home."

"Has she moved to Santa Barbara?" Jane asked. "You came in at five o'clock this morning, because the night clerk told me so."

"But, Jane," he protested, his innocence outraged, "I did it for you. I thought it would help you in pictures if I could get next to her. She has a lot of drag."

"For me!" she snarled. "Catting around with

everything from sheep to elephants. You're just a tramp."

Whereupon she shoved him violently from her apartment and slammed the door.

Returning to his own room, Whitey sat disconsolately on the bed and contemplated the dismal future. Yesterday he had had more than three thousand dollars. Now he had less than twenty-five. The five thousand dollars had vanished in three weeks. Whitey had nothing to show for it save a fairly extensive wardrobe, and his prospects of employment apparently were no brighter than before.

He called Paul Bannon in the hope that a position as scenario writer might be possible on the strength of his having written *Gun Man*.

"I'm sorry, Whitey," Paul said, apologetically. "I'd like to get you a job here, but the place is over-run with writers now. If you've got another original story I'll try to sell it for you."

In desperation, he telephoned Lucille Jettifer. At least, he thought, she would be the source of some meals, and he possibly could persuade her to use her influence in placing him somewhere about the studios. If I got over in a big way last night, he reflected, I might even get Bobby DeSales' job—both of them.

Lucille was a Puritan at heart. The morning found her remorseful and regretting her amorous escapade of the previous night. She had returned penitently to the empty arms of Bobby, who knew better than to jeopardize a good spot by becoming hypercritical. The coolness of her telephonic reception chilled White's heart and made him wonder if he were losing his charm.

McGinnis, he knew, could do nothing for him. Joe Greet was still jobless and impoverished, in fact had been supported by Whitey for the past few weeks. Hoffberger was still warning his associates against the cherubic adventurer. Sylvester was sure to put in a bad word for him wherever possible.

The saddening realization of his spectacular thriftlessness, of his unfortunate and stupid encounter with the Pyramid Club, of his falling out with Jane and of his failure to capture the fancy of Lucille Jettifer, brought to Whitey a mood of hopeless despondency which his raging hangover did nothing to improve.

The future looked dark.

II

To make it darker, the blight of talking pictures descended up Hollywood just at this period, and turned the town into more of a maniac colony than ever.

Talking devices had kicked around the studios of Hollywood, friendless and unwelcome, for more than a year. No one would venture a trial of them. Silent pictures were still returning enormous profits. An experiment with the new invention meant large investments for equipment, and even larger investments to wire theaters with transmitting devices. It meant, moreover, a period of unsettlement, experimentation and woe.

Then came a third-rate company, heavily in debt,

staggering toward bankruptcy, its pictures stumbling along to mean returns in small theaters. The talking device was a feeble straw at which the drowning organization clutched frantically. Hollywood and Culver City are still trembling from the ensuing earthquakes.

Within a few short weeks, the tentacles of the talking octopus coiled about Culver City studios, Beverly Hills mansions, and Hollywood apartments. In passing it laid an oppressive finger on Whitey.

Voice culture schools sprang up, as thick as bootleggers. Dubious technical "experts" arrived from nowhere, and were engaged by studios at fat salaries. Broken down playwrights and dialogue writers leaped from every westbound passenger and freight train, to the terror of the literary master minds of the Writers' Club. Famous film stars, without voice or real ability, saw reputations crumble before them. Directors who lacked education, or stage experience, or both, confronted the abyss. Scenario writers whose culture and literary ability had handicapped them for years, came into their own. Actors who had been labelled "All Through" in silent pictures, suddenly found themselves in demand, their salaries sky-rocketing as the microphone revealed their real talents.

Many Rolls-Royces and Beverly Hills estates changed hands in a few months.

Players who had received three thousand dollars a week were glad to take a job in talking pictures at any price. Fortunes were dissipated. Fortunes were made. The business was in a chaos, the town in a panic. One could no more control the future than one could control the winds that whistle through Cahuenga Pass.

Producers and studio executives were bewildered and terror-stricken. Huge and unnecessary sound-proof stages reared up from every studio. Thousands of dollars were spent for the mysterious sound equipment which no one understood or could operate.

Those fortunates who had caught the first boat and could boast that they were working in the talkies strutted pompously, talked importantly, and advertised heavily in publications of the trade. Those studio workers still assigned to the despised silent pictures slunk about, concealing what they were doing, pleading with executives, pulling wires to clamber aboard the band-wagon.

Hundreds of greater and lesser personages about the studios—executives, directors, writers, cameramen, production managers, supervisors—found themselves swept from jobs in which they had felt secure. A man without a contract was a man doomed.

And all because a New York mammy singer had gambled his time and money on a third-rate picture for a third-rate company.

In the sea of economic disaster bobbed Whitey, bewildered, confused, and helpless. He had barely learned the tactics of survival in the old era. Now he was as a little child, crying in the dark. He haunted the studios, looking for any sort of work, and could not contrive an audience with anyone who might have hired him. He tried to find a place on one of the downtown Los Angeles papers, and on the smaller Hollywood dailies as well. Too many ex-newspapermen had fled back to journalism from the talkie panic already. There were five reporters for every job. He tried to do extra work, and found he could not get even one day's check. There were not only thousands of professional extras, but hundreds of established actors as well, hungry and willing to work for the seven dollar and a half daily fee.

Jane would have none of him, and apparently had made Paul Bannon equally wary. Grace, now cast off by Hoffberger, was sympathetic, but in desperate straits herself. McGinnis, reduced to a minor executive position, was without influence.

Joe Greet, whose last escapade had been marked as one too many by the comedy studios, had been jobless for weeks. Whitey and Joe were far behind in their rent, eating infrequently, and mostly at the expense of the generous but unconcerned Straubel or Rocco.

Romaine Randolph made them occasional small loans, but he was having no great success in the talkies and was living economically on his savings.

With what dimes they could scrape together, Whitey and Joe smuggled loaves of bread and tins of meat into their room—they had moved in together as a means of economizing—and managed to keep alive. Whitey sold his evening clothes to Johnny Rocco and, day by day, pawned articles of apparel until he was down to one pair of shoes and one shirt.

One evening Whitey strolled along Hollywood Boulevard and saw *Gun Man* in electric lights at a neighborhood theater. He searched his pockets and found two dimes. The price of admission was a quarter. He could not even see his own picture, and had to content himself with looking at the display photographs in the lobby. He saw his name, as the author of the story, in small type on one of the posters. It gave him a momentary thrill, but did little to relieve the pangs of hunger.

On another occasion he encountered Dorothy Irving sitting in a smart roadster parked by the curb in front of Musso-Frank's. She was smartly and becomingly gowned, and still the most beautiful girl in Hollywood.

"How's Hoffberger treating you, Dorothy?" Whitey asked.

"Just fine," she answered. "They've given me a little part in Sonia Varon's next picture."

"That's great," he grinned. "Any time they're not nice boys over there, you just tell Uncle Whitey. He'll fix 'em."

"Whitey, you're too good to be true," she said, putting an affectionate little hand on his arm. "What are you doing now?"

"Oh, I've got a swell job out at First National," he lied glibly, and then, to avoid further questions. "Whose car is this?"

"Albert Blynn's."

The answer startled and dismayed Whitey.

"Are you running around with that guy?"

"Not running around with him, exactly," she answered. "He's been very nice to me. I've gone to the theater and to dinner with him several times."

Whitey's voice became solemn.

"Dorothy," he said, "listen to me. Stay away from that mug. I know him. He's a worthless, ignorant, conceited, two-timing four-flusher."

Dorothy pursed up her lips in comic amazement.

"My! My! As bad as that?"

"Worse than that, only there are a number of appropriate adjectives ruled out by etiquette. Don't believe anything he says, and don't trust him. Wear brass knuckles."

Whitey would have continued, but he saw Blynn approaching. He bowed stiffly to the director and strolled away.

III

Even in his darkest days, Whitey clung to his lifelong theory that something would always happen. This philosophy was corroborated, in a measure, for one day he received through the mail a check in payment for a vacuous article on Hollywood which a fan magazine had accepted three months before. It was for forty dollars, more than Whitey and Joe had possessed between them in two months. He dared not cash it at the Major, for his bill alone was three times that. With Joe, he tramped down Hollywood Boulevard to the bank where he had been a depositor during his brief period of affluence.

There were so many things to consider that the two

forlorn comrades knew not where to begin expenditures. They discussed them over an enormous luncheon of steak and potatoes, the first really complete meal either had eaten in a week.

"We could make a payment on the rent," Joe said.

"It wouldn't do any good," Whitey argued. "We're in there for more than two hundred now, and we'd be broke again."

"We might get a furnished room somewhere," Joe suggested. "It would be cheaper than the Major."

"No," said Whitey, who had maneuvered his way through many a similar crisis in even less friendly towns. "Once we leave there, we're sunk. We can't get our clothes out anyway, and I think they'll carry us awhile yet."

They ate in silence for some time.

"I know what I'd really like to do," said Joe.

Whitey looked at him.

"So would I," he agreed.

So they did it.

IV

Madame Frankie Lee is a Hollywood institution. Many a famous star, many a celebrated director, and not a few prominent producers have slipped furtively up the dark stairs to her gaudy establishment. Many others, who have never visited her personally, have made business arrangements by phone for the delivery of her shop-worn merchandise. She has been discussed at many a Hollywood fireside—a sinister but fascinating legend to the women, a speciously vague figure to the men. She moves often, as is the custom of such markets of ancient trade. Just now she was located in an old mansion on Fountain Avenue, a street of Hollywood on which almost anything might happen.

It was at the spacious quarters of Madame Lee that Joe Greet and Whitey hilariously called, a good many hours after the luncheon. They had some twenty-three dollars left after a visit to Johnny Rocco and subsequent personal calls upon a number of Hollywood apartments. Now they were in just the proper mood for Madame Lee.

Whitey was the life of the party once more. He seized hungrily upon the piano in the parlor, for it had been weeks since he had touched the keys. Many customers came in and joined the circle of rapt listeners, to sing lustily and beat upon the floor to Whitey's barbaric rhythms. Gerald Normandy arrived and was so delighted with Whitey's version of *The Bastard King of England* that he bought many rounds of drinks and telephoned for friends.

The girls flocked about, dizzy with Whitey's inspired minors and his crooning of bawdy blues.

Madame Lee beamed. She had not seen business so rushing since the last Shriner's Convention. Drinks were a dollar, and Whitey's music had sold many rounds.

"Keep it up, kid," she whispered in his ear as Normandy excused himself for a trip upstairs and there was a period of relative calm. "Keep it up," she repeated. "The place is yours—anything you want."

Whitey had not been so happy since the last of his five thousand dollars had disappeared. He was truly in his element. Here were people he could understand thoroughly. He banged away steadily at the piano for three hours. He sang until his throat was raw. He had been the non-paying participant in nineteen rounds of drinks for the house, and managed to wheedle a good many more separately from the Madame by threatening to stop the music.

The film star's friends arrived and called for more drinks. The cop on the beat came in to join the party. The cash register jangled constantly. There was a never-ending procession up and down the stairs.

At three o'clock in the morning, Whitey went soundly to sleep, with his head upon the keys. Joe Greet was unable to arouse him. Kind, grateful hands stretched him out upon a sofa. One of the girls threw a blanket over him, and there he slept, wrapt in pleasant dreams, until morning.

v

Whitey was somewhat surprised to awaken in the parlor of Madame Lee's next morning, and to find that genial dame smiling at him benignly. He shook his muddled head, and slowly the events of the night before came to him.

"How do you feel?," Madame Lee asked.

"Not so good," he grinned. "The life of the party seldom does."

She fetched him a long, cool drink of orange juice, loaded with gin. "This'll pick you up," she said, and was right.

Having swallowed the eye-opener, Whitey struggled to a sitting position and surveyed the room about him. Empty glasses stood about everywhere, the dregs of alcohol in them. A dozen white rings atop the piano testified where others had been. Gerald Normandy had forgotten his vest, and Joe Greet his glasses.

"Reminds me of the time they held the Democratic National Convention in Frisco," Madame Lee said.

"You've never seen anything," Whitey remarked, "until you've covered a World's Series."

"Have you been in Hollywood during a Wampas Frolic?" she asked.

"No."

"Then you don't know anything about a party."

"Well," said Whitey, "it's a great life. I was in Paris when they signed the Armistice, but I've never seen anything like Hollywood. They don't need anything to celebrate here. It just goes on, week in and week out."

Madame Lee lead him to the dining room, where a mighty Negress brought them scrambled eggs and coffee.

"Listen, kid," Madame Lee began, after some thought, "what do you do, anyway?"

"Me?" he asked. "Why I'm a newspaperman, and a press agent. I worked in a carnival in Memphis once for three weeks and I used to play the piano in a cabaret in Chicago. I did that for a month. I drove an ambulance during the war, and I fought a four-round bout in Dallas, Texas, once for ten dollars. Just now I'm trying to make a living in Hollywood, with practically no success."

"How'd you like to work for me up here?"

Whitey considered this, over a swallow of coffee.

"At what? I don't know all the things they might expect a man to do in a Hollywood cat-shop."

Madame Lee laughed.

"Nothing like that. I need an entertainer here, and you're a riot. I'm an old-fashioned sport, I guess, but I never feel right unless I have a professor."

"You mean just play the piano?"

"Sure, and sing some. You don't have to do as much as last night. You couldn't keep it up."

"What's the inducement for all this?"

"Forty dollars a week. Dinner every night free. I always feed the girls about seven o'clock. A place to sleep, if you want it. And if you can get in on the free list with any of the kids here, it's all right with me."

Whitey wandered out some time later. He had wheedled a ten dollar advance out of his new employer, and declined the offer of a free room, deciding to stay at the Major.

"If that isn't something to write to your maiden aunt about," he said aloud to the morning air. "Professor in a fancy house in Hollywood."

CHAPTER SIXTEEN

WHITEY had never found a job to which all of his peculiar talents were fitted so aptly. He was just slightly embarrassed for the first few days when he found that so many of his acquaintances were regular patrons of Madame Lee. He observed, however, that most of them believed him to be a customer instead of an employee.

"After all," he told himself, "the line between working in such a place and patronizing one is very finely drawn."

He continued to live at the Major, and found time for considerable diversion when off duty, despite his unusual hours of employment, which, after all, did not differ much from those of a morning newspaper. He ordinarily reported about seven o'clock at the Lee brothel, where he dined on rough but wholesome fare and listened, with considerable interest, to shop talk. He found the girls a friendly, congenial, and generous lot, on the whole. They were thrifty and industrious and never drank during working hours—traits seldom found in either newspaper men or actors.

Occasional quarrels and differences, of course, were bound to occur in any such gathering of attractive young women. Thelma, a rugged Kansas blonde, was charged by others with stalling on the job. Ruby, a vivacious little soul, was covertly accused of being up-stage because she had once worked in the chorus. But Whitey found her to be the most generous of all.

He failed to discover among them any of the intel-lectual traits with which ladies of the profession have been credited in so many works of fiction. He recalled having read somewhere that a man had found, to his astonishment, a professional lady who could discuss Ibsen intelligently. It was really a source of secret relief to Whitey that these conditions did not obtain here, as his knowledge of Ibsen was sketchy indeed.

Most of the girls, he found, read the Confessions magazines in large and eager doses. The various mo-tion picture magazines were always to be found in Madame Lee's parlor, but they were for the benefit of the trade rather than the employees.

One of the girls professed to be an admirer of the works of Jim Tully, but most of the others said he was no gentleman and refused to read him. Their favorite novelists, in the main, were Elinor Glyn, Michael Arlen, Jeffrey Farnol, and Fannie Hurst.

The evening rush began shortly after dinner, as a rule. The studios generally closed about six o'clock and Madame Lee, as a consequence, adjusted the din-ner hour to suit that time. Whitey was generally in top form by nine o'clock, when the heavier spenders arrived. By twelve o'clock, when he had been primed liberally with drinks for the house, the place was going full blast and he was the center of attraction.

His easy familiarity, his wit and his superb performance on the piano soon ensconced him firmly in Madame Lee's heart. She even made a few tentative amorous advances toward him, which he repulsed, because of a long-standing rule never to have any intimate dealings about the office.

Except for unusually boisterous evenings, which generally occurred after the fortnightly Wampas dinners or following the sessions of the Academy of Motion Picture Arts and Sciences, Whitey's work was over by one-thirty. Arrivals after that time did not ordinarily come to be entertained with music.

Unless he was unusually tired, however, Whitey rarely departed at this hour. After the house was cleared for the night, Madame Lee, a generous soul, served a nightcap to all hands, and the girls remained for a farewell cigarette. They often fell to discussing the events of the evening, and compared notes on customers. Whitey learned a good many curious and illuminating facts about a number of prominent Hollywoodians during these get-together chats.

As Whitey's connection with Madame Lee's establishment became known about Hollywood, the rosy-cheeked professor was subjected to considerable banter by his friends and acquaintances. He bore it smilingly, knowing that envy inspired most of it.

"The only job I ever had," he was wont to say, "that combined business with pleasure."

Madame Lee was soon to discover that Whitey was not only a pleasant addition to the entertainment value of her house, but actually the source of considerable income as well. He attracted a good many customers who came merely to listen and drink, and the sale of drinks was no small part of her revenue. Whitey became an attraction, also, because of his versatility at singing close harmony. He excelled at tenor, although he could manage a passable bass, and it became a well established custom for roistering Hollywood trios to visit Madame Lee's and pay her exorbitant prices for drinks solely to fill out the quartette.

Whitey was still at outs with Jane, who had been even further infuriated when she learned of his rather surprising employment. This did not concern him overmuch. He felt that he could win Jane back in due time, and that, at this period, she would be a particularly small and non-combustible bit of anthracite to carry to Newcastle.

As the weeks went on, he gradually paid off his bill at the Major, and most of Joe's as well. He redeemed the garments he had pawned and even began to save money. His salary was not large, but his expenses were almost nothing, for his evening meal and most of his hilarity were taken care of in the line of duty. He provided Joe with spending money and kept him on the rounds looking for employment at the studios, either as an actor or director. They often discussed their futures.

"How do you really like that job?" Joe asked him once. "Is it better than a studio?"

"Well," Whitey replied, "you work with a better class of people."

Although Whitey was in particularly good voice, and regular practice had advanced his pianistic ability almost to perfection, it started out like a dull evening. It was Monday, for one thing, and as there was an opening at Grauman's Chinese, any rush that might develop could not be expected until rather late. At nine-thirty there was not a customer in the house. Whitey amused the girls by playing request numbers. They were mainly ballads of the moment, which he sang after the Jolson-Richman manner. The ladies were a sentimental lot.

Madame Lee, tired and sleepy after a riotous Saturday and Sunday, and discontented because her cash register had clanged so infrequently, was considering an early closing when sounds of revelry came from without. There was a heavy, insistent pounding on the door, and she went to peer through the look-out gate. Apparently strangers were seeking admittance, for those inside could hear a considerable argument— Madame Lee quiet and firm, the strangers argumentative and noisy. After a time she returned to Whitey.

"There's a drunk out there with another guy," she told him, "who says he's Sol Snifkin, of the Snifkin Studio. Do you know him?"

"I don't know him," Whitey said, "but I've seen his

pictures. He resembles an unfriendly hedge-hog. I'll take a look."

He peered through the wicket. The Snifkin hallmark was unmistakable. Whitey unbarred the door and admitted the producer and his guest into the sacred presence.

"How'd do, Mr. Snifkin," Whitey said. "Good thing I was here. I just dropped in to play the piano for a while. My name's White."

"Glad'a meetcha, Mr. White," Snifkin said. Whitey observed that he was very thoroughly drunk.

"Thish," said Snifkin, waving a hand at his companion, "is Mr. Pappadoulous, bigges' theater-owner in souse-west. Bigges' theater-owner in whole damn worl'. Joe, thish ish m' ol' frien', Mr. White."

Whitey shook hands and surveyed the stranger. A Greek he was, short and swarthy, kinky of hair, with shrewd, beady eyes buried in huge pouches, a nose that had been broken one time by a heavy hand, a crooked, jutting chin, and a jagged slit of a mouth.

"Glad t' know you," he said, in a croaking voice, and looked over the Lee household appraisingly, with the air of a professional.

"Nice li'l place you got here," he said. "Best I've seen in a long time."

"Hollywood's best," said Whitey, putting his heart in his work.

"Cat-houses not what they usta be," said Mr. Pappadoulous. "When I was young feller, gettin' started, they had houses as was houses.

"Why, young feller," he went on, tapping Whitey on the breast-bone with a heavy fore-finger, "twenty-fi' years ago I had bigges' first-class parlor house in Seattle. Any of the ol' timers up there'll tell you. Just ask 'em, sometime, if they don't remember Joe Pappadoulous' place. Fact."

"Was that before you got into the theater business?" Whitey asked.

"Before? Young feller thass *how* I got into theater business. Usta have a burley-que house right next door to my place. They hadda long intermission, and fellers usta come to my place for drinks and what-not between acts. Theater went broke and my business fell off. I'm smart, see? Can't make ten million and be dumb. I opened theater of my own, in same place. Better yet. Instead of fifteen minute intermission, I had twenty-fi' minute intermission. I pack 'em in both places. Get 'em coming and going. Early customers go to show. Customers at show go to cat-house afterwards. Those who gotta catch early car home come in durin' intermission. I clean up."

During this recital, which apparently he had heard before, Snifkin ordered drinks, including Whitey in the round, whom he had taken up immediately as an old and trusted friend. They seated the garrulous magnate of the drama on a divan between Ruby and Thelma, while Snifkin weaved about the room taking charge of things. He sidled over to Whitey, who had taken his customary post at the piano.

"Listen," he said, "whazz your name?"

"Whitey."

"Well, Whitey, this guy's big shot, see? Bigges' shot in whole souse-west. I'm entertainin' um, see, like all big exhibitors gotta be entertain'. Means a big contract for me. You help me, see, an' we'll give ol' hyena time of his life."

Whitey nodded, cast about swiftly in his head for a tune that might appeal to Mr. Pappadoulous, and launched into the ancient but always torrid, *Chicago*, putting in all his tricks.

Pappadoulous and Snifkin listened, enraptured. As Whitey wound up with a fantastic combination of minors, Pappadoulous slapped his knee in ecstasy, and roared.

"Hot dam, thass swell! Haven't heard any good saloon music since I left Seattle!"

"You're a riot," Snifkin murmured in Whitey's ear. "You're gettin' him sentimental."

Whitey's encore was his most popular vocal number, *Frankie and Johnnie*, rightly assuming that it had been a favorite when Pappadoulous was lord of the manor in Seattle. He did a very good job of it, sliding to an impressive height on the line "He was her ma-a-a-a-a-a-a-n," and descending to a rumbling smash on "But he done her wro-o-o-o-o-o-ong." Tears came to Pappadoulous' eyes when the song was ended. Before him danced delightful visions of his youth, when he was a gay young blade, with all Seattle at his feet. In his ears again rang the lusty choruses which had shaken the beams in his spacious, red parlor. Those were the days when the police let an honest business man alone and no one bothered about the noise. It took him back to an ancient custom, too, and, snatching a handful of silver dollars from his pocket, he hurled them where the kitty should have been.

"More! More!" he yelled. "Drinks for the Professor! Drinks for the Madame! Drinks for everybody!"

He had not enjoyed himself so much since he had jobbed a partner out of his rights to a theater in St. Louis and realized his first million. Snifkin seized Madame Lee and slipped a fifty-dollar bill into her hands.

"Lock the door and keep everybody out for the night," he ordered. It was done immediately.

Whitey had never been so magnificent. He played and sang *The Gay Caballero*, *The Ballad of Samuel Hall*, *The St. Louis Blues*. He howled seventy verses of *Mademoiselle from Armentières*, improvising as he went, and followed this with the unabridged life history of *Stacko Lee*. He played *Rhapsody in Blue* as George Gershwin has never heard it played. He told bawdy stories. He flattered Pappadoulous and Snifkin. He did a tap-dance. He privately determined to demand a salary increase from Madame Lee. He got drunk beyond all previous efforts.

About him roamed Madame Lee, deliriously happy, not only over her own good fortune, but also because Pappadoulous had spoken highly of her house, which was, indeed, praise from Sir Hubert.

Pappadoulous, after many drinks, became sentimental, and wept on Ruby's shoulder. He bared his dreams and ambitions. He was going back to his old business—his first love—he declared. He planned the biggest and best parlor house in Kansas City. He'd have a hundred foot bar, fifty girls, a ten-piece orchestra, and Gene Tunney as the bouncer. Crowning touch of all—he'd have Whitey as master of ceremonies! Good ol' Whitey! Dear ol' Whitey! He'd given an ol' man the happiest evening in fifteen years.

With the instinct of the true showman, Whitey shifted from bawdy lyrics to lachrymose ballads, as he saw Pappadoulous drifting toward alcoholic sentimentality. He chose his songs with the fine precision of a psychologist. Songs of an earlier day, they were, ballads that were popular when Pappadoulous was young —*A Bicycle Built For Two, Mother Machree, After the Ball Was Over, I Wonder Who's Kissing Her Now*. Pappadoulous bawled until the rafters shook, and achieved the greatest crying jag ever known to Madame Lee.

Snifkin, unbalanced in his joy, crowded many bills into Whitey's hands, and later charged them to "Production Costs." Thus does Art become expensive.

Hours later, when Snifkin had ascended and descended three times from the quarters above, surprising even himself, the producer had his great idea. He approached Whitey craftily, as one might address a temperamental diva.

"You workin' now, Whitey?" he asked, thereby in-

[213]

forming Whitey that Snifkin was not aware of his business association with Madame Lee.

"Not right now," he answered cautiously.

"You wanta work for me?" the producer asked.

"What at?"

"I wantcha to sing—sing for Gilbert Vance. We just signed him. Gotta great story for him. Supposed to play a piano and sing—in the story, that is. Vance's great actor but he'sh gotta nance voice, an' he couldn't play piano if he took lessons for ten years."

"I might," Whitey said. "How much?"

"Hunnerd an' fifty—aw, what the hell, two hunnerd a week."

"When do I start?"

"Right away."

"But," said Whitey, "how can I sing for him?"

"Cinch," said Snifkin. "He makesh faces, just like the words of the song. You sing 'em. We record your voice. Same way with piano. We show him poundin'. You play."

At three o'clock the two of them managed to carry the unconscious Pappadoulous into the waiting limousine. As they departed, Whitey found himself seventy dollars richer, and with a promise to visit Snifkin next morning at the studio for confirmation of his employment.

Whitey watched them go, chuckling to himself.

"Things go faster and faster on this Hollywood merry-go-round," he said. "The centrifugal force is going to get me eventually."

Then he fell down.

Chapter Seventeen

Madame Lee wept bitterly when Whitey resigned. She offered him a partnership in the business and numerous other personal concessions. He was almost swayed, but the vast increase in salary, together with a position which offered additional respectability, however slight, decided him.

Snifkin, when Whitey called upon him the next morning, had not forgotten his alcoholic promises. After an hour's conversation, Whitey was placed on the studio payroll at the stipulated salary of two hundred dollars a week. Snifkin exacted a promise from Whitey not to reveal his duties, as the producer hoped to conceal from the public the fact that Vance did not possess the golden voice his handsome visage seemed to indicate.

It was ridiculously easy for Whitey, particularly after his strenuous musical feats of the past few months with Madame Lee. He lolled about the studio for weeks while Vance's first picture for Snifkin, *The Singing Man* was being made. He could have done all the singing necessary in two days, except that that would not have conformed with the Snifkin standards of efficiency. When he did finally sing, it was not on a set, but in a darkened projection room. While the recording instruments listened, Whitey watched the close-ups of Vance's lips forming the words of the song. As Vance pantomimed the ballads, Whitey sang them synchronously. Three or four repetitions were enough to produce one fairly perfect recording. The piano episodes were finished in another day.

Meanwhile, Whitey was idyllically happy. He was completely out of debt, and saving money. Joe Greet, too, had been engaged to direct some two-reelers for a fly-by-night company on Poverty Row, and had his head above water once more. A reconciliation with Jane made Whitey's happiness complete. She was now definitely at outs with the voice culturist, and even the generous Paul Bannon had wearied of investing so much, when Whitey was the sole beneficiary.

Whitey's employment with Snifkin ended after several weeks. With one of the bursts of economic caution which infrequently overtook him, Whitey had saved several hundred dollars, and was confident that he could find similar work either with Snifkin or elsewhere.

The Singing Man was rushed through the process of cutting and editing and was cast upon the public hurriedly, for Snifkin was behind his competitors in talking pictures, and was anxious to keep abreast of the times. The picture speedily became a sensation. Flappers and grandmothers, alike, raved over it. The songs were tremendous hits, due, as those on the inside were aware, not to the handsome Vance, but to the invisible Whitey.

Lucille Jettifer said in her review:

"The contrast between Mr. Vance's speaking voice

and his singing voice is astounding. Hollywood has
never suspected this popular star of any such vocal
ability, and it is safe to assume that his golden voice
will be heard often in the future."

It was about as accurate as most of Lucille's profound cinematic opinions.

It was no surprise to Whitey that a week after the
release of *The Singing Man* at a Los Angeles theater,
he should receive an excessively cordial telephone call
from Sol Snifkin.

"Whitey, old man," beamed the unctuous producer
over the wire, "I'd like to talk to you. Drop over and
see me, will you?"

"What about?" Whitey asked, suspecting what was
coming, and preparing to bury the knife to the hilt.

"Why . . . just a little matter I'd like to discuss
personally."

An hour later, mentally rubbing his hands, Whitey
was seated in an enormous chair in the private lair of
Sol Snifkin, a fat Snifkin cigar between his pudgy
fingers.

"Well, Whitey," Snifkin began, "here's a break for
you. *The Singing Man* was such a hit we've decided to
make another singing picture with Vance."

"Yes?" Whitey commented.

"Yes. So it looks like another job for you."

Whitey rolled the cigar between his fingers, study-
ing it intently.

"At how much?"

Snifkin sensed trouble.

"Well, say, two hundred and fifty a week. That's fifty more than we paid you before."

White arose, seemingly about to depart.

"I believe not—for two-fifty a week," he said. "Try Tito Schipa."

Snifkin ran to the door to intercept him.

"Now, Whitey, that's no way to talk," he wailed. "That's a lot of money."

"It's not as much as you pay Gilbert Vance."

"Yes, my boy, but Vance is a big star. You're nobody," Snifkin argued.

"I'm nobody but the guy who sang his songs and played the piano for him," said Whitey, hotly. "That's what made his picture a hit. You can't kid me about it. Vance is a big ham, and he was all through. That's why Colossal let him go. He hasn't had a hit for years, and *The Singing Man* would have been just another shooting-gallery picture without my singing."

Snifkin appeared almost on the verge of tears. He did feel a bit like crying.

"Whitey, my boy, after all I've done for you . . . after I pick you up from nowhere . . . after I treat you like a son . . . you do this to me?"

Whitey snorted.

"Yah! What did you do for me? Found me in a good sporting house and put me to work in a bad one. What did I do for you? You paid me twelve hundred dollars for six weeks' work. What'll you do? Make a million dollars on a picture that didn't cost two hundred thousand. And you rejuvenate that ham Vance from a broken down has-been whose hair is falling out, to a big star again. I want a lot of dough, or I won't play."

Snifkin tried one more approach, smiling craftily.

"Of course, my boy, I was only trying to give you a chance, because I like you. I can get someone else to sing."

"Oh yes," White agreed, "you can get someone else. Better than I am, too. I'll grant that. But you won't get another singer that sounds like I did. And you won't get a singer of any prominence to keep his mouth shut about what he's doing."

Whitey paused, to let this sink in thoroughly.

"And another thing you won't do; you won't keep me quiet about Vance's singing in the first picture. I'm no half-witted coon-shouter you're talking to now. I'm a smart guy. I've been a newspaperman, and a press agent. You fooled the critics and the public once, but I won't let 'em stay fooled—not without a great many Jewish flags—right on the line."

Snifkin's face saddened.

"Blackmail, my boy. That's blackmail."

"Maybe it is. I've done it before. Who hasn't, in the picture business? You've done it so many times you look like a member of the Mafia. Half the guys in this town get their jobs that way. Don't try to scare me with any chatter about blackmail, or I'll show you what a Chicago newspaperman can do with it when he really tries."

Snifkin walked back to his desk and sat down, slowly.

"How much do you want?" he asked, meekly.

White made rapid calculations, trying to arrive at the top figure his squeeze play might produce.

"For how long?" he asked.

"One picture—six weeks."

"I'll tell you, Mr. Snifkin," White said. "I've talked pretty rough to you. Now I'm going to give you some good advice. The best thing for you to do is to put me under contract—a long one. Insert a clause, if you like, that the agreement is broken if I ever tell anybody what I'm doing for you. I'm warning you, if we turn out another hit with Vance and you haven't a contract with me, I'll take your studio away from you for the third one."

"Well . . ."

"Yes, just that. A lot of smart guys, you button-hole makers, aren't you? If you were as cagey as you think you are, this would have occurred to you two months ago, and I'd still be getting two hundred a week—and liking it."

Whitey departed some time later, bearing a signed and notaried document, which he immediately deposited in a safety vault.

II

Jane and Whitey, rich again, as happy as newlyweds, over-dressed in customary Hollywood fashion, money in every pocket, were dining and dancing at the Montmartre.

Except for such odds and ends as Jane could pick up from what few victims remained in a thoroughly harvested field, Whitey was now the sole provider for the firm. He had been completely forgiven for all his transgressions and infidelities of the past. Indeed, he was already contemplating new ones. Jane was even hinting at marriage, having been separated by law from her Manhattan husband. To all such guarded suggestions, Whitey replied by allusions to a thoroughly fictitious wife in South Bend, Indiana.

Into the Montmartre that night swept two striking figures. The girl was Dorothy Irving—a new Dorothy. Her gown must have cost several hundred dollars, and the fur coat about her could not have been purchased under two thousand. Her brown eyes danced and sparkled, and her smile was as warming and gay as ever. She was still the most beautiful girl in Hollywood.

Behind her came Albert Blynn, faultlessly attired, handsome in a raffish, dissipated way, the possessive glint strong in his eye.

"Jane," said Whitey, "there's Dorothy Irving. Let's ask them over to our table."

Much as he detested Blynn, he wanted to talk to Dorothy, whom he had not seen in more than a month. He overtook them before they reached a table. Dorothy greeted him warmly, Blynn with supercilious coolness. The invitation was accepted, despite the animosity between the two men, and a few moments later Whitey was pouring highballs.

"You want one?" he asked Dorothy.

"Certainly."

He mixed a fourth, saying nothing. He had never seen Dorothy drink before.

Jane, the instinct of the huntress still strong within her, fastened upon Blynn immediately, and a few moments later the orchestra summoned them to dance. Dorothy and Whitey remained to talk.

"How are they going at the studio, Dorothy?" he asked.

"Wonderful. I've got the lead in *The Love Market*."

"That's Blynn's new picture, isn't it? Is it a good part?"

"The best in the picture. And you did it, you fat, little scoundrel. I'd still be hashing in Henry's except for you."

"Not you," Whitey protested. "You're the real thing. I just helped a little."

He paused to gulp at his highball.

"Dorothy, you look swell tonight—a little too swell."

"You're always flattering me."

"I'm not flattering you. I'm talking about your clothes."

"Do you like them?"

"I like to look at them."

"What do you mean by that?"

"I mean I'd rather see them in a store window than on you."

Jane and Blynn returned to the table just then, perspiring from the Montmartre scrimmage. White sat silent, wondering why he always assumed the rôle of guardian toward Dorothy. "I wonder if I'm jealous of

Blynn because I want to make her myself," he speculated, "or if it's because I dislike him so much?"

Whitey was not a philosopher. He had never heard that the ordinary person concerns himself more over one he has helped, than over one who has helped him. Dorothy was puzzled, but could not find an opportunity to ask him his meaning until the orchestra began to play again.

"What are you getting at about my clothes, Whitey?" she asked.

"Just this: Have you signed a new contract, or something?"

"No."

"Then you're getting—let's see—you're getting a hundred and a quarter a week, aren't you?"

"Yes."

"Are they selling fur coats for a hundred and twenty-five a week?"

Dorothy tried to be indignant, but could not manage it. Her lip trembled, and she said, reproachfully.

"Whitey!"

"Dorothy," he went on, "I like you one hell of a lot. It annoys me terribly to see you around with a guy like Blynn."

"What's the matter with Al?"

"Everything's the matter with Al. I warned you against that dope when I saw you with him months ago. He's no good. In fact, he's as bad as I am."

"I'm in love with him," she said, quietly.

"I don't doubt it. That's what I was afraid of. I suppose he's in love with you, too?"

"Yes."

Whitey sought for convincing phrases, although knowing that there are no convincing phrases for such an argument.

"Dorothy," he began, "you wouldn't fall for a man like Hoffberger. He made you a proposition on the up-and-up and you got insulted. But you go for a soft-spoken guy like this, with some water-front good looks and a reputation. You've made a worse bargain than the other would have been. I'd rather trust even a kike than the shanty Irish any time."

She was really indignant.

"I haven't made a bargain with anybody."

He tried to soothe her.

"I'm a funny looking godfather, but I want to be yours. I'm not trying to be insulting. When I met you, you were the sweetest kid in Hollywood. There are a lot of 'em, but I don't meet many. You're still the head girl in this town. That's why Blynn is making a play for you."

"We're going to be married."

"When?"

"As soon as he gets his divorce."

"That's an old stall. I've used it myself."

The dance ended, and they returned to the table, where Blynn was describing to Jane the wonders of his latest picture and the transcendant glories of his coming one. Dinner arrived, and they ate and drank heartily. The hatred was strong between the two men, and they fell to firing insults, thinly disguised as small talk.

"Still working for Frankie Lee, Whitey?" Blynn asked, maliciously, smiling significantly at Jane.

"No," said Whitey. "Why? Don't you go up there any more?"

"What are you doing now?" Blynn asked.

"I'm working at the Hal Roach studios," Whitey lied, not wanting to reveal his real employment, "but don't tell my family. They still think I'm working for Frankie Lee."

Blynn swallowed several mouthfuls of steak.

"I didn't see you at the opening of my picture at the Cathay Circle," Blynn said. "I suppose you are waiting until you can get passes."

"I was there. You should remember me," White said. "I'm the sap that laughed at the comedy touches."

Blynn drank deeply from his highball, and decided to cease firing. A moment later he danced away with Dorothy.

"Quit smart-cracking him," Jane reproached. "I've almost got him talked into putting me in his next picture."

"Such innocence," Whitey said. "Do you think you're the only blonde cutie that ever tried to fast-shuffle him?"

Whitey grudgingly consented to dance with Jane, assuming quite naturally the rôle of the bored husband, and they milled about the ever-increasing throng of movie merry-makers. Whitey made a praiseworthy attempt to trip Blynn, but missed by inches.

It was almost an hour later before Whitey and Dorothy sailed out on the dance floor to talk once more. Whitey opened the conversation bluntly.

"So Blynn is buying your clothes now?"

She flared back at him.

"He is not. And besides, who buys Jane Wilson's clothes."

"That's a typical feminine argument," he answered. "A lot of people buy Jane's clothes. I've bought some myself. That's not what we're talking about."

"It's none of your business."

"Of course it's none of my business, except that I like you so much. Blynn won't do anything for you but make a bum out of you. I'm trying to prevent it. Can't you see that?"

She patted him on the shoulder.

"Of course, I do. But you're wrong, Whitey."

"Am I? You're wearing about three thousand dollars' worth of clothes, and I saw you on the Boulevard the other day driving a La Salle roadster. Is it yours?"

"Yes."

"All right. You can't afford it. I know it, and everybody else knows it. Everybody also knows you're running around with Blynn, who makes four thousand a week."

"I don't care what people think."

"All right, don't. Forget about the morals of it, because that's not what I'm talking about. This is a small town, and everybody gossips about everybody else. The same producer who cheats on his wife and supports a dame in every apartment house in town will fire a girl because of the 'morality clause.' Blynn is dynamite. He has the worst reputation in the whole village. He's had a dozen girls since he left his last wife—and what's become of them? His last one was Sally Wilbur. She's not even in Hollywood any more. If you'd been through the chorus racket and knew how to deal with guys like Blynn, I wouldn't object. But he'll play you for a while. When he gets tired of seeing you around, he'll use his drag to get you booted out of the studio."

Dorothy did not reply for a long time. Then she said:

"But, Whitey, I love him."

They glided a few more steps. Whitey silently acknowledged defeat, and the evening suddenly went flat.

"Let's go back to the table," he said. "I want a drink."

III

Despite his concern over Dorothy, Whitey was finding life a thoroughly enjoyable procedure. It was not altogether because of the lazy nature of his employment or the magnificent salary. He was firmly in the driver's seat at the Snifkin Studio, and he made himself as offensive and irascible as his naturally pleasant disposition would permit.

Vance he detested for his posturing and conceit. Snifkin he disliked for his imperial arrogance, and the cruel manner in which he abused those employees who could not strike back.

"To think," he said of Snifkin one day, "that the ideas and creative work of intelligent men should be filtered through the mind of a Snifkin."

Consequently, he filled the days with discomfort and dread for Vance and Snifkin. He was the studio's official little old man of the sea, snapping at their heels, muttering sinister threats of exposure, breathing sarcasm and ridicule, and destroying morale wherever possible. He was sure of his position, and confident in the realization that every day the deceit went on made him more impregnable. Some strange quality in his voice as it was recorded captured the fancy of film followers, and saccharine fan letters poured in upon Vance. No longer did they rave about his classic features, but about his superb singing, which was naturally a source of some annoyance to the star.

Whitey envied Vance his bizarre mansion atop the hills where he had caught his first glimpse of Hollywood almost two years before. Consequently, he made it his headquarters, moving in for days at a time. Vance could find no means of dislodging him. He protested, loudly at first, and whimperingly later, neither having the slightest effect on Whitey, whom nothing in this world could abash.

"All right. All right," Whitey would reply to every protest. "I'll not come here any more. I'll tear up my contract, too. You can just sing for your own supper."

Peanuts Oliver was a fairly permanent guest, although she maintained a residence elsewhere until Vance's divorce had run the legal year. She found Whitey's almost constant presence a bit embarrassing, but there was nothing to be done about it. Had Vance been good-natured about Whitey's actions, which began as nothing more than genial, if misguided, raillery, the torment would have ended soon. The actor's storming indignation only added to Whitey's unholy delight.

Whitey made it a practice to fetch to Vance's home an odd assortment of associates, including minor actors, bootleggers, reporters, gagmen and others of that ilk. Without exception, they were raucous, Rabelaisian fellows, precisely the sort to look on Whitey as a ringleader. In swarms of six and eight he let them in, and generously served them Vance's liquor, food and tobacco. If they were not received with the utmost cordiality, Whitey would pretend to fly into a tantrum and refuse to work when they needed him most. This halted production, of course, and Snifkin added to Vance's misery by abusing him for having offended Whitey.

Whitey also blandly insisted upon accompanying Vance on many of his social engagements, and managed to alienate most of the star's friends by his hilarious buffooneries and amorous advances toward wives and fiancées. The women looked much more favorably upon his conduct than did the men.

Whitey, at this time, hit upon one of his most annoying traits so far as Vance was concerned. He made it a practice, in social gatherings, to demand loudly that Vance sing the theme song from his latest picture. Inasmuch as the secret of Vance's voice-doubling had been carefully concealed, others would join the requests, thus inadvertently lending support to the campaign of bedevilment. On a few occasions, when Whitey outdid even his own customary efforts, Vance lost control and threatened assault.

"Go ahead and poke me," Whitey would urge. "It would look fine, a great big athlete hitting a poor little fellow like me, who never hurt anyone. You'll see a nice story about it in the papers."

Sure of his position, Whitey was unafraid.

His conduct on the set never pleased Vance to any great extent. Although he was not needed there, Whitey made it a point to drop in unexpectedly several times a week. His calls were just irregular enough to keep Vance in a constant state of uneasiness. On these visits, he delighted in demanding whatever chair Vance happened to be occupying. He also enjoyed standing just beyond the lights to leer at Vance whenever the actor was performing.

"That's great," he would mutter under his breath as the scene ended. "How do you do it, you great big ham? That's a fine occupation for a grown man. Too bad you have that chorus man's voice, isn't it?"

This always helped Vance greatly with his acting.

Chapter Eighteen

Four months later came the Los Angeles premiere of *Harmony Hearts*, the newest Gilbert Vance singing picture. Came almost simultaneously a new residence for Whitey and Jane.

They decided that the Major Hotel was no longer sufficiently palatial and engaged a rambling bungalow far up in Hollywoodland. It was of Spanish style and would have completely bewildered any Spaniard.

Jane selected the furnishings after her own bizarre style. There was a grand piano, of course—the only standard article. There were a number of trick lamps, and some futuristic furniture which looked slightly odd in a Spanish house, and a great many gaudy hangings to thrill Jane's chorus-girl heart, and some rather pornographic objects of art, and not enough dishes.

Whitey decided to stage a house-warming following the opening of *Harmony Hearts*. He did it in his own peculiar way, inviting friend and foe alike. Johnny Rocco, always seeking, with an eye to furthering trade, to widen his circle of Hollywood acquaintances, agreed to provide three cases of his best Scotch in return for an invitation. Jane had suggested that a buffet supper also be provided, which Whitey laughed to scorn.

"Why ruin a million dollar jag," he protested, "with ten dollars' worth of food?"

The house-warming started to gather momentum immediately after the showing of the picture, when the lobby of the theater was jammed with thirsty Hollywoodians. A parade of automobiles, ever increasing, set out toward the queer hillside mansion. Passing Sunset and Hollywood boulevards two carloads of extra men fell in line. Four assistant directors and two cameramen joined them unbidden at Van Ness avenue, and seven residents of the Villa Carlotta, hearing the cavalcade, ran, partially clad, from their apartments, to trail the procession on Franklin avenue.

Automobiles were lined far down the winding, narrow road which led to the White-Wilson residence.

It was a moment of supreme triumph for Whitey. He had never been paid so well, although he had enjoyed two weeks of affluence after the sale of his story. He had never lived in so magnificent a dwelling since his pre-college days. And he had never achieved so decorative a consort as Jane for a permanent possession.

Joe Greet was there, of course, with his flame of the moment, a sloe-eyed extra girl. McGinnis was present, too, with Peggy Lewis, as were Paul Bannon and an exotic foreign actress from the Bronx, Max Wagner, the most spectacular of all the Wagners, Grace Harper and a handsome Latin juvenile on whom she had clamped, Bob Carey and most of the other fantastic residents of the Major, Jim Mitchell and his wife, and a lot of other nondescript guests, some of whom were not even known to the host and hostess.

Gilbert Vance and Peanuts were there, having been invited in a burst of magnanimity. Whitey had invited Dorothy Irving and Blynn, too, when he found them in the lobby of the theater, and they came, despite the protests of the director. Johnny Rocco and his dark-eyed, gangster girl were waiting for them, brown bottles of refreshment temptingly arrayed in the dining room, flanked by crocks of ice and rows of ginger ale and seltzer bottles.

The party completely filled the house and eddied out into the sun porch which overlooked Hollywood, and into the kitchen and breakfast nook. The bungalow rang with unrestrained conversation, laughter, oaths, and whispered proposals of assignation. Bottles were dropped. Glasses were broken. The party was on.

Peanuts Oliver, skirts pulled high, revealing shapely, tanned limbs, danced what she called the "Hollywood Strut." She claimed it as her own invention, though Whitey had seen it done better at Madame Lee's.

Joe Greet and the gloomy Straubel draped themselves in a corner over a bottle and discoursed upon all the many things they found awry in the picture business.

Whitey played the piano vigorously, closed his eyes, and dreamed happily of his halcyon days in Hollywood's famous brothel.

An extra man, apprehended in a fairly successful attempt to lure the wife of a director into the seclusion of an unoccupied bedchamber, was booted off the porch and rolled some distance down the steep hill.

The exotic foreign actress from the Bronx wrapped her flaming red cloak about her and sneered loftily at the antics of the canaille. Her contempt did not restrain her from consuming vast portions of the Rocco Scotch. About her hovered the kind-hearted but ineffectual Paul Bannon, breathless with anticipation.

They were observed by Greet and Straubel.

"Why is it," Greet asked, "that as good a guy as Bannon will fall for a chippie like that?"

"You must remember," Straubel sighed, "that Anatole France married his cook. What can you expect of a scenario writer?"

A haughty correspondent (female) for one of the yellower of the New York tabloids, cornered a press agent and attempted to cross-examine him concerning the marital troubles of his star. She got nowhere, and at length became exasperated at his evasions.

"I'm glad," she said with venom, "that I'm not sitting on a garbage can."

"And I'm glad," he answered, with perfect good humor, "that I'm not working for one."

The guests milled and shoved about, the table of Scotch being the axis. They danced, with the radio and phonograph playing simultaneously. A number fell down. They talked of marriages, divorces, personalities, random and permanent fornications. They lampooned their employers, ridiculed competitors, bewailed fancied and real misfortunes, wept on sympathetic shoulders over old wrongs, and laughed over old jests. There were arguments, a few incipient fights, necking in the corners, and pawing in the clinches. As the night advanced, one or more of the bedroom doors seemed permanently locked, and the traffic in the hall was enormous.

A simpering brunette asked her drinking companion of the moment, "Did you know that Albert Blynn is engaged to Dorothy Irving??"

"Why, no," he answered, grabbing frantically for a chaser. "I didn't even know she was pregnant."

"That's the trouble with these platonic friendships," a listener added. "The girls are always getting pregnant."

It passed midnight, passed one o'clock, passed two o'clock.

Some of the guests went home, some went to sleep, some went Hollywood.

The exotic foreign actress from the Bronx, her fifteenth highball overcoming her stated aversion to the party, flipped aside her flaming cloak, stepped easily from her gown, and leaped into a twisting, writhing dance, confirming Hollywood's suspicion that she had once been a carnival performer.

Max Wagner emerged from the darkened hallway with a black eye and casually ascribed it to his own mistake in a matter of female identity.

Jim Mitchell, trying to revive a colorful custom of his native Kentucky, was dragged home by his good-natured but, by this time, apprehensive wife. He had merely been attempting to ride to the hounds in the living room.

McGinnis, his Irish belligerency inflamed by alcohol, called Moe Fishbein out of bed and resigned in a long and profanely derogatory tirade, then went quietly to sleep with his head on the telephone stand.

Straubel, aroused at last from his conference with Joe Greet, began to pursue divers unattached women about the house, pawing them awkwardly but with disconcerting fervor.

The house thinned out. The more respectable and timorous guests departed. Those remaining settled down amid dimmed lights to a party of the sort which occurs so seldom and is attributed so often to Hollywood. Passion flared in every corner. Embraces were arduous and unconcealed. The demoralizing, sensuous atmosphere became heavy—hypnotic.

Finally they began to go, frankly worn out or eager for what might follow. Joe Greet managed to subdue Straubel and arouse McGinnis, and drove them both home. McGinnis bawled weakly for Peggy, who had departed some hours before with Grace's dark-eyed Latin. Gilbert Vance, maudlin in his cups, took twenty minutes to bid Whitey farewell, weeping on his shoulder, forgiving past wrongs, pledging undying friendship.

The neighbors phoned twice to say that the police would be called if the uproar were not brought to a close. There were a number of wrinkled fenders and cracked headlights as the drivers extricated themselves from the untidy mass of cars. Whitey found one belated guest sleeping on the lawn, and loaded him into the last automobile.

Lights burning brightly again now, the rooms looked strange and empty. Bottles were strewn everywhere. All the ash-trays overflowed upon the floor. A director had forgotten his toupée. The exotic foreign actress from the Bronx had forgotten her evening gown. Gilbert Vance had forgotten his top hat.

Whitey and Jane stood together in the midst of the battlefield and surveyed the wreckage.

"What a party!" he said.

"Do you think they had a good time?" she asked, womanlike.

"If they'd had any better one, the house wouldn't be on its foundation."

A dull, booming noise, coming from a bedroom, startled them.

"What's that?" Jane asked in terror.

Whitey ran to the room whence the sound had come and swiftly threw open the door. Dorothy Irving, eyes wide with horror, turned to stare at him. A revolver was in her right hand. At her feet lay all that was left of Albert Blynn.

"Give me that gun," Whitey said, and grabbed it from her hand. He hurriedly examined Blynn. The bullet had penetrated his temple. The director had died instantly.

Dorothy, dazed, stood rigid for an instant, then sank to the bed, moaning and crying hysterically.

"I killed him! Oh, I killed him!"

"Pull yourself together," Whitey said, shaking her. "You've got to get out of here."

"What am I going to do?" she sobbed.

"You're going to quit crying," he said. "Jane, take her out of this room."

Between them, they dragged Dorothy into the living room. Whitey's brain, completely cleared now, was racing madly.

"What happened in there," he said, shaking her by the shoulders. "You must tell me quick!"

"I killed him! I killed him!" she continued to sob. "They'll hang me for it. I know they will. I'm glad of it!"

"What did he do to you? Tell me, please! Tell Whitey all about it."

Her sobbing ceased for a moment. She looked up at him, madness in her eyes.

"He didn't do anything. He laughed at me."

Whitey knew he was dealing with a person temporarily insane. He put his arms around her, drew her down on the divan, and nestled her head upon him.

"Now, Dorothy," he began, "you must tell me all about it. I'm going to fix everything. It'll be all right. Just tell me what happened, so I'll know what to do."

"I shot him. I'm glad of it," she said, obedient as a little child who has crept into the protecting arms of its father. "You were right, Whitey. Right about everything. He was going to throw me out. I—I lived with him for six months. Today they tore up my contract, just as you said they would. I found him in there with another girl. He got ugly. Swore at me. We talked for an hour. Oh, Whitey, you don't understand! He got me to taking something—cocaine, I think it was. That's why I did it, I guess. I was wild. I found that gun in your bureau. Something happened. Something he said, and the way he laughed ——"

Whitey released her and sprang up.

"Jane, get her out of here," he ordered. "Somebody will come. They might have heard that shot. Drive her away in your car. Come on, snap into it!"

Dorothy, now completely dominated, started out with them.

Jane protested.

"What are you going to say?" she asked. "They'll think you did it."

"Don't argue with me," he snapped, pushing them toward the door, "I'll take care of myself. They'll never hang anything on me. I've been in worse jams than this."

As they approached the front door, Whitey stopped them. A car was whining swiftly up the steep hill. Their bungalow was the last on that road, and the machine was undoubtedly coming there.

"Out the back way," Whitey said. "Wait till they come inside, then beat it around the house. The car's headed down hill. You can get away without starting the motor."

They hurried out through the kitchen, Jane reluctant, but following orders, Dorothy sobbing softly, but obedient.

Whitey waited for the callers in the living room, lighting a cigarette to test the steadiness of his hand. The strange car drew up outside. He could hear men coming up the cement walk, and a determined pounding on the door. He hurried to open it.

Two uniformed policemen stepped inside.

"What's coming off here?" one asked.

"Just a little party," Whitey smiled. "You're too late to join it. Everybody's gone home."

As he talked he strained his ears for any sound of Jane's car. He thought he heard it leave, but wanted to be sure.

"Have a drink?" Whitey asked.

The police looked at each other quizzically.

"We've had several complaints about a wild party and a lot of noise going on here," said one, peering about.

"Sorry we disturbed anybody. It's all over now."

"What's your name?"

"Theodore White."

"You live here?"

"Yes."

"What'll we do, Joe," one of them asked, "lock him up?"

"Why don't you have a drink instead?" Whitey said, stalling for time.

"Let's do," proposed the thirstier of the two.

Whitey led them hastily to the kitchen, wanting them as far from the road as possible. As they drank a neat one together, the grinding of automobile gears was heard on the hill below.

"What's that?" asked one of the policemen. "Some of your guests coming back?"

"I hope not," Whitey said.

There was a silence. They drank again. The girls are safe now, Whitey thought.

"Listen, men," he said slowly. "I'm damned glad you came. I was just going to phone you. We've—we've had an accident."

"Accident?"

"Yes—just a minute before you fellows came."

"Well, what is it?"

"Come here."

He led the way to the bedroom, and they saw Blynn's body on the floor. One of them rushed to the body, the other turned to Whitey and shook him roughly.

"Come on! Come on! Spill the story!"

"He's dead," came from the policeman on the floor.

"Who is he?"

"Albert Blynn."

Both policemen gasped.

"The director!"

They came menacingly close to Whitey.

"Better talk fast, son!"

"It was an accident."

"Who shot him?"

"I did."

CHAPTER NINETEEN

WHITEY found himself next morning in the famous murder cell of the Los Angeles County Jail, which has confined so many notorious prisoners.

Nervous and shaking from the night's debauch, he had been dragged there at dawn from the Hollywood station where they had taken him first. He had been bullied, questioned, abused and beaten, but he had steadfastly refused to say anything save the unadorned statement that he had shot Albert Blynn accidentally as the climax to a drunken argument.

Screaming black headlines in hasty extra editions that morning told the world of Los Angeles' newest murder and Hollywood's latest scandal. Telegraph wires sizzled with the news. It was the best story in months.

Jim Mitchell arrived at the jail at seven o'clock. He had been aroused by the day city editor and had hurried, breathless and breakfastless, to the aid of his friend.

"What can I do?" was his first question, after he had used his reporter's badge to browbeat the jailers into a private audience.

"Call McGinnis and Joe Greet and get them down here right away," Whitey said tersely. "Then call

Jane and Dorothy and tell them to lay low—not to talk to a soul—until they hear from us later."

"What really happened last night?"

"I plugged Blynn. I'm in a mess, but I'll come out of it."

Mitchell hurried to an outside telephone. Forty-five minutes later the four of them, McGinnis, Greet, Mitchell and Whitey, were in secret consultation.

"Here's my story," Whitey told them. "It's the only one I'll ever tell, and they can't break it. After everybody went home last night, I found Blynn passed out on the bed. I woke him up by slapping him in the face with a wet towel. He got nasty and started a fight. In the scuffle, he was shot. It was an accident, and anyway, I was only fighting in self-defense."

"Where'd the gun come from?" McGinnis asked sharply.

"He had it in his hand and I tried to take it away from him."

"Whose was it?"

Whitey hesitated.

"It was mine."

"The hell it was!" Greet broke in. "It was his. He pulled it on you."

"Certainly," McGinnis added. "There's nothing on the gun to tie it to you, is there?"

"Not a thing."

"Here's another thing," said McGinnis, looking at Whitey searchingly. "Where were Jane and Dorothy all this time?"

Whitey hesitated again, longer this time.

"Jane had driven Dorothy home to spend the night with her."

"O.K.," Joe summed up, "that's the story. Nobody else was in the house. Blynn was on a fighting jag and pulled a gun. You tried to take it away from him and it went off."

"That's it," said Whitey. "Now you fellows have got to do something else. Find Dorothy and Jane. They're at Dorothy's apartment. Get Dorothy out of sight and keep her out of sight and tell Jane to keep her mouth shut."

"We can't hide Dorothy," McGinnis protested. "They'll find her, sure."

"It's only for a few days," Whitey said. "They'll never bring this to trial. What the hell can they do. They've got nothing on me. I was the only one there."

"They might get tough," Mitchell argued. "The District Attorney is a hound for publicity. He might try to stick you."

"Nuts," Whitey scoffed. "The only thing they'll ever know about it is what I tell 'em. And who's going to say I'm lying? Everybody else had gone home. All you have to do is keep Dorothy out of sight until after the inquest. The thing is this: Blynn put the poor kid on the hop, and if the cops ever get hold of her, they'll break her sure and make her say a lot of things she shouldn't. It would look bad, because she was his girl."

They all paused to consider this difficulty.

"That *is* bad," McGinnis said. "I heard Blynn was

taking hop, but I never believed it. You can hear that about anybody in Hollywood."

"I've got it," Greet cried. "I know a doctor and his wife who run a little sanitarium, 'way out on Ventura Boulevard. I've got plenty on him, too—an illegal operation. I'll make him hide Dorothy and do it for almost nothing."

"Oh, wonderful," Whitey said, almost tearful in his gratitude. "You guys are the real thing."

"Let's get going," said McGinnis, springing up. "We've got to beat the cops. Joe, you get hold of that doctor. I'll start for Jane and Dorothy. Jim, suppose you phone Dorothy's apartment and tell them I'm coming. I'd better not meet them there. Somebody'll see us. Tell them to drive up Laurel Canyon to Mulholland Drive. I'll come up the other way to meet them."

The three valiant friends started on their errands.

II

Whitey had not reckoned with the then District Attorney of Los Angeles County when he predicted so confidently that his case would never be brought to trial. The young prosecutor, relentlessly ambitious, was as insatiable for publicity as a film star, as scheming as a pawnbroker, and as lacking in ethics as a prohibition agent.

That same afternoon, Whitey jauntily faced a coroner's jury, and glibly told the tale of the accidental shooting of the director. The verdict was what he expected: that Albert Blynn came to his death from a gun-shot wound inflicted by Theodore White.

What he had not expected was that he would be led once more to the County Jail. But he regarded it only as a formality.

Two days later he faced the Grand Jury and rattled off the story of Blynn's shooting once more, carefully avoiding any variations. He even managed a deliberate yawn while the outcome was in doubt.

His nonchalance, however, was rudely dissipated when that august body of retired farmers indicted him for first-degree murder.

"What's the matter with those dummies?" he complained petulantly, back in his cell once more. "They can't stick me for this."

"Oh, no," said Mitchell. "They can't make you wear chains, either—clank, clank!"

"Whitey," said Joe Greet, "we're all with you—win, lose or draw. But if you're holding anything back you'd better get it off your chest right now. This guy Burrows, the District Attorney, is after your fat little hide."

"That's swell advice," Whitey replied. "But if I broke down now and told 'em that Lindbergh or somebody killed Blynn, they'd have me right where the hair is short—for perjury. I've told this story to the Grand Jury under oath. Remember what happened to Earl Carroll? I'd rather take my chances on beating this rap than meditating up in San Quentin on the sin of telling a lie."

"There's only one thing to do," McGinnis counselled.

"I'm going to send Mark Herron up here to talk to you. He's only a young fellow, but he's one of the smartest lawyers in town."

Herron came, and listened to Whitey's story gravely. He did not believe it to be strictly the truth, but he did not say so.

"I might point out, Mr. White," he commented, "that you weren't compelled to testify before the Grand Jury. You could have refused on the ground that it might have incriminated you."

"More fine advice," Whitey countered. "But did you ever try to scrape milk off the floor? And besides, if I said anything about incriminating myself, what chance would I have making 'em believe it was an accident?"

Herron shrugged, courteously refraining from pointing out that nobody seemed to believe his story, anyhow.

"It's a widespread habit," the attorney remarked, "to call both the doctor and the lawyer too late. However, things might be worse. You say there was no one else in the house?"

"Not a soul."

"Can they disprove it?"

"No."

"All right," Herron advised. "Don't say another word until we come to trial."

III

Just at this period no one was flying the Atlantic, swimming the channel, contesting for the heavyweight championship, running for office, or splitting the Four Hundred apart with scandal. No evangelists were drowning in the desert, and even Chicago was quietly bivouacked for the moment. Consequently, Whitey stayed on the front page for days and days.

Hollywood ran to cover, hiding its head in the sand, as it always does. Blinds were drawn on the most circumspect Beverly Hills social events. Elder Will Hays lifted pious, prehensile hands in characteristic, Presbyterian horror.

The New York tabloids smacked their lips over this savoury dish, yelped with glee, and sent special representatives to Los Angeles by plane. Whitey chatted with them pleasantly, gave them the telephone numbers of several bootleggers, and managed to sell his "exclusive" life story to all of them, demanding cash payment in advance. They all happened to start serial publication of his confessions simultaneously, but stopped the first day, when his deceit was discovered. The various editors complained bitterly that it was not ethical, though Whitey wondered where they had discovered that word.

Donald Henderson Clarke, biographer of some of America's most lurid heroes, rushed westward to do a Hollywood novel that would carve a niche for Whitey's pudgy torso in the same Hall of Fame that houses Rothstein and Frank Tarbeaux.

Photographers mugged him, artists sketched him, sob sisters interviewed and wept over him. Adela Rogers

St. Johns was engaged by the Hearst papers to do a series of articles on the affair.

Whitey's mottled career, his strange employments, and his amorous escapades were revealed for columns and columns. His fan mail became prodigious, with many suggestions of future assignations, in case of acquittal, and several *bona fide* proposals of marriage.

An unknown extra girl, hoping publicity of any sort might get her a better chance on the screen, finally managed to be photographed laying daily wreaths on Blynn's grave. She claimed to be the slain director's secret love, although he had never seen her in his life.

District Attorney Burrows spent considerable time and a great amount of the taxpayers' money to uncover Whitey's past. He said he was searching for criminal records. He found a number of curious things, among them:

That Whitey had been expelled from a middle-western college for ordering twelve barrels of beer delivered at the home of the dean during an afternoon lawn party.

That Whitey had been pulled, protesting, from a freight train in Omaha and had served ten days for vagrancy. Burrows neglected to discover, however, that Whitey had merely seized this means of flight to avoid parental wrath in Salt Lake City.

That Whitey was remembered distinctly in all the cities where he had worked as a newspaper reporter, and that all his former employers were unanimous in the opinion that he was a good man when sober, but that to trust him with a loan, however small, was sheer foolhardiness.

That Whitey had once run a shell-game with a travelling carnival troupe through Texas.

That Whitey had been named as co-respondent in divorce suits by prominent business men of three different cities.

Burrows tried to make each one of these incidents appear as damning as a prior felony conviction.

The reputation of the late Albert Blynn did not come unsullied through the fire of official investigation. His personal friends were amazed to discover how little they knew of the director's past life.

His real name was Watson, for one thing. He had been cashiered from the British army for cheating at cards. He had dealt faro in a gambling house at Juarez. A man answering his description was reported to have been a fugitive from justice in Canada some years before. He had wives in Montreal, and in Mobile, Alabama, in addition to his several ex-spouses in Hollywood.

Moreover, he had been a drug addict for years, and his connection with professional narcotic peddlers in Los Angeles was found to be unsavorily intimate. A package of cocaine had been found on his person the night of his death. All of this more or less substantiated Whitey's claims that the director had pulled the revolver from his pocket, for Blynn might easily have been one to carry a gun.

The District Attorney revelled in this opportunity to

achieve gaudy prominence in the public prints. He bellowed grandiose statements. He hinted at damning, mysterious new evidence. He denounced the vice and wickedness of Hollywood. He dragged in everyone who had attended the house-warming, and even managed to besmirch the names of several prominent stars who had never had anything to do with either Whitey or Blynn.

Briefly, he did everything in his power to convict Whitey in the public mind before the case came to trial.

The disappearance of Dorothy Irving kept the story running and added a wealth of scandalous material. Burrows screamed loudly for her presence, and investigators from his office scoured all Southern California. She was reported to have been seen in a hundred towns and cities, and a number of girls who happened to resemble her remotely were chivvied and harassed. Her parents in Newton, respectable Iowa folk, were humiliated and annoyed by swarms of photographers and reporters.

The District Attorney professed to be working on a theory that she, too, might have been murdered, and searched all the remote canyons of Griffith Park and the Hollywood hills, to Whitey's intense delight.

The suggestion of a love triangle—to quote the headline writers—the implication of so many famous names, and the alluring vista of Hollywood as a backdrop for all this, gave the story tremendous national prominence.

Through it all, Whitey kept his nerve and his silence. In reality, he enjoyed the spectacle thoroughly. The instinct of the actor was strong within him. He liked the limelight. Wherever he went he had always been the life of the party, but never before had he been given the opportunity to do it on such a magnificent scale.

True, he had occasional periods of doubt, and a few moments of genuine panic. He distinctly did not want to go to prison, and in his years as a reporter he had seen many miscarriages of justice—convictions on flimsier evidence than this. But it was too late to change his story, anyway. And besides, there was a certain stubbornness in his affection for Dorothy.

"I've been a bum all my life," he would tell himself. "This is the first decent thing I've ever tried to do, and I'm going through with it."

Whitey found that life in jail was not so bad, with all the privileges which his inner knowledge of jails, and the influence of his friends, managed to provide. From the sale of his confessions to the tabloids, he had received enough money to provide him with restaurant dinners sent to his cell. Occasionally his friends managed to smuggle bottles of cheer to him, and even to stage reasonably decorous parties inside the lockup.

Of all his guests on that fatal evening, not more than half a dozen came to his aid, or even visited him. Mitchell, Joe Greet, McGinnis, Johnny Rocco, Romaine Randolph and Straubel alone stood by him.

To McGinnis he turned over most of his money, with instructions to dole it out to Jane for her living expenses and to provide Dorothy with whatever she needed. He received regular reports on Dorothy's health and safety from his friend.

One morning during his incarceration, Whitey read in the *Times* that Israel Hoffberger and Ruth Michaels were to be married in the new synagogue on Wilshire boulevard. The ceremony was to take place the following week.

Whitey pondered over this for some time and decided upon a wedding present which, at least, was novel. He directed Joe Greet to the safety vault where the photographic copy of Hoffberger's check to Grace Harper was hidden, had it wrapped becomingly and tied with baby ribbon and mailed to the Michaels home.

"Just let him put that on the table among the pickle-forks," Whitey chortled to himself, and sorrowed that he would be unable to witness the bride's reaction upon receiving the gift.

Whitey's greatest worry was Jane. Terrified by the bombastic declarations of the District Attorney that he would hang Whitey upon his purported new evidence, Jane threatened to tell the real story and reveal Dorothy's hiding place.

"Jane," Whitey pleaded, "please keep quiet. I'm running this show, and I'm going to get out of this. You'll only mess up the detail."

"They'll hang you, I know they will," she wept. "I love you, and I'm not going to let you do this."

Whitey laughed, although he did not feel particularly mirthful.

"You're a good kid, Jane, and I'm for you," he said.

[253]

"But talk sense. They can't hang me. Even if I were to be found guilty, the worst it can be is manslaughter. That's only ten years, at the maximum, in California."

"Ten years!" Jane moaned.

"And besides," he pointed out, "I've got my foot in this now, anyway. I've told this story under oath, can't you understand? They've got me, either way. This hyena, Burrows, would cheerfully ship me off to the pen for perjury if I repudiated my statement. I wouldn't be any better off, and neither would Dorothy."

"You're in love with her," said Jane.

"No, I'm not," he answered. "Yes, maybe I am, too, in a funny sort of way. I wouldn't marry her, and I never tried to make her. But it burned me up to see her with that heel, Blynn. I got her into this mess, anyhow, in a way. If I hadn't horned into her affairs, she'd still be hashing at Henry's. That's better than being a ham actress on the snow."

"I'm going to tell where she is, I swear I will!" Jane threatened again.

Whitey became almost sinister.

"Jane," he said, "I'm going to get tough. The only thing now is to go through with this. You open that painted pan of yours just once, and I'll have Johnny Rocco and his gang of yeggs take you for a ride. I mean that."

IV

Whitey's trial for the murder of Albert Blynn was as grotesque a circus as Burrows could make it.

The Prosecutor had insufficient evidence for a charge of first degree murder, and knew it. But he also knew that an impassioned appeal for Law and Order, and a ringing denunciation of Hollywood's decadent immoralities and debaucheries, as he so neatly phrased it, would align the church element behind him for future elections. Hollywood is a favorite bogey for Los Angeles reformers to attack, because it cannot fight back. By packing the jury with bigots and fanatics, and by beclouding the facts with details of Whitey's unsavory past, Burrows felt that a conviction might be possible. Justice never concerned him overmuch.

Hundreds battled to find a place in the courtroom the day the trial opened. There were reporters from all the Los Angeles papers, representatives of every wire service, special writers from the eastern press. Whitey, Burrows, the judge and the celebrities who were called as witnesses were sketched by artists and snapped by photographers. What Whitey ate for breakfast, the color of his tie and the state of polish on his shoes, became matters of national importance.

H. L. Mencken was in town and stayed over for several days in order to witness a portion of the comedy. He departed, shaking his head in delighted amazement, and pronounced it even gaudier than the Scopes trial.

Everyone who had attended the fatal party was summoned to testify for the state, although none of them was able to give any direct testimony concerning the shooting. All of them lied, moreover. Not one would admit having taken a drink at the party. All had "dropped in for a few minutes" on their way home from the theater.

Burrows tried desperately to show that there had been bad blood between Blynn and his self-admitted assassin. He managed to insert in the record some declarations that Whitey had expressed a violent hatred for the director. He launched into frequent, bitter, editorial comment in his questioning. He attempted to show that Whitey had been in love with Dorothy, and that this constituted his motive for the killing. He hinted that the defendant had deliberately lured Blynn to his party for the express purpose of slaying him, presumably to do it in as public a spot as possible.

Burrows wound up his case smugly, with a parade of character witnesses to blacken still further Whitey's already thoroughly soiled reputation.

Herron called but four witnesses.

The first were Greet and McGinnis, both of whom testified that they were intimates of Whitey, that they had never known him to possess a gun, that he was not of a quarrelsome or vindictive nature, that he had never told them of any trouble with the director, that when they left the party Blynn had been snoring peacefully on the bed.

The third witness was Jane, who corroborated the stories of McGinnis and Greet, and added to them. She testified that she had driven Dorothy to her apartment after the party and spent the night with her.

"Where do you live?" Burrows asked, in cross-examination.

"At the Major Hotel."

"Where did you live the night Albert Blynn was murdered?"

Jane hesitated.

"At 3656 Hanson Way."

"That is where Blynn was killed, isn't it?"

"Yes."

"That was also the residence of Theodore White?"

"Yes."

"Then, in other words, you were living with Mr. White?"

"Yes."

"Why didn't you stay there that night? Did you know a murder was going to take place?"

"Of course not. I didn't stay because Mr. Blynn was asleep on my bed, and we couldn't get him up."

"On your bed? How many beds were there in the house?"

"Two."

"I take it, then, that Mr. White occupied the other one?"

"Yes."

"And when you found Mr. Blynn asleep on your bed, I suppose you couldn't have shared the other one with Mr. White?"

The judge over-ruled Herron's objection to this.

"Naturally I could have," Jane answered. "But Dorothy had come in Blynn's car, and she had no way to get home."

"You drove her home?"

"Yes."

"At what time?"

"I don't remember the exact time. It was about three o'clock."

"Blynn was alive when you left?"

"Yes. He was asleep."

"You're quite sure you didn't leave until after the murder had been committed."

"Certainly."

Burrows harassed her for an hour over this point, attempting to establish some discrepancy in her account of the time, and struggling to prove that she had been present during the shooting. His line of questioning made Whitey nervous and uneasy, for he had no great confidence in Jane's mental processes. The point was passed over, finally, however, and Burrows learned nothing of importance.

"When you drove Dorothy Irving home, you spent the night with her?"

"Yes."

"Where did she go the next morning?"

"I don't know. She left before I was awake."

"Where did she go?"

"I don't know, I told you."

"Didn't it strike you as odd that she should leave like that?"

"Why, no. I supposed she had gone to the studio."

"She didn't say anything about it the night before?"

"No."

"Was she intoxicated at the party?"

"I don't believe so."

"Were you?"

"No."

"Don't you think it rather strange, Miss Wilson— or perhaps I should call you Mrs. White—that although there were several dozen empty liquor bottles found after the party, apparently no one drank anything? How do you account for that?"

"Well," said Jane, after a pause, "I understand the police came after I left."

The cross-examination of Jane lasted several hours. Burrows made her admit, again and again, that she had lived with Whitey, and uncovered her career in the chorus and in night clubs. But she was too proficient a liar for him, and he could not shake her on an essential detail.

The fourth and final witness for the defence was Whitey himself.

Simply and convincingly he told the story of the party—how he had found Blynn there after the others had gone, of trying to arouse him. His account of the ensuing fight and fatal accident did not vary from his first statements.

Herron gave the witness to the prosecution and settled back to listen to Whitey's own fight for freedom.

"I think he can do it," the lawyer whispered to McGinnis. "He'll be a tough witness to tangle up."

Burrows tore at his victim like a hungry wolf.

"How long have you been in Los Angeles?" he demanded, and made even that question sound accusing.

"About two years."

"Where were you first employed?"

"On the *Examiner*, as a reporter."

"How long did you work there?"

"About six hours."

"Why did you leave?"

"Mr. McGinnis gave me a better job."

"Isn't it true that you got that position under false pretenses?"

"Partially true. He hired me under the impression I was someone else."

"So you lied to him to get that job?"

"I lied to him as a joke, and he took it seriously."

"Where were you next employed?"

"By Moe Fishbein, who was making a picture with Rethea Clore."

"Albert Blynn directed that picture, did he not?"

"Yes, sir."

"You were discharged from that position, were you not?"

"Yes, sir."

"Isn't it true that Albert Blynn had you discharged because of incompetence."

"No, sir. It wasn't for that, and Blynn didn't have the authority to discharge me, anyway."

"Why were you discharged, then?"

"As far as I know, Israel Hoffberger asked Fishbein to fire me."

"Why?"

Whitey smiled benignly at the judge.

QUEER PEOPLE

"If I answer that question, it is likely to cause embarrassment to several people, and it will have no bearing on the trial."

"Answer it," the judge ordered.

"Very well. I called on a girl one evening, rather late, when Mr. Hoffberger was there. He didn't seem to like my coming, and ran out the back door as I came in the front."

The crowded courtroom roared. Burrows ragged him about the incident for half an hour, and uncovered all the details, to Mr. Hoffberger's subsequent personal embarrassment.

"Mr. White, after you left Mr. Fishbein's employ, where did you work next?"

Whitey saw what was coming, and smiled.

"I worked for a woman named Frankie Lee."

"What was her business?"

"She operated an establishment where entertainers were employed and liquor was sold."

"As a matter of fact, it was a house of prostitution, wasn't it?"

"You could call it that."

"And what were your duties?"

"I played the piano."

"Ah! So you were the professor?"

"Yes. As a matter of fact, I think I met you there once."

Burrows grew red, and the courtroom roared again. The charge was utterly untrue, but the Prosecutor

[261]

knew that a denial would only make him more ridiculous.

"Do you know Dorothy Irving?"

"Yes, sir."

"Do you know where she is now?"

"No, sir."

"You have no idea of her whereabouts, or how to find her?"

"No, sir."

Burrows paused dramatically.

"Suppose I should lead her into this courtroom, now."

"Suppose you should? That's not a question."

"If Dorothy Irving were present, do you think she could shed any light on the shooting of Albert Blynn?"

"I don't see how."

"When did you first meet Miss Irving?"

"About a year and a half ago, when she was a waitress in Henry's."

"How well do you know her?"

"We were very good friends."

"Did you ever live with her?"

"I did not."

"You were never intimate with her?"

"No, sir."

"Do you expect a jury to believe that a man of your reputation and habits could have a respectable friendship with any woman?"

Herron bounced to his feet. The question remained

unanswered, after a lengthy wrangle, but its effect was the same.

"In other words," Burrows went on, "although you worked in a house of prostitution, although you lived with one woman to whom you were not married, your relations with Miss Irving were quite respectable?"

"They were."

"Didn't you declare in public that you made Miss Irving a film star?"

"I may have. I helped her get started in pictures."

"Were you in love with her?"

"No, sir."

"Did you know that Albert Blynn was engaged to her?"

"Yes, sir. She told me so."

"And you weren't at all jealous?"

"No, sir."

"Did you know that Blynn was paying the rent on her apartment, and had given her an automobile?"

"I didn't know it; I suspected it."

"Didn't you warn her against Blynn?"

"Yes, sir."

"For what reason?"

"I disapproved of her going with him."

"Oh, you disapproved of it, did you? You appointed yourself a guardian of her morals?"

"Not exactly that. I didn't think he was a proper person for her to associate with."

"You considered yourself an eminently proper associate for her?"

"As far as my conduct with her was concerned, yes."

"And what were your objections to Mr. Blynn?"

"Well, he was a man of the world, a great deal older than she was, and he already had wives all over the country."

"Did you think Mr. Blynn's reputation any worse than your own?"

"I don't suppose it was any worse, but it couldn't have been much better."

Burrows badgered him for a day and a half, dragged up all his past, hammered upon every escapade for which Whitey was celebrated, dwelled again and again upon the fact that he had worked for Madame Lee, and insinuated that he was concealing much of his former life. Whitey had listened to too many courtroom dramas as a spectator to lose his temper or permit his story to be shaken. When Burrows, through sheer fatigue, ended his bitter inquisition, Whitey had not swerved from his original account of the shooting.

The District Attorney spent three hours in a vicious harangue to the jury. He worked himself into a frenzy, shouted in full voice to make the jurors hear from a distance of four feet, denounced Whitey as a dishonest libertine, called upon high Heaven to strike Hollywood with a divine thunderbolt, and finished at last, completely hoarse and clammy with perspiration.

Herron talked barely half an hour, pointing out calmly that despite the efforts of the prosecution to becloud the issue and blacken his client, the fact remained that Whitey was the only living person who had been present at the shooting, and that the state had failed utterly to produce the slightest refutation of his story. The mere fact, he pointed out, that Blynn had been invited to Whitey's home and had accepted, removed any possibility of there having been previous trouble between them.

Herron, McGinnis, Greet and Jane sat in the almost empty courtroom while the jury pondered.

"What do you think of it, Mark?" McGinnis asked, again and again.

"It's a good bet," Herron contended. "Unless that jury goes suddenly insane, they can hardly get around the fact that it was an accident."

"I don't like the looks of some of those blue-noses on the jury," Greet said.

"The deacon from Pasadena might be liable to hang it on Whitey," McGinnis said.

"The mental processes of a juror," Herron observed, "are beyond comprehension. They might hang him, or they might come out and pin a medal on him."

Whitey, back in his cell, smoked many cigarettes. His nerve was unshaken, but he could not refrain from recalling the gruesome executions he had witnessed as a reporter, and the deadly dullness of prison cells.

"I've seen a lot of poor mugs hanged," he told himself. "It may be my turn now."

In the crowded jury room, at this precise moment, the deacon from Pasadena was Whitey's staunchest supporter, on a unique theory of his own.

"Albert Blynn deserved death for his sins," he argued to his fellows. " 'The wages of sin is death'. White was only the Lord's instrument of vengeance."

"I'm going to vote for acquittal," said another juror, who had been a gay dog. "But not for that reason. White looks like a nice kid to me. He certainly doesn't look like a killer."

"Personally," said the youngest of them all, who was much impressed with the importance of his task, and with his extraordinary powers of perception, "I don't think White killed him at all. I'll bet he's protecting someone."

"I think so too," said the gay dog. "I'll bet that Irving girl knows something about this. Funny the way she disappeared."

"The Lord works in mysterious ways," said the deacon.

"So do these people out in Hollywood," commented the youngest member.

The gay dog wondered, privately, if, in the event of acquittal, he should ask Whitey for Madame Lee's present address.

A grizzled Babbitt from Glendale led a stubborn fight for conviction, due chiefly to his private envy of Whitey's carefree career.

But the three mothers on the jury, won over by Whitey's moon face and pink cheeks, had been convinced of his innocence from the first. All had secretly wanted to take him on their laps and darn his socks.

After an hour's discussion and three ballots, Whitey was adjudged innocent of the murder of Albert Blynn.

Chapter Twenty

A WEARY but joyous gathering sat that night in Henry McGinnis' apartment and discussed the fantastic events of the past month. Whitey was there, the guest of honor, surrounded by Jane, Jim Mitchell, Joe Greet, Romaine Randolph, and McGinnis.

Now that the trial was over, the strain was showing its effects on all.

Although he was happy to be free once more, Whitey felt completely worn out. The constant worry that Dorothy might be found, or that some loophole might develop in his carefully constructed story seemed for the first time to have shaken his carefree attitude toward the universe. For weeks he had been planning a spectacular celebration upon his release. Now that the occasion was at hand, he felt no desire for it.

The others chatted jubilantly, praising Herron's conduct of the trial and complimenting Whitey on his splendid performance under Burrows' venomous questioning. The object of their praise sat quietly in a corner, saying nothing. He was trying to peer into the future. It seemed none too bright. Snifkin had joyously torn up his contract. The producers had blackballed him from all future employment in Hollywood, acquittal exonerating him no more than it had exonerated Arbuckle.

Drinks were served, but Whitey could find neither exhilaration nor comfort in them.

"What are we going to do about Dorothy Irving?" he asked, during a lull. It was more a statement than a question.

"That's what I've been wondering," Mitchell said. "We can't keep her in that sanitarium the rest of her life."

"What does the doctor say about her?" Whitey asked.

"I talked to him yesterday," said Joe. "She can leave whenever she wants to. She's completely cured."

"She couldn't have been taking dope very long," Mitchell said. "I think she hardly had the habit at all."

"Poor kid," Jane said. "She's had a lot of tough breaks she hasn't deserved."

"She's had some good ones, too, if you ask me," McGinnis observed. He had never believed Whitey's story of the shooting.

"Do you think Burrows would try to do anything to her?" someone asked.

"I don't see why," Mitchell said. "After all, Whitey stood trial and was acquitted. They've nothing on her."

"I'm going to take a chance and see her tomorrow," Whitey said. "Where's her clothes and stuff?"

"The manager of her apartment house is holding them for her," Jane said.

The next day Whitey and McGinnis drove to the secluded sanitarium with Dorothy's belongings.

She wept with joy and gratitude when she saw the man who had jeopardized his own liberty to shield her. He refused to listen to her fervent thanks.

"Whitey," she said, "I've felt rotten out here, so safe, with you on trial for something you didn't do. I'd have come in and stopped it, only they wouldn't let me."

"I told them not to let you go, you little mug," Whitey grinned. "I knew you'd spill the beans. And I was sure I'd come out of it. No fat-witted cop will ever pin anything on Whitey."

He pulled an envelope from his pocket.

"Here," he said, "is a ticket and Pullman reservation to Newton, Iowa. The train leaves at six o'clock to-night and you're going on it."

"Whitey," she said softly, "will you never stop doing things for me?"

"Never while I'm conscious," he said, and pulled a roll of bills from his pocket. "Here's fifty dollars to feed you on the train and buy you magazines. Don't give it to the first hungry-looking panhandler you see."

She would not accept the money and ticket.

"I can't take that," she said. "You've done too much for me already."

Whitey lifted her head with a finger under her chin, until their eyes met. He looked positively stern.

"You can't take what?" he asked. "Don't tell me what you can't do. I'm the boss of this outfit. You're going on the train if I have to put you in a strait-jacket."

"You can't afford it, Whitey."

"Can't afford it? I'm filthy with money."

At six o'clock that evening, after tearful farewells, promises of correspondence, and a paternal goodbye kiss, Whitey stood in the station, watching the train roll out, Dorothy aboard. He had done it in grand style to the last, dining with her regally at the Biltmore, and taking her to the station in a taxicab. He had calculated finances almost to the dollar. Now that it was over, he had barely more than carfare to Hollywood. He walked wearily back to Hill street and boarded a Gardner Junction car, just as Van Ettisch had told him to do on that eventful first night in Los Angeles.

The town seemed different, almost strange to him, as he stepped off the car at Hollywood Boulevard and Cahuenga. It was almost as if he were arriving in some distant city, for the first time in his life. He did not analyze his feeling, nor realize that his weeks in jail had sobered him, temporarily.

It was early evening, and the Boulevard was crowded with traffic. The street was the same as it had always been. The same signs flashed, the same theaters beckoned to crowds, the same restaurants fed the same diners. Only Whitey had changed, and the street seemed to possess an air of unreality.

He had no place to go except the Major Hotel, where

[270]

he had stored his baggage with Joe Greet, and to that
eccentric hostelry he trudged.

Joe was working that night, and Whitey sat alone in
the room. With his feet propped up on the window-
sill, he stared out into Cahuenga Avenue. Steady pro-
cessions of automobiles and trucks moved up and down
the narrow, steep thoroughfare. Across the street he
could see the tall apartment buildings, and farther still,
the hills of Hollywood, splotched irregularly with the
lights of homes perched precariously upon them. The
Gargantuan "Hollywoodland" sign, flashing intermittently, was barely visible.

He had no money, no prospect of a job, no plans for
the future. The only ones to whom he could turn were
the friends who had done so much already. The thought
occurred to him that he should leave Hollywood, yet he
knew of no place to go and had no means of getting
there.

Jane burst into the room, pop-eyed with excitement,
brandishing a telegram.

"Whitey! Look!" she shrieked.

It was a money order for a thousand dollars from
her parents in Buffalo, instructing her to return east.
They had gathered, from the telegraphic accounts of
the trial, that perhaps their little Jane needed succor.

"Mother of Moses!" Whitey said. "A thousand
bucks to leave Hollywood. I'd do it for nothing. When
are you going?"

"Day after tomorrow. I just looked it up, and a

boat leaves then for New York by way of the Panama Canal."

The prospect of parting with Jane left Whitey vaguely upset. Despite his frequent, prancing infidelities, she had captured a definite portion of his elusive heart.

"Gee, that's fine," was all he could say. "I'll get Jim or somebody to drive you down to the boat."

Next day they cashed the money order, and Whitey helped her pack. Toward evening they bought two bottles of Scotch and drank quietly for some time. Neither could achieve the gay spirit of old. That night they went to the Roosevelt for dinner. They listened to the music and sat without dancing, talking quietly until after midnight. Whitey had borrowed Joe's car for the evening and parked it on a side street. He went to fetch it while Jane waited at the hotel. In doing so, he passed the forecourt of Grauman's Chinese Theater, dark and silent after the evening performance.

It is the custom of that theater to pave the floor of the outer lobby with cement blocks in which the leading film stars have made their footprints and written their names. Charlie Chaplin, Doug and Mary, Norma Talmadge, Marion Davies, Harold Lloyd, and several others have left here their marks of immortality.

A block of concrete had been removed, Whitey observed. He remembered having read in Louella Parsons' column that Gilbert Vance was to be so honored because of the signal triumph of his recent talking-singing pictures. Whitey smiled to himself.

As he started on, he noticed that an office building was in process of construction nearby, and that a night shift was rushing the work. He approached one of the workmen, handed him a dollar—Whitey's last one—and conversed earnestly for a moment.

Jane waited impatiently on the curb before the Roosevelt. Whitey seemed to be taking a long time, but finally he returned with the car, and they drove back to the Major in silence.

Early next morning, Jane, Whitey, and Jim set out in the Mitchell Chevrolet for the harbor at Wilmington. There was little conversation—most of it supplied by Mitchell. Jane and Whitey dreaded the parting which was to come.

At last they had embraced and breathed farewells. She was on the deck, weeping a little, surrounded by travelers. He was on the pier, grinning feebly, surrounded by a noisy, waving mob. Tears were shed. Confetti was thrown. Advice was shouted.

Jane, unable to restrain her tears, retired to her stateroom. With less than five minutes remaining before sailing time, she rushed out to the rail excitedly.

"Whitey," she screamed, "why don't you come along?"

"A great idea," he shouted, "but you know I'm broke."

She threw him a roll of bills, all that remained of the thousand dollars.

"Buy yourself a ticket," she shouted.

He picked up the money and looked at it curiously.

The crowd on both deck and pier, who had overheard the shouts, laughed and cheered.

"I'm a pink elephant if I don't!" he said, and rushed toward the office of the passenger agent, followed by the mildly curious Mitchell.

Just as the gangplank was being pulled up, Whitey bounded aboard, grinning like a Cheshire cat.

"Are you really going?" Jim yelled.

"Every inch of the way!" Whitey answered.

"But you haven't got your clothes, or any money, or anything. You haven't even got your hat."

"No," Whitey yelled, as bells and whistles began to sound, "but I've still got my sanity. Many a man has left Hollywood without that."

Whitey stood at the rail as the big ship slipped easily down the harbor and put out to sea. It was a beautiful, clear morning. In the background he could see the blue hills of Hollywood standing sharply against the distant, pale sky. He thought of many things as he watched them dwindle and fade.

He thought of Rethea Clore and Fishbein, of Jake and Sam Schmalz, of Grace Harper and Israel Hoffberger, of the erratic, generous Joe Greet, of the saturnine Straubel, of the rugged and dependable McGinnis, of the handsome, conceited Gilbert Vance, of friendly Romaine Randolph, of smiling Jim Mitchell, with his southern drawl, of the exotic Sonia Varon, of kind-hearted Madame Lee, of all the strange tenants of the Major.

A parade of queer people passed before him.

He sighed. It had been a good show while it lasted. Now Hollywood was no more for him. It was only another town added to the list of those in which he could never set his foot again. He had risen to heights; he had sunk to depths. He had posed as a famous author; he had broken up a banquet for Sam Schmalz; he had worked for Rethea Clore; he had chased a powerful producer from an apartment and later blackmailed him to start a girl toward stardom; he had been the professor in a sporting house; he had sung for a movie star and made him famous; he had confessed a murder he did not commit, and had heard a blood-hungry prosecutor demand his life on the gallows.

He thought of the beautiful girls in the studios, of loyal friends he had had, of riotous evenings in the Major, of long, sunny afternoons on the sands at Santa Monica, of comfortably informal dissipation on the fringes of the Hollywood hills, of warm, friendly ladies in many an apartment and bungalow.

He thought, too, of the scene when he had come upon Dorothy Irving, terror in her eyes, standing over the body of the man she had loved too well.

Then he thought of something else.

"I wonder," he said to himself, "how soon they will open the bar on this boat."

II

About the same time that morning, there was a bother in the forecourt of Grauman's Chinese Theatre.

Gilbert Vance, attired in a morning coat, purchased

for the occasion, came smirking and leering to place his footprints among those of the cinema great and thus become immortal.

Sid Grauman, long hair gleaming in the sun, was there with a silver trowel, to act as master of ceremonies at this portentous occasion. Present, too, were film stars, theater officials, photographers, an orchestra, and bored representatives of the press.

Gathered together there, they saw a curious sight.

During the night someone had filled with concrete the space which had been hollowed for Vance's footprints. The concrete had hardened by this time. In the space were two footprints. The heel was worn away on the right shoe. A large, gaping hole in the left sole had made its mark. Below the footprints, a stubby forefinger had scrawled:

WHITEY

AFTERWORD

by Budd Schulberg

Leaving Hollywood thirty-five years ago for the first of my habitual defections, I chose, symbolically, the opposite end of the continent, a pastoral hamlet in Vermont just across the Connecticut River from Dartmouth College. Having been raised in Hollywood and having put in three years there as an apprentice screen writer—"junior writers" they called us in those days—I had decided I would rather be a novelist than a thousand-dollar-a-week big-studio employee. What I would have to write my novel about of course involved Hollywood. Almost every writer works outward from his home town and Hollywood was mine—almost uniquely mine, it seemed to me then.

In the Stanley Rose Book Shop on Hollywood Boulevard that had become our literary headquarters in the 30s I had mingled with *book* writers for whom I held a special awe not reserved even for twenty-five-hundred-dollar-a-week screen-playwrights who twirled their hats or reread *The Hollywood Reporter* while they waited and waited for an Irving Thalberg, a David Selznick or a B.P. Schulberg to admit them to the inner sanctum. At Stanley Rose's, the writers who made an indelible impression on me were William Faulkner, John O'Hara, William Saroyan, Nathanael West, Scott Fitzgerald among the better known, and Guy Endore, Michael Blankfort, Aben Kandell, Jo Pagano, Daniel Fuchs, John Fante, and perhaps half a dozen other gifted men whose contribution to our national letters may exceed their present reputations.

I was a natural target for their questions on the seemingly inexhaustible subject of Hollywood, because in those days it seemed to them such a curiosity that Hollywood (a self-contained duchy dedicated to printing moving pictures on celluloid) should produce a sport who was far more excited by the printed word than by the ten reels of glossy film that was literally canned and served up to a hungry public. At that time I had written a number of short stories about Hollywood for *The Saturday Evening Post*, *Collier's*, *Liberty*, *Esquire* and other magazines, and everyone—from Pep West to the taciturn (even when profoundly intoxicated) Bill Faulkner— was telling me that I ought to try my hand at "the Hollywood novel."

The Hollywood novel, of course, like the Great American Novel, is a conceit, a mirage, a reach for a sense of totality that exists more in the literary imagination than in any actual achievement. Where for instance is *the* Russian novel? Is it *War and Peace*? *Crime and Punishment*? *Oblanov*? Each is a master work, each is Russian to the core, and each could not be more different from the other. There are tempting comparisons between Russia and Hollywood: there are czars, ruling families, secret agents, major domos, struggling masses, and occasionally a sacred cause—like a war or an epic motion picture—that temporarily unites all the contending factions.

Unless a giant's giant came along—a Tolstoy-cum-Dostoyevsky-cum-Turgenev, a Fitzgerald-cum-Wolfe-cum-Faulkner-cum Hemingway—*the* Hollywood novel would have to be a collection of novels, treating all levels of the geographically simple but culturally complex motion picture industrial society. Nathanael West had just polished his cameo, his small gothic tale of Hollywood's lower depths, *The Day Of The Locust*, and had received the dismal reception that he had come to accept as his ironic fate. Pep West's dour, patient, sardonic resignation had become his public personality. Scott Fitzgerald was working from the other end of the spectrum, writing his own sensitive, romantic, ambitious spirit and heart into the creation of an unusual motion picture tycoon who bore more than a casual relationship to "the boy-genius of MGM," Irving Thalberg.

At the end of the 30s we were not yet aware of the scope of Fitzgerald's conception and we were still mourning the "failure" of West's unappreciated *Locust*. "Why," we Stanley Rosers used to speculate over our generous proprietor's bottomless pitchers of orange wine, "was there such a dearth of novels about Hollywood? How could so many good writers—Dorothy Parker, Dashiell Hammett, Lillian Hellman, Ben Hecht, Aldous Huxley —from Theodore Dreiser to Robert Benchley—come to Hollywood and not be moved by its urgency, its outrageously American dynamics, its symbolism as the super capitol of the Great American Rat Race?

When I holed up in Norwich, Vermont, I prepared myself for the writing of *What Makes Sammy Run?* by taking on a major distraction—the reading of every Hollywood novel I could unearth. I must have read at least two dozen, beginning with one of the more literate, that early tongue-in-cheeker, Harry Leon Wilson's *Merton of the Movies*, and working my way through a three-foot shelf of lively trash, things like *Hi Diddle Diddle* by Charles Saxby and Louis Molnar, and *Sky Rocket*, the rags-to-riches saga of a movie star by that prolific sob-sister happily still with us, Adela Rogers St. Johns. I would walk down the middle of the deserted main street of Norwich with all those Hollywood sugar plums dancing in my head. For the most part they were a helpful guide as to how not to write *the* or even *a* Hollywood novel. Oh, they reflected the Hollywood of the great silent days, no doubt about that. But in a cliché-ridden town where every hit picture had its score of pale carbon copies, they seemed to be largely a collection of used movie plots pushed into prose. The Hollywood community, chock-a-block with dramatic illiterates who could thrive in the hyped-up atmosphere of advertisements-for-myself, tended to inspire insipid tales with sentimental turning points and happy endings to match the most splendid bathos that MGM, Universal and Fox could foist upon us.

After a month or so of this scholarly procrastination, I came to the conclusion that there was only one novel that stood out among the cold porridge of fiction I had collected. It was called *Queer People*, by the brothers Carroll and Garrett Graham, and when it was published in 1930 it was the sort of thing you would not dare to bring into a motion picture studio unless you hid it in a brown wrapper and locked it in your middle desk drawer. Like *Ulysses*, it was considered something unclean and unfit for respectable studio eyes. The moguls and the mogulettes were eminently respectable in those days. Like the exalted Louie B. Mayer, they believed in God, in Country, in Mother-love and the Sanctity of the Home. Their mistresses and their casting couches were none of your goddamn business.

[280]

Well, the Grahams dared to break the Commandments, not only Moses' but, even more dangerously, L. B.'s. In *Queer People*, as you have just observed, the studio bosses have names like Jacob Schmalz, his insufferable young son Sam, Israel Hoffberger, Moe Fishbein, and Sol Snifkin. The *goyim* who work for them refer to them (behind their backs) as *kikes* and *yids*, and money is described as "Jewish flags." The book was a Hollywood scandal in the early 30s, when I first read it as a high school boy, and indeed its anti-semitism, even in those pre-Nazi days, was a burr under the saddle cloth of the sensitive. Still, the main thrust of the book was refreshingly irreverent, the first Hollywood novel I had come upon that had the courage of its irreverence—and in "The Industry," as I knew from youthful experience and would soon know more directly after the publication of my Hollywood novel, you had to be prepared to pay for your courage with banishment, if not the firing squad.

The Grahams' anti-hero, "Whitey," an archetypal newspaper reporter of the period, in the Hecht-MacArthur tradition, hard drinking, irresponsible, amoral, opportunistic, arrives in Hollywood with symbolic baggage: a frayed beach robe, five short stories all unfinished, two novels of James Branch Cabell, Ben Hecht's *Count Bruga*, a revolver removed from the body of a slain Chicago gangster, a gin bottle he had drained on the trans-continental Sante Fe—and thirty-six dollars and change. What more—the Grahams have asked with tongue sometimes in cheek and sometimes thrust forward from sensuous lips with evil glee—does a man need to scale the high walls of the Hollywood castle, and what more does he need to fall from those walls back into the moat where the human

[281]

piranas wait to eat him alive? Or to vary our metaphor, the unprincipled, fun-loving, ever-ready "Whitey" may remind us of Alice fallen down the rabbit hole to find herself in a wonderland as inviting as it is daft and dangerous. Whitey participates in a story conference as insanely logical as the Mad Tea Party; he is in turn gloriously drunk, gloriously rich, gloriously broke, gloriously free to accept Hollywood on its own terms in the old era of three-day parties and big studios that combined the hierarchal authority of the Vatican with the morals of Reno—or Tijuana. And finally Whitey is gloriously free to say goodbye to all that, as he impulsively jumps on a ship heading East through the Canal.

Whitey stood at the rail as the big ship slipped easily down the harbor and put out to sea. It was a beautiful, clear morning. In the background he could see the blue hills of Hollywood standing sharply against the distant, pale sky. He thought of many things as he watched them dwindle and fade.

Everything about that paragraph is so beautifully dated that *Queer People* takes on an added quality with age. It becomes a racy testament to an era as totally vanished as the civilization of the Aztecs. Nobody leaves Hollywood by rushing up a gangplank anymore. What were once mornings beautiful and clear are now a moondust smear of fog. Never again will "the blue hills of Hollywood" stand sharply against the distant, pale sky. Now those hills are sun-baked brown in those rare moments when you can see them. And "the parade of queer people" among whom Whitey adventured in this picaresque novel—alas they have all gone on to Forest Lawn or to an even gaudier

Coconut Grove of the fabulous Hotel Ambassador where
the great Abe Lyman Jazz Orchestra plays "Ain't Misbe-
havin" on and on and on . . . .

So, for all its flaws and simplistics, it's good to welcome
this high-spirited nose-thumber of a novel back into print
again. It's a salutary idea, this project of rediscovering and
republishing "lost novels," and in *Queer People* we
have—if not *the* Hollywood novel—at least a truly seminal
work on Hollywood in which may be found the seeds of at
least three of the longer-lived Hollywood novels, *The Day
Of The Locust*, *What Makes Sammy Run?* and *The Last
Tycoon*. You may also recognize "Whitey" as a forerunner
of Scott Fitzgerald's "Pat Hobby," the irrepressible studio
hack, part heel, part victim—an All-American, inter-
changeable with All-Hollywood in those hilarious and desperate days when the Whitey–Pat Hobbies lived off the
crumbs from the banquet tables of the queer people who
combined the decadent flamboyance of Louis XIV with
the stupidity of George III.

Brookside
November, 1975

Textual Note

The text of *Queer People* published here is a photo-offset reprint
of the first edition (New York: The Vanguard Press, Inc., 1930).
No emendations have been made in the text.

M.J.B.

LOST AMERICAN FICTION SERIES

published titles, as of October 1976
please write for current list of titles

Weeds. By Edith Summers Kelley. Afterword by Matthew J. Bruccoli

The Professors Like Vodka. By Harold Loeb. Afterword by the author

Dry Martini: A Gentleman Turns to Love. By John Thomas. Afterword by Morrill Cody

The Devil's Hand. By Edith Summers Kelley. Afterword by Matthew J. Bruccoli

Predestined. A Novel of New York Life. By Stephen French Whitman. Afterword by Alden Whitman

The Cubical City. By Janet Flanner. Afterword by the author

They Don't Dance Much. By James Ross. Afterword by George V. Higgins

Yesterday's Burdens. By Robert M. Coates. Afterword by Malcolm Cowley

Mr and Mrs Haddock Abroad. By Donald Ogden Stewart. Afterword by the author

Flesh Is Heir. By Lincoln Kirstein. Afterword by the author

The Wedding. By Grace Lumpkin. Afterword by Lillian Barnard Gilkes. A Postscript by the author

The Red Napoleon. By Floyd Gibbons. Afterword by John Gardner

Single Lady. By John Monk Saunders. Afterword by Stephen Longstreet

Queer People. By Carroll and Garrett Graham. Afterword by Budd Schulberg

[285]